Out of the Storm

by

Kevin V. Symmons

Out of the Storm

Cover Art by *Kim Mendoza*

The Wild Rose Press, Inc.
PO Box 708
Adams Basin, NY 14410-0708
Visit us at www.thewildrosepress.com

Publishing History
First Crimson Rose Edition, 2014
Print ISBN 978-1-62830-029-1
Digital ISBN 978-1-62830-030-7

Published in the United States of America

He looked back at Ashley as she lay on the blanket, wrapping herself in her arms. He'd build a small fire to keep her warm. To take care of her. Ashley was funny, pretty, and showed every sign of caring for him. A lot. A dangerous combination? Maybe, but for the first time in months he felt good.

"But how about you?" he asked as he approached the blanket. "Don't you...?" He stopped in mid-sentence. Through the twilight he saw her, tightly curled up with a pleasant look on her face. Her eyes were closed. Ashley lay asleep, purring softly.

Eric knelt, watching her. He smiled, touching the scar on her cheek. It was almost healed. As he touched it, she curled tighter and made a gentle sound. A soft murmuring like she felt happy and safe. Her hand moved, finding Eric's, squeezing it in her sleep.

She looked so sweet, so innocent, so content. As he stared at Ashley, Eric knew why he avoided being alone with her, spending time with her. He knew it was happening. He'd done everything he could to avoid it.

Eric lifted her slender body and walked, cradling her tenderly in his arms. When they reached the path leading to his house, she put her arms around his neck in her sleep and nestled closer to his chest. He followed her lead and pulled her tighter. He liked the feeling. Safe. Warm. At home. He stopped, watching her, wanting to pull her lips to his.

Eric shook his head, angry with himself. Very angry. Because he knew why he'd felt uncomfortable about being alone with her. Since that first day at the hospital he'd been falling in love with Ashley.

Praise for *OUT OF THE STORM*

"Kevin Symmons' latest novel, *OUT OF THE STORM*, has something for everyone: action, adventure, romance—and a clever premise involving political conspiracy. His protagonist is a classic hero: wounded in love, world weary, yet resourceful and capable. Cape Cod makes for a great setting, and the nefarious villain will frighten even the most stout-hearted readers. A perfect book to read in front of the fire on a stormy New England night—with your doors securely locked!"

~C. E. Lawrence, award-winning author

"A breathtaking blend of action, romance and terror in an idyllic Cape Cod setting. Symmons ratchets up the tension to full boil while providing readers with intriguing characters they will cheer for."

~Arlene Kay, author

"Kevin Symmons has hit the target again with his latest novel, *OUT OF THE STORM*. A thriller with strong romantic flavor, Symmons snatches his story from the headlines as his hero and heroine battle a sinister domestic terrorist. A classic novel of misdirection set in his Cape Cod home. It will keep you turning pages well into the night. This novel has it all!"

~Chip Bishop, author

Dedication

To my wife,
whose patience and loyalty has helped to make this
and my other works possible,
and to my loyal and enthusiastic readers.

Chapter One

Late April

The luminous dial on his chronometer said 3:10 a.m. Perfect. The family inside the small ranch house should be asleep, lulled by the gusting wind and the gentle rain falling against the dull aluminum siding. The man nodded to his accomplice sitting in a van close by.

The man scanned the small yard. Everything was where he expected. The ten-year-old Camry rested its tired frame in the driveway, its drab finish showing no reflection from the streetlamp fifty feet away. From behind a gnarled maple the man couldn't see into the garage. He didn't have to. He knew the new Dodge pickup would be parked inside.

Using the fence along the property line for cover, he moved quickly, coming abreast of the Camry. He bent low, making his way between the car and the building, coming to rest when he reached the corner of the house nearest the garage.

He surveyed the surrounding houses. No sign of life. Good. Very good. Fitting his back tightly against the old siding, the man slid the automatic from his waistband. He slipped the silencer from his pocket, expertly threading it onto the muzzle of his 9mm SIG Sauer, then replaced the weapon in his belt.

The cool, slim blade of his knife pressed against his forearm. Approaching the rusty screen door that lead to the porch, he slipped the weapon into his right hand. In one fluid motion he twisted the knife into the old lock that secured the door.

The lock groaned and surrendered without a fight. Once inside the screened-in porch, the man held his position for a full sixty seconds. Satisfied the small noise had awakened no one, he made his way to the back door. The top half was glass with no curtain, the bottom a thin wooden panel. He peered inside. No movement. He knelt, waiting. Patience had kept him alive. Still nothing. Not a sound. *Perfect.*

Knife in hand he deftly jimmied the old lock on the porch door and pushed his way into the small kitchen. Once inside he scanned the interior, putting his hearing on high alert. The kitchen faucet dripped, keeping time with a cheap pendulum clock over the refrigerator. The faint scent of dinner—hamburger, he thought, maybe cheap steak—hung in the thick, humid air. Satisfied his entry had gone undetected, the man rolled up his jacket sleeve, replacing the knife in its cradle.

He'd studied the floor plan of the small ranch—had watched the house for a long time. His gaze swept the tidy interior to find the location of his targets. That was the easy part. But something gnawed at his gut. It was the child. He'd watched the small family. *His* life had been spent in a fucking cesspool. Taking the kid went against everything he believed in. He knew what they intended. Same fate as the older girl. The kid was bait…leverage to get their target to talk. He cursed a second time, knowing he had no options. It had to be done.

The older girl was the key. Hot and smart. Damn smart. Too smart for her own good. Some kind of wizard his employers had said. If she'd just minded her own business...And she could be a handful, too. He'd seen her in action. Tapping the pocket of his camo vest, he felt the syringe. That would keep her under control till they got her where they needed.

He'd do the old man quickly, signal his partner, and get his ass out of there with the girls.

But as he pulled the SIG Sauer from his belt, chambered a round, and released the safety he felt uneasy. Something was wrong. Very wrong. He held fast and scanned the kitchen and the hallway again. They had a dog. Where was the damn mutt? Asleep in the living room? Crated in the basement? He hated dogs. Mangy, smelly, drooling things. He wasn't about to look for trouble but loose ends bothered him. Putting his doubts on hold, he crept across the scratched vinyl floor, heading for his first target.

He tiptoed down the hall. When he reached the room where the man slept, he turned the doorknob quietly. He pushed the door inward. It creaked loudly. He swallowed deeply. Squaring his stance, the man held his breath as he pointed his weapon at the bed. Curtains were drawn tightly across the small window. As his eyes adjusted to the sparse interior he stared at the bed. *What the hell?*

How could this happen? They'd watched the house to make sure they got the girls and no one got away.

This was not possible, but... He tiptoed to the older girl's room. Then the kid's. No one! He ran through the rest of the house, searching, growing more desperate and angry with every step. He scoured the basement,

the crawl space above the living room.
   This could not happen.
   But it had.
   The house was empty.

Chapter Two

Friday night. Mid-May.

The nor'easter assaulting the Cape's South Shore showed signs of surrendering. Maybe the six-pack of Sam Adams had dulled Eric's senses. The Red Sox were in Baltimore, kicking the Orioles' ass. He paid little attention. The TV was on mute.

It would have been a special occasion at the Montgomerys'. Eric's third wedding anniversary. Debussy's *La mer* floated through the damp air. Elaine loved classical music. Debussy was her favorite. She always corrected Eric, explaining charitably, "Debussy isn't really classical, darling."

An immaculate Baldwin upright piano stood against the far wall. Elaine's prized possession. She'd spent so many hours at it, happy hours, playing and teaching, even during her pregnancy.

Eric stared at the empties lined up on the coffee table. Rising unsteadily from the couch, he headed across the cluttered living room to the kitchen, stopping in front of the wedding picture: Elaine in her wedding dress by their pond. His eyes burned. Turning away, he set his jaw and headed toward the refrigerator. Almost empty. Some milk, a loaf of bread from earlier in the week, and a block of cheese. Not what he wanted. No beer.

"Shit," he mumbled. His primary supply was exhausted. Time for reinforcements.

Eric made his way to the garage and the small fridge Elaine had bought two weeks before her accident. Opening the door, he grinned as he saw his supply of Sam Adams lined up like little soldiers. He came to attention and saluted. Reaching in, he took one, then, seeing a bottle of champagne, put the Sam back. *My God.* Could the champagne have been sitting there this long? Had he forgotten it? It was the good stuff too, real good—pricey. Elaine had been the connoisseur. She'd bought it to celebrate their second anniversary. They'd never opened it, because Elaine had been pregnant. He wrestled with the cork, twisting it out and under-handing it into the stack of dirty dishes in the sink.

Eric bumped around the kitchen. Had to be a clean glass somewhere. After all, you couldn't drink champagne out of the bottle. That was just plain tacky. Finding a glass that looked clean, Eric went back to the living room. He took a couple of hits from the bottle, leaving the unused glass on the coffee table. His cheerless celebration was having its effect. Pushing a week's worth of *Cape Cod Times* off the couch, he leaned back for just a second, closing his eyes…

…There she was, sweet, beautiful, passionate. His princess. His French professor at Williams would have described her as his raison d'être—*his reason for existence. Why he'd resigned his commission and put saving the world on hold. She came toward him, lips parted, flawless smile engaging him. But the light behind Elaine was so bright he lost her face and features. She beckoned. But something else was there in*

the dream, a noise, a distraction. Something pulling her away...

Eric jumped to attention. It wasn't the dream. It was something else. A noise. At the front door. Not the wind but a knock. At the front window. A voice with it. He dropped the half-empty champagne bottle. Damn it. There it was again. Another knock. More forceful this time.

He stood, trying to figure out who'd be coming to his front door on Friday night. His buddies were working or at home. He didn't owe anyone money. And it was too late and too stormy for Jehovah's Witnesses.

The third knock was accompanied by a muffled "Hello?"

Eric called out, "Yeah, keep your shorts on. I'm coming." Zigzagging toward the door, he hefted the baseball bat he kept behind it. "Who is it," he slurred, angry someone was interrupting his Friday night date with oblivion.

"Open the door. *Please?*" The voice was soft and female. Back at the door again. She had an accent. Sounded southern. Definitely southern. Barely audible above the gusts of wind.

"Who is it?" he repeated.

"Uncle Eric, *please.* Open the door." The drawl sounded plaintive. *Uncle?* He had no nieces. Who'd be calling him that? His brother Ralph came to mind—a petty officer stationed in Norfolk. Ralph was Eric's only family. Had a live-in girlfriend and gentle young daughter. At least she had been the only time Eric had been there. The girl had played a welcome counterpoint to Ralph. She was a sweet kid—cute and soft-spoken. He remembered her from the visit.

"Please," Eric heard the voice from outside.

Eric flipped on the spotlights and opened the door. A girl stood shivering, silhouetted, like the woman in his dream. But this was no dream. And she was no angel. She looked thin and soaked through, poor kid. And unless the alcohol was playing tricks on him this *was* a grown-up version of that teenager he'd met ten years ago.

The poor girl shivered as the hood of her slicker fell back, pushed by a gust of wind, revealing short, damp hair. It was dark-brown, close cut, and clung to her head. Her right cheek showed a serious bruise. Swollen, fresh, and painful looking. Very painful. Eric understood pain.

"Hello," she spoke in a soft drawl. "Don't know if you 'member me. I lived with your brother Ralph. Melissa's daughter. I'm Ashley. Ashley Jean." She pulled her hood up, wrapping her thin body in her arms, tightening the slicker around her waist as the wind howled and the rain resumed.

"'Course I remember you, Ashley," Eric said. And he did. She had the same pretty face. But she'd been all arms and legs at fourteen. This Ashley was tall and lean, but beneath the wet, weary clothes he could see it. She'd grown into a woman. Her pale face looked drawn and tired. "What's going on? Why are you here?" Eric asked. Ashley looked away and stood frozen.

"Momma had an accident. Died a while back."

"Okay." He shook his head, still trying to grasp why she stood at his front door. "Come inside and tell me about it."

"Things were hard before, but they took a real bad turn since then." Ashley stood in place. Looking away, she shivered.

"Why? What happened?" Eric asked. "And for God's sake, come in." He grabbed her slender arm through the old slicker. She resisted.

"Last week Ralph said we should git out." Were those tears or the rain? She brushed the moisture aside and clenched her jaw, fighting hard to control whatever emotion lurked behind her large brown eyes.

"What do you mean?" he persisted, hand still on her arm.

"We didn't know many folks. So when he told us we should leave, I didn't know what to do, where to go."

"So you came here?" Eric asked in amazement.

"We had nothin'. No money. No real friends. No car." She stared at him, her face betraying something. Eric could only guess. *Damn you, Ralph*, he cursed silently. "So, yeah. I remembered meetin' you years ago. Know we're not exactly close but you were so nice and everyone on Momma's side is dead. I figured…guess I hoped maybe you'd help us."

Eric stared at Ashley, trying to come to grips with what she'd said. None of this made sense. She looked so pale and fragile. Her hands and nails were dirty. "Come on in," he insisted, trying to pull her into the front hall. The last thing Eric wanted was a young roommate, certainly not a female one, but he couldn't leave her shivering in the rain. And if Ralph had thrown her out he had some sympathy.

The girl took a halting step and stopped, taking his arm off her sleeve as she looked in the direction of the detached garage. "Thanks, but…" Ashley hesitated, playing with her bottom lip.

"Jesus, Ashley. The weather's terrible." He studied her. She looked tentative, frightened.

"Well, you see, I...I'm not exactly alone." She continued biting her lip and studied the steps.

The wet darkness pelted him as he leaned into it. "What do you mean—not alone?" Sobriety was making a rapid comeback. Adrenaline could do that.

The girl looked toward the garage, then back at him. "I can't leave them out here. We walked a long way. From the highway." Her words were muffled by a gust of wind. Had she said "them"?

Eric pushed past Ashley and looked toward the garage. In the lee of the building sat a frail-looking little girl and a small cocker spaniel. Both looked spent and cold. Even from his vantage point Eric could see their eyes. They looked hollow and devoid of emotion. Each wore a tattered garbage bag to shield them from the rain.

He looked at Ashley Jean, then at the child and the dog. "Jesus Christ," he swore and ran toward them. He lifted the little girl and brought her inside. She weighed less than nothing. Eric lowered her gently onto the living room sofa.

Ashley walked toward the dog and called him. "C'mon, Rusty." Eric watched the poor little guy stumble under his protective cover, then followed Ashley into the house.

Eric shook his head, studying the girls. Both looked like they needed a good meal and a bath.

The young woman followed Eric inside and shut the door behind them. He took her worn slicker off. It was heavy and utilitarian. Looked like Navy issue. Eric threw it over a kitchen chair and ran to the hall closet where he kept spare blankets and towels. When Eric returned Ashley knelt beside the little girl on the couch. She took the plastic bag off the child, gently putting her head on a pillow. The little girl's teeth were chattering. The spaniel tried to shed his cover, too. When Eric pulled it off, the dog ran to the little girl and nuzzled her tiny, soiled hand.

Eric shook his head. "Did you say you walked from the highway, from Route 6?" She nodded. *Jesus! It's three, maybe four miles from my house to the Mid-Cape Highway,* he thought as he heard the wind and the rain...

"Yes, sir. Nice lady gave us a ride for a little bit but..." Ashley shook violently. Eric wrapped her in one of the blankets. Sitting on the carpet next to the child, she took the little girl's hand, surrounding it with her own, singing a lullaby in a soft, pleasing voice. The dog continued to hover, settling down next to the girls and wagging his tail.

"When did you eat last?" Eric asked, trying to comprehend this surreal turn of events.

No answer.

"Be right back," Eric threw over his shoulder as he went into the kitchen to put on the tea kettle and shove some bread in the toaster. When he returned, the little girl and the spaniel were asleep. Ashley Jean lay face down sprawled on the carpet, unconscious.

Chapter Three

Eric opened the front door and let his mother-in-law in. Louise Crawford lived ten minutes away. She came as soon as he called. Lu had been his rock, the one person he could count on after Elaine's death. Tall and striking like her daughter, Louise had the same heart-shaped face and pale-blue eyes. Only telltale age lines and the graying of her dark-brown hair hinted at her age. She looked beyond Eric into the living room where the little girl and the dog lay asleep. Ashley Jean lay motionless on the floor. Eric had covered her with a thick quilt.

He gestured toward Ashley, the little girl, and the spaniel. "They just showed up. In this damn monsoon," he whispered. "I brought 'em inside. While I was getting them something to eat this happened." Eric stopped and swallowed hard, looking toward the girl lying on the carpet. "When I saw Ashley—that's the older girl—passed out like that I didn't know what to do." He frowned. "I checked her vitals. She's breathing and got a pulse. Should I call 9-1-1?" He'd handled three tours in the Middle East as a Special Forces Team leader. Handled them well. A fragile young woman fainting in his living room was new territory.

"Who are they?" Elaine's mother whispered as she tiptoed into the living room.

"They lived with my brother. The older one was

his girlfriend's daughter. Met her once. Seemed like a real nice kid but that was years ago. Not sure about the little girl. Could be a sister"—he paused as the thought took hold—"or her daughter. Ashley said my brother told them to get out last week."

"I remember you talking about your brother but what could have happened? Why would they show up here?" Louise asked, shaking her head slowly.

"Wish I knew." He shrugged. "I have no clue. All I know is they arrived soaked and exhausted at the front door. Couldn't turn them away."

"'Course you couldn't." She gave him a reassuring smile.

Eric frowned.

Lu bent over Ashley, checking her vital signs. "Go call, *right away*. She's burning up, her breathing is shallow, and her pulse is weak. When the EMTs get here, you go with her." She gestured toward Ashley. "I'll take care of the little girl. Eric. Here. Chew some gum, honey. Take two." She pulled a pack of Trident from her purse. It wasn't a criticism. Louise never passed judgment. She put her hand on his cheek and smiled softly.

"Thanks." He knew he smelled of beer. But this crisis had brought him back to reality. The mind-numbing buzz of an hour ago was a memory.

While Eric placed the emergency call, Lu took out her cell. After hanging up, she took his arm. "I called the hospital. They're expecting you." His mother-in-law was a senior ER nurse. She was calling in favors. The way she had the night of Elaine's accident. Eric prayed the result would be better.

****

Eric entered the doctor's office and cleared his throat. The place smelled of floor wax and antiseptic. This man was tall. He carried himself with dignity, had a full head of thick gray hair and a goatee to match. The doctor showed Eric a neutral smile as he gestured toward a chair. Eric watched him. This was no medical student. His name tag said Chief of Obstetrics. He knew his business.

We had no real friends. Didn't know where to go… Ashley's words echoed as the doctor flipped through her chart. The implication confused and angered Eric. His brother had never been a stand-up guy, but he wasn't *that* low, was he? He wouldn't throw these sad girls out with no money and no place to go. At least Eric hoped he wouldn't.

"How is she?" Eric asked, working to push the suspicions about Ralph from his mind.

"She had a miscarriage."

"A miscarriage," Eric said in a whisper. "Jesus."

"Generally, Ashley's a healthy young woman," the doctor continued. "She's dehydrated, exhausted, and could use a good meal. That combination brought this on, but she's a strong girl. That cut on her face is pretty nasty, though. We'll keep her for a couple of days to make sure she's all right. "

"A miscarriage," Eric repeated as a torrent of thoughts flooded his mind, none of them pleasant.

The doctor nodded, closed her chart and turned, studying Eric. "What can you tell me about Ashley? Do you know her? Who the father is? We found an ID in her pocket that indicates she came from Virginia?"

As the doctor questioned him, a middle-age woman knocked and stuck her head in the office. The doctor motioned her inside. Eric didn't recognize her. When he saw her name tag, his stomach sank. It read: Barnstable County Social Services.

Eric sat, eyeing the woman. He wasn't sure how to describe Ashley's relationship with Ralph. "She lived with my brother. His girlfriend's daughter." He shrugged. "That's all I know. She showed up on my doorstep tonight. Had a little girl and a dog with her." He shook his head. "Said that my brother threw them out." He stumbled over the words, not wanting to believe them. "Look, Doc. I only met Ashley once. It was years ago, I..." Eric stopped in mid-sentence.

"I'm sorry you're stuck in the middle of this. Lu called here. I know she was your mother-in-law and—" The doctor showed a sympathetic smile as he turned toward the woman standing next to them. "The ID we found was a Virginia driver's license. It fell out when they undressed her. Said she's twenty-four. Does that sound right?"

"Guess so." Eric nodded and looked at him.

The doctor gestured toward him, then turned toward the woman. "I think this lady has some questions for you."

A miscarriage? My God! This just keeps getting better. Eric had a mind to jump on a plane, find Ralph, and beat the shit out of him. Except this didn't fit Ralph's MO. He was a schmoozer not a bully.

"Mr. Montgomery?" the woman interrupted. The doctor had left the office. Eric sat facing the social worker. She looked around, then tilted her head as she studied Eric. "I know you—by reputation. You own the South Coast Marina. I have friends who keep their boats there." She smiled, finding his eyes. "And I know

Louise was…"

The woman's words stopped, hanging in the still, antiseptic air between them. The walls, painted institutional green, seemed to close in around them.

Eric sighed and nodded slowly. "Yes, ma'am. That's my place. And Lu is…was my mother-in-law."

"Sorry we have to meet like this. My name's Rebecca Walsh." The middle-aged woman held out her hand.

Eric shook it.

"BCSS—Barnstable County Social Services has a staff member on site at the hospital. It's policy," the woman explained then paused, giving Eric a charitable smile. The social worker twisted in her plastic chair. "Your wife." The woman's eyes focused and narrowed. "Lu's daughter—had that hit-and-run last spring."

Eric's throat tightened as he felt the familiar burning in his eyes. He nodded again.

"I'm so sorry. That must have been—" She shrugged as her words died again. She nodded and passed her card across the table.

Eric said nothing. Just heard the fluorescent ballast buzzing overhead as he studied the light reflecting on the waxed tile floor.

"I'll keep this short," the woman promised. "The medical staff tells us that Ashley, the young woman you brought in, shows possible signs of abuse. That's one reason they called me." The woman did her best to maintain a neutral expression. Sadly, Eric assumed problems like this were all too commonplace. "Some evidence of old bruising, a couple of healed fractures."

Old signs of abuse? Fractures and bruising? This kept getting worse. Eric didn't want to think what the next revelation might bring.

"I tried to talk to Ashley, but she was pretty groggy," the social worker continued. "What she said didn't make much sense. Mumbled something about a bag? I thought maybe you could help."

"Ms. Walsh, I really don't know anything about her. I told you. And I have no idea what she's talking about." Eric sighed and stared at the woman across the table. His frustration mounted. "Can you answer a question for me?"

"I can try," she agreed with a non-committal smile.

"This alleged abuse." He paused, mustering his courage. "You said it looks old?"

She looked down at her report and nodded. "According to what the report says. Hard for them to tell without more tests and input from Ashley."

Eric sighed deeply.

"Honestly, Mr. Montgomery. Without something from the potential victim—from Ashley, we may never know."

He'd let this poor girl and her little band into his life. Despite the fact that no one accused him of anything, somehow, Eric felt responsible. "She showed up tonight," Eric repeated defensively, picturing her standing in that downpour when he opened the door. "In that storm. All the way from Norfolk. Damn tough travel for a couple of girls and a little dog." Eric swallowed and shook his head.

"I'll speak to Ashley tomorrow about what may have happened." Rebecca twisted her lips and found Eric's eyes again. "The other reason I have to get involved is that she's an adult with a child apparently in her care and has no place to stay when she's released.

She's got no evidence of insurance and no means of support for her or the child, whatever their relationship. From what you've told me she went to a lot of trouble to find you. That and the potential abuse almost guarantee she's not going back to Virginia. I'll have to talk to DCF—the Division of Children and Families. They handle cases like Ashley's."

Eric heard the words. They took a moment to register. He knew nothing about the Social Service system but had the gnawing feeling that unless he took these girls and their dog into his home they were going to be thrown under the bus—into more chaos. Maybe a shelter or a foster home for the little girl.

"What if they came to live with me? If I assumed responsibility for them?" The words spilled out too quickly. But when a smile brightened Rebecca's face he knew it was what she wanted to hear. Easier for her and better for the girls.

"That's between you and Ashley. She's an adult. We'll have to determine the relationship with the younger girl before making a determination. If she's related to Ashley, a sister or daughter"—Rebecca put on a pleasant face—"I think that would work, but we'd have to get approval, of course. I still need to follow up and make out a report on what the doctors found. But with your background and reputation it *should* be just a formality."

"About the insurance?" Eric began. He wasn't sure how to handle the second issue. If he agreed to take them into his house the burden of payment would fall on him. He had memories of the bill from Elaine's hospital visit on the night of her accident. Well into the five figures.

"You'll have to address that with the billing department." Rebecca shrugged and held up her hands. "Sorry." Her eyes showed she felt his anxiety.

Eric had his own insurance, but that wouldn't cover a stranger of legal age. He had the $100,000 from Elaine's life insurance sitting in an account at the Cape Cod Five. Would it be a violation of trust to use some of that to pay for Ashley? Was he ready to take responsibility for her, the child, and their pet? If he agreed to take them in, Eric knew he had to pay.

"If you want to talk to my brother, the man she lived with, I'll give you the last phone number I have for him. The last time I saw him was ten years ago when Ashley was a kid. Ralph and I were never close," he added. "What do you do to someone who...who mistreats a girl?" Eric asked.

"In Massachusetts we take domestic violence very seriously. If Ashley swears out a complaint, we'd call Virginia and get the police involved but..." Her words trailed off again. Eric thought she was hoping he'd take them under his wing and avoid that. "She's an adult. If you take her in and she doesn't pursue a complaint, our hands are tied. So we may not need that number. I'll let you know." They exchanged glances. Eric wasn't sure how to feel about that. If Ralph had anything to do with this, he wanted the SOB punished. He'd try to find out from Ashley when she was better.

"Are we through here?" Eric asked. Exhaustion was overtaking him.

She looked at him. "I think so." The social worker held out her hand. "We'll be talking to confirm this conversation when Ashley's back on her feet. She may have other ideas."

She gave him a weak smile.

I'd like to have a talk with Ralph myself, Eric thought as he stood to leave.

A long and painful one.

Chapter Four

By the time he pulled the Jeep into the crushed stone driveway it was after one. Eric parked in front of his garage and trudged across the gravel. Lonely raindrops chased him as he made his way to the kitchen door, but the nor'easter had spent its fury. He couldn't remember feeling this drained. Not since the fire-fights in Afghanistan and Iraq.

Now, as his adrenaline faded, anger and frustration mixed with fatigue. He thought his head would explode. These girls needed someone. Eric didn't doubt that. A picture of young Ashley—the sweet, innocent girl he'd met ten years ago—stuck in his mind. What happened to turn her into the solitary, desperate creature he'd left at the hospital?

In four hours I've inherited a family. But not the family he'd envisioned. Eric's dreams were filled with Elaine and the beautiful little girl he expected to watch grow in her image, not this sad, broken young woman and her followers. *Fucking Ralph.* If he really had thrown them out, Eric would put his brother in the hospital for a month.

Before he arrived at the door, Louise opened it quietly and put her fingers to her lips. "Shhh. They're both asleep. The girl's in the second bedroom down the hall. I did the best I could to clean them up and gave them something to eat. They were both exhausted," she whispered, smiling as she nodded at the small spaniel, eyes closed and snoring on a makeshift bed in the corner. "I figured I'd keep an eye on them and give the little girl a bath in the morning. I have the day off. The dog is your job," she added.

"Thanks for everything," he said, pulling her to him and giving her a generous hug. "You're always there when I need someone."

"I always will be." She nodded and blushed. "You know that." Lu cleared her throat. "What happened with Ashley?"

"A miscarriage," he said quietly, shaking his head and flushing as he studied the floor.

"I figured that." She patted his shoulder.

"They're going to keep her for a couple of days. Make sure she's all right and the cut on her face heals. A social worker showed up. Rebecca Walsh. Said she knows you."

Louise nodded.

"Ashley was..." Eric hesitated, wanting to spare Angie the details. The thought that Ralph might have hurt Ashley sickened him.

His mother-in-law seemed to sense his discomfort. "It's okay. Tell me the rest tomorrow. If you want." She picked up the overnight bag she'd brought. "I threw some things in when you called. Figured I could stay for a couple of days if you needed me to. It may take you a while to figure out your next move."

Next move? Eric tried to get his mind around it. Suddenly, something nagged at him as he looked at Lu's bag. "They had nothing? Right? No suitcase, knapsack, a plastic bag with clothes, a toothbrush— nothing?" he asked, remembering Ashley had mentioned a bag to the social worker.

Louise stopped and looked at him curiously. "No. Funny. Now that you mention it, they didn't."

Eric tiptoed to the kitchen door and stuck his head outside. He flipped on the spotlight and looked around the garage area where the little girl and the puppy were huddling when Ashley rang the bell. "Nothing," he said quietly. "Think about this," he began. "They were leaving for the rest of their lives. They had no money and packed *nothing?*" He raised his eyebrows. "Unless my brother just kicked them out of the house with no warning. It doesn't make sense."

"I guess not," she whispered, watching him. "Eric, what are you trying to say? Do you think that something isn't...?"

"I don't know what to think," he interrupted. "This doesn't add up. Norfolk is 600 miles from here. And it's been pouring for a week. These girls travel all that way and suddenly appear on my doorstep as if by GPS. All they had was Ashley's wallet, a few bucks, and a Virginia driver's license."

"I guess I see your point." Her words trailed off as she sighed. "But it's been a long night."

Maybe it was exhaustion, anger, or the residual alcohol in his system. All could fertilize the seeds of suspicion. Eric needed a good night's sleep. He wanted to ask about the little girl and the dog, but he was dead on his feet. He yawned and gave Angie a peck on the cheek. "Thanks for everything," he repeated and dragged himself up the stairs to his bedroom. "I've got no idea where this is going. We can talk about it tomorrow," he called back softly.

When he slipped between the sheets at 1:20 he

should have fallen asleep in seconds. It had been a tense evening. Elaine had been brilliant, the person with the twenty-five-dollar vocabulary. "Surreal" was one of her favorites and the word that kept coming to mind as he thought about the past four hours. When he closed his eyes all he could see was an image of Ashley standing cold and wet in his doorway. How had the sweet, precocious fourteen-year-old he'd met at Ralph's become the hungry, broken young woman who'd knocked at his door? And more importantly how did she, the little girl, and their ragamuffin dog manage to get from Norfolk to Cape Cod with three dollars, no baggage, and no car? He needed answers.

Two questions kept him awake: If everything Ashley said was true, why him? They'd met once—for ten days a decade earlier. Yes, she *had* followed him around like a puppy. Maybe even developed a crush on him. But this leaving home when she was pregnant and making a pilgrimage with a child and a dog to find him—why? What was she running from—an abusive boyfriend, the child's father, something criminal, Ralph? Could he have made that much of an impression? Would he be the one she ran to when her life fell apart? There had to be someone else—a friend, lover, the father of her child, certainly somebody closer and easier to find. Someone more connected to their lives. Could Ashley really be so desperate and alone she had nowhere else to go? Were the bruises another clue, a more sinister reason she might come looking for him? Her mother was dead. Was she afraid to be alone with Ralph?

And then there was his brother. They'd never been close. Eric's father had remarried and Ralph was a teenager when Eric was born. He was always in trouble. Eric had been the model son. But lying there, despite the urge to find his brother and kick his ass, Eric had to admit that Ralph had never been violent. He'd never abused anyone or done some of the other sick things that lurked in the recesses of Eric's mind. His brother was smooth and slick, a good-looking schmoozer who charmed his way into women's hearts and men's wallets. Had he changed or was Eric's dislike for Ralph coloring his judgment? Was there another explanation? Had he thrown Ashley out *because* of her condition or something that had happened? But that raised a more sinister question. If he *had* thrown her out what did that say about Ashley? At two o'clock Eric got up. He didn't want to think anymore. He couldn't. He went to the bathroom, took one of the prescription sleeping pills his Army shrink had given him. In ten minutes he passed into a deep, dreamless sleep.

****

Nine a.m. Sounds filtered in through his open bedroom window. Eric jumped up. He never slept this late. Seagulls called their comrades and the sound of a distant outboard hummed somewhere. More sounds—working gently up the stairway from the kitchen mingled with the smell of freshly brewed coffee as Eric rubbed his eyes and stretched. He wanted to curl up and pull the quilt back over his head. He thought he'd heard the sound of the phone earlier but couldn't be sure. He searched the bedroom, realizing he'd left his cell in the kitchen.

He'd awakened at 4:30, sleeping in restless fits after that. Images of Ashley's large, desperate eyes haunted him. Now, he sat up and rubbed his own, still hoping the whole thing had been a bad dream. The hoarse sound of barking from the kitchen told him otherwise.

Pulling on his jeans from last night and a clean sweatshirt Eric headed downstairs. When he arrived in the kitchen he saw the cause of the barking. Louise had placed a fresh bowl of dog food on the floor by the door and the little spaniel was gobbling it up. She must have gone shopping as soon as the stores opened. While he was still asleep. *An amazing woman*, he thought as he had so often in the months since the accident. Sadness washed over him. Elaine had been the kindest, most caring woman Eric had ever known. Louise had been her role model.

"Hi," she said, smiling at him. "How'd you sleep?"

"How do you think?"

She laughed softly. "The little girl's still in bed. Poor kid was exhausted. Bobby called from the marina. I told him you had an emergency. Said you'd get back to him by ten."

Eric nodded. Bobby was his head mechanic, foreman, and best friend. Had been since their days in Afghanistan. A genius with gasoline engines, diesels, generators—anything. Bobby was the best on the Cape's south shore and he worked for Eric. They had good men for the mechanical side of the business. What the marina needed was someone to run the office. Eric liked being where the action was—on the water or the dock, meeting the customers, tending to the boats, not spending his days at the computer or processing payables.

"Thanks," Eric said, closing the distance between them and giving his mother-in-law a hug. He'd known

Louise for most of his thirty-one years. Had fallen in love with her daughter when they were twelve. After Eric's mother died a few years later, his father was never the same. Lu had taken care of him like her own.

"I'll get back to Bobby." Eric held up his cell and nodded.

"And Becky called." Louise raised her eyebrows. "Rebecca, from BCSS. She needs to talk to you." She backed away and studied him. "Been quite a year, eh, LT?"

A lump formed in his throat. LT…Lieutenant. His rank as a Green Beret Team Leader. No one had called him that since Elaine.

"I've had better," he whispered, finding her eyes.

Lu   studied   him,   acknowledging   the understatement. His wife and high school sweetheart—Louise's only child—had been killed in a hit-and-run on the way home from her baby shower last spring. Their little girl had been born as a result of the accident, surviving for six heartbreaking hours.

Eric hadn't taken it in the stoic way his friends expected of a hard, seasoned veteran. Alcohol became his elixir. Not all the time or every day. But an occasional balm to soothe his lonely soul and fill the long, empty evenings. Now, a girl he'd met once had descended on him with her little family. It was the last thing he needed.

"Look, I'll go, get washed up, brush my teeth, have some of that fine-smelling coffee of yours, and make the calls."

"Eric." The halting quality of Lu's voice caused him to turn. "There's something else." She hesitated, watching him.

"Okay. Shoot," he whispered.

"It's about Kylie. That's the little girl's name."

Eric nodded.

"She's not Ashley's sister."

Eric got a hollow feeling. He knew where this was going.

"She's Ashley's daughter."

"I figured that." He sat down heavily on a cane-back chair and shook his head. "How old is she?"

"Seven," Louise told him. "She's adorable. A real doll. Polite, kind." She squeezed his shoulder.

"Seven," he whispered.

Eric stood and walked down the hall to the bedroom door, opening it quietly. He stared at the child's face. Her image mirrored the fourteen year-old he remembered. *Seven*, Eric thought as he closed the door. *Ashley would have been seventeen.*

"And they had no bags, no clothes, or stuff with them?" he repeated his question from the night before. It made no more sense this morning.

She turned. "No," she said, looking curious. "You're right. I never thought about it until you mentioned it, but they didn't."

He headed for the stairs. The thought nagged at him. Maybe he was being too analytical, too cynical. Combat made you that way. Assess every detail, look at everything. Especially the ones that seemed trivial. They were usually the most important, the ones that could mean the difference between life and death.

No backpack, no change of clothes, toothbrush, not even a stuffed animal for the little girl. It just didn't make sense. There had to be an explanation. But it could wait. It had too. Ashley was in the hospital, there was a seven-year-old sleeping in his guest room, and he had a business to run. He stopped. Maybe Ralph really had pushed them out the front door. If that was the case, Eric wanted to know why.

"Be back in a second," he said as he changed directions and turned toward the living room. Eric went to the generous nook that had doubled as a home office and Elaine's sewing room. Small but cheery, sunlight poured in through the sheer curtains from the east-facing windows. It did nothing to brighten Eric's mood. A phone sat on the small desk, and he could close the door for privacy. He pulled a yellowed slip of paper from the bottom of the top drawer. The last number he had for Ralph.

As he was about to dial, Eric looked at the phone. The message light blinked. He never came into the room to use the phone. He always used his cell or the land-line in the kitchen. Eric picked up the handset. He had a strange premonition. Swallowing hard, Eric pressed play.

A scratchy voice spoke to him. "Eric..." his brother's voice whispered. "I know we...we didn't always get along. But there's something I have to ask you. You remember Ashley, Melissa's daughter? You don't owe me anything, but I got a funny feeling she may show up at your place. Please, if she does, take care of her. Real good care. She's a great kid and she's in bad trouble." Silence followed. "She got into something that..." Ralph started then stopped suddenly. The line went dead. He covered the receiver. Maybe Eric had misjudged his brother.

Chapter Five

Eric replayed Ralph's voice mail three times. Nothing. Not a clue. He stared at the phone, remembering one of his professors defining stupidity as repeating the same thing with the expectation of different results. There was something in his brother's voice, an intonation he'd never heard from Ralph— regret, fear, a plea for help? Eric tried returning the call twice. The number on caller ID was the same one he had in his drawer. A recorded message told him the number was no longer in service.

Ashley was running away from something and Ralph knew about it. He wasn't the reason. An abusive boyfriend, the police, bad guys? What could have happened to bring her to his door. Leaving everything and dragging her daughter six hundred miles through a monsoon wasn't a schoolgirl whim. This was something heavy. Had she brought the danger with her? What about him, Lu, and everyone she came in contact with? He needed answers.

"Eric." Lu opened the door, holding a cup of steaming coffee. "I thought you forgot this." She brought the mug in and stopped, studying his face. "You okay?"

"Yeah, I'm fine." He took a deep breath and cleared his throat. "Just an old message I missed."

Eric took the mug.

"Could you bring your coffee into the kitchen? Please." She gestured. Her eyebrows were raised, but she wore a soft look. "There's someone I want you to meet."

Eric swallowed and nodded, following his mother-in-law as he ran through his options. When they arrived in the kitchen, Eric stood facing the little girl he'd seen the night before. The child was very thin. She had Ashley's large, dark eyes and dimples carved into her shallow cheeks. In the daylight her short hair looked dark-brown, like her mother's. Kylie looked so frightened and alone. His throat tightened. She sat at the table, eyes downcast, wearing the same worn clothes she had the night before. She was without a doubt the most adorable little girl he had ever seen.

"Eric. This is Kylie." The child stood and approached him slowly, her lips pushed together tightly.

"Hello, Kylie," Eric said, holding out his hand. "It's very nice to meet you."

The little girl looked at Louise, then put her tiny hand in Eric's and shook it. Her grip was so strong it caught Eric off guard. "Hello," she whispered in a voice that mimicked her mother's soft drawl.

"Did you sleep okay?" Eric said, unsure what to ask this sad little stranger.

"Yes, sir." She nodded. "I did."

Eric looked at his mother-in-law. "You rest here with Aunt Lu, today. Your mommy's sick, but I promise she'll be home real soon."

"Yes, sir. I will," Kylie repeated, her small face deadly serious as she moved behind Louise.

"Now, come on. Sit down and have some eggs and

pancakes." Louise pushed Kylie gently and pointed to the table, putting a bottle of maple syrup in front of her. The little girl glanced at Eric and sat down. She closed her eyes and mouthed a silent prayer. Louise raised her eyebrows and looked at Eric. He shrugged as a smile crossed his face.

Kylie attacked her breakfast. Eric watched, sipping his coffee and picking at a piece of cinnamon toast. He wondered how long it had been since this little girl had eaten a good meal. When she finished, Kylie inhaled a full glass of orange juice, then sat quietly, hands folded as she looked back and forth between Eric and Louise.

"Would you like some more?" Lu offered. Kylie's face lit up.

"Yes, ma'am. If it's okay?"

"Of course, honey." Louise nodded and filled her plate.

Kylie hesitated. "Back home none of us ate till everyone had food."

Eric touched her soft, silky hair and smiled. "You eat your fill."

He motioned for Lu to join him in the hallway. "Look, I know it's asking a lot, but could you look after her for a few hours. I have some things to check on."

"Sure," she said. "Do what you have to. We'll be fine. She needs a bath and I'll see if Cuffy's has some clothes her size. I washed what she had on but they could still walk away on their own." Louise shook her head.

"You're too good to me." Eric kissed her forehead. He went to a drawer next to the stove and pulled out two one-hundred-dollar bills. "Here. This should cover whatever you need."

"Okay, but it may cost you. I'm feeling like Chinese take-out tonight." She grinned at him.

Eric ran upstairs to get cleaned up. He took his cell phone and speed-dialed the marina.

"What's happening, boss?" Bobby asked when he heard Eric's voice.

"Some strange shit. You wouldn't believe it if I told you. I gotta ask you to handle things today, at least for a while." Eric knew Bobby loved being left in charge. He could imagine his friend's wide grin.

"You got it. Call me later, and tell me what's happenin'."

"Thanks, Bob. Will do." He pushed the button to end the call.

After he downed the cup of coffee and brushed his teeth, Eric ran downstairs and retrieved Rebecca Walsh's number. He put it into his cell while he thought about Ralph and the cryptic phone message. Expecting Rebecca's voice mail, Eric was surprised when she picked up on the first ring.

"Hi, Eric?" she asked.

"What's up?"

"Can you bring Kylie over to my office? I'd like to talk with her."

"I guess. Since you know her name I assume you've spoken to Ashley this morning?"

"First thing." Rebecca confirmed. "She acted withdrawn. Secretive. Almost surly—like I was prying. Look, I'm no detective. But what you were saying last night about them arriving so unexpectedly got me thinking."

"And?"

"Like I said. I wasn't satisfied with her answers.

When I asked her about the potential abuse and how she got to your house her answers were vague. She wanted to get rid of me."

"What do you mean?"

"Said she just happened to find your address and decided to take off and find you. Does that make any sense?"

"Of course not." Eric's mind was working overtime. "What about that bag comment? Did you ask about that?"

"Yep." Another short silence. "Said she had no idea what I was talking about. Claimed it was the pain-killers."

"That's possible." Eric agreed. "That stuff can give you crazy dreams or hallucinations."

"It could except for one thing." She paused. "I asked the nurses. They told me they didn't use any. Just an IV drip and a sedative. And when I asked about the abuse, Ashley dodged the question. When I tried to press her she stonewalled me."

"Maybe it was something she wanted to forget. You said the injuries were old."

"It's possible, except for that nasty cut on her face."

Eric remembered the fresh bruise and swelling on her face last night.

"I'll get Kylie and bring her over when she and Louise get back."

"Maybe she can help. I hate to use a child, but sometimes they can shed a light on a situation. Like what happened and why they appeared at your house. I'm pretty good with kids. I promise I'll be gentle with her.

"You said last night you were willing to take them in. To let them stay with you," Rebecca said before she hung up. "We have some paperwork you have to sign. We can do that when you bring Kylie by."

He thought for a moment. "I did." He *had* promised to look after them. "Okay. We can talk later." Eric knew he sounded tentative, even reluctant. Everything he was hearing raised more doubts.

There was silence on Rebecca's end. "You're not changing your mind, are you?"

"No," he told her. But Eric had so many questions. He wanted to talk to Ashley himself.

First, he had two more calls to make.

****

"Dennis Police Department, Officer Monroe. You're being recorded," the officer said with rehearsed precision.

"Can I speak to Detective Flaherty, please? Tell him it's Eric Montgomery calling."

"Yes, sir. I'll try his line."

Fifteen seconds of dead air was followed by a robust, "Hello. Been too damn long, buddy. You doing okay?"

"Yeah, better all the time. Thanks for asking."

"Okay. What's the deal? You need a parking ticket fixed?" The heavy voice at the other end gave a throaty chuckle.

"No. Wish it was that simple."

"Well, just ask. I'm your man."

Eric and Buzz Flaherty went back to elementary school. Both had been champion wrestlers in high school. Buzz enlisted right after 9/11 and ended up as a warrant officer assigned to the Army's Criminal

Investigation Division. Eric finished college and went the OCS route; both served multiple tours in the Middle East and had a long-standing friendship. He was one of the few Eric let inside the wall he'd built around himself after Elaine's accident. Buzz had been a willing shoulder more than once.

"I need something that may stretch your rules, Buzz. Nothing illegal but I need info about someone who arrived at my place last night. She needs help, but before I get involved I want to make sure I'm not harboring a fugitive or God knows what else. If it's asking too much I understand."

Eric heard the echo of footsteps and a door close on his friend's end.

"I believe as a decorated veteran and leading citizen you're showing good judgment and trying to protect the public from possible risk."

A grin worked its way across Eric's face. "Thanks, Buzz. I couldn't have said it better myself."

"What's the name you want searched?" Buzz asked.

"Ashley Fitzhugh. Twenty-four. Lived in Norfolk, Virginia."

"Any SSAN?"

"Sorry, no. She appeared on my doorstep last night in that nor'easter. Used to live in my brother's house. The address is 24 South Eucalyptus in Norfolk."

"And you think she might be in trouble?"

"I don't know what to think. This is right out of a mystery novel. I just want to make sure she's not public enemy number one before I take her in."

"Anyone else I'd turn down flat, but you, man. No question."

"Thanks, Rodney."

"Eric, use my given name once more and the whole deal goes south!"

Eric heard his friend laugh.

"Scout's honor...Buzz. It'll be our secret."

"Sounds good. Besides, you know the chief is Bobby's godfather. He loves you."

"That's the trouble with the Cape. Too damn incestuous. And thanks."

"As soon as I know, you'll know."

Eric grinned at the exchange and hit End. His next call would be more difficult.

He sat staring at the cell before making the call, knowing this one would bring back memories. Not all of them as pleasant as his casual banter with Buzz.

He called up the name from his address book and hit Send...

"Naval Intelligence. Commander Lipton." The voice was exactly the way Eric remembered it. Soft and mellow with a lazy drawl—from a small man who could outthink you or kill you half a dozen ways and never leave a trace.

"Lip?"

"Holy shit." There was a pause. "Is this who I think it is?" The soft laugh brought a tight feeling to Eric's throat. He swallowed hard. He and Commander Ronald Lipton had teamed up on half a dozen missions. Lip outranked him by a stripe, but it never got in the way of their friendship. They'd hit it off the day they met and never looked back. Eric called up the image of the RPG that would have vaporized his buddy and blown his ashes into the stratosphere... until he pushed Lip behind a building.

"In the flesh."

"You retired, remember? Supposed to be living the easy life." Lip sighed and paused. Eric could anticipate his friend's question. This seasoned, hard-as-nails officer had a soft spot for special friends. Few ever saw it. Eric was one of the lucky ones. "How're you doing? We tried calling you...a lot." Lip's words were quiet and compassionate.

He and his wife Jennifer had come up for Elaine's funeral. They'd called a dozen times. But like so many of Eric's cadre of friends, Eric had shut them out in the months following the deaths.

"I feel terrible, Rick. Jen and I've wanted to invite you..."

"Don't sweat it." Eric had no time for apologies. "It's my fault. I got lost for a while. I'm getting better."

And though it went against all logic Eric felt a change happening. The appearance of Ashley and her daughter had been like a cold shower after a long night of drinking. Confusion and curiosity mixed with a possible dose of anger. But more than anything, Eric felt energized. Since the girls' sudden and unexplained arrival, he had reason to think of something other than the death of his wife and unborn daughter.

"I need your help with something."

"Okay. Just ask. I'm your man," his friend said evenly. "What are you looking for?"

Eric swallowed and whispered, "My brother."

Chapter Six

Early May. Damp and drizzly with Norfolk's characteristic humidity. The nondescript sedan sat in the Wal-Mart parking lot just off the beltway that skirted the city. Best place for the business at hand. Eleven p.m. The only vehicles belonged to the handful of employees inside. The Director lit his third cigarette of the hour. His window was cracked open, letting the smoke exit and the pungent fragrance of exhaust, asphalt, and the distant Atlantic in. He checked his watch. His visitor was late. Maybe he'd skipped town. Not a bad choice since he and his associates were not lenient with failure.

As he was about to abandon his vigil a single headlight appeared in his mirror. Somehow his quarry had found the back entrance, emerging from behind the mammoth department store. Perhaps this man was more resourceful than he thought. The vehicle approached cautiously. The driver had good reason for caution. The Director suffered no fools—failure was unknown in his vocabulary.

The vehicle, a scarred utilitarian van, approached, slowed, then parked twenty feet away. The Director threw his cigarette on the damp pavement as he opened the door. He gave the driver of the van a nod and smiled for reassurance. A passenger slumped low in his seat. Backup. The Director assumed the passenger had a

MAC 10, 12-gauge, or something equally lethal, poised to cut him in half at the first sign of trouble.

Good luck. He smiled.

"Got a headlight out." The Director pointed at the driver's side as he approached the van slowly. He shook his head. "Not a good idea in our line of work. It attracts attention."

The man in the van nodded, sitting up, and stiffening in his seat. "Yeah. I'll take care of it."

"You missed the targets?"

"Can't figure it." He nodded toward his companion. "We watched that damn house for two weeks. Had their routine down. Can't figure how the girls or the old man got away," he repeated with a hint of frustration in his husky voice.

"Shit happens sometimes. Can never figure *every* detail. But I am surprised." The Director studied the driver. "You came highly recommended," he said as he arrived at the van. He stumbled and shook his head. He bent, pretending to examine the driver's side tire. A small device emerged from his sleeve. The Director kept it concealed in his left hand. "Tire needs some air, too." He pointed.

"Take care of that, too." The driver stared coolly, adding, "You own an auto repair shop or something?"

The Director smiled. "No, just trying to help. Got half your money in the car. I'll get it. Wanted to make sure it was you," he said casually. "I'll give you the rest when you bring us the girl and her daughter." As he stood he moved his hand skillfully, placing the sticky side of the compact package on the wheel.

The Director walked back and opened his door, picking up an envelope. It contained paper cut in the size of bills with twenties at each end in case the man checked. He returned to the van and tossed it to the driver. "Make sure you finish the job this time. You want to count it?"

The man in the van looked at his partner and shook his head. "No. I trust you," he answered and handed it to his partner.

Your mistake, the Director thought as he gave a nod, got into his vehicle, and slowly headed for the exit. After a hundred yards he extracted a small detonator from the sedan's glove box, counted to five, and pressed the button. As a blinding burst of orange flame lit the sky the driver departed the Wal-Mart and headed to the ramp that lead to Interstate 95 and back to Washington. He'd switch vehicles at the coffee shop where he'd picked this one up. Just in case someone spotted the meeting.

He shook his head as the glow illuminated the parking lot and the dull gray of the building beyond.

"Fuck-up," he muttered to himself, knowing he should have dealt with the girl himself. "I don't give second chances!"

Chapter Seven

Eric sat in the Cape Cod Hospital parking lot, considering his options. He was an adrenaline junkie—lived for tense, hard-hitting situations that demanded split-second timing and courage. Melodrama was not in his repertoire. And the last eighteen hours had played out like an afternoon soap opera.

He'd told Lip the story of the girls' arrival and the strange call from Ralph, leaving out the more graphic details like Ashley fainting in his living room and her miscarriage. It was irrelevant—or so he surmised. His friend sounded as dumbfounded as he was. He agreed to do a search for intel on Ralph, find out his status, and call back ASAP.

Eric found Bobby's cell number on speed-dial and pressed Send. "Hi, Bob. What's happening'?"

"Got the new fuel pump for the Bertram. And Ronny fixed the exhaust system on that thirty-foot Duffy."

Eric nodded. That big Bertram was a high-end luxury cruiser. Sleek, comfortable, and expensive. It was for sale. If Eric could find a buyer, he'd make a nice commission. Multiple five figures. The Duffy was different—a classic fishing vessel. High, sharp bow, beamy and seaworthy. Something you could ride out a storm in.

"Sounds good," he told his friend. "I'll be back as

soon as I can. Probably tomorrow. Anything else?"

"Well, yeah." Bobby hesitated. "Got a couple of calls about some overdue bills and another one that said we overpaid by two hundred bucks. I tried to talk to 'em. Didn't know what you'd want me to say."

"It's not your fault." Eric groaned inwardly. "Bad enough being behind with the vendors. We can't be overpaying on top of that. Not this time of year. I'll straighten it out. Who was it?"

"Reynolds Fuel Oil, our local supplier."

"Well." Eric shrugged. "If we've got to be in anyone's good graces, better them. When gas and diesel prices go through the roof and supplies get tight mid-summer maybe they'll remember we paid in advance. Oh, did that new kid start today?"

"Rocco? Yeah, Rick. Hell he was here before I was at seven. He's all over the place. Nice kid."

"Yeah. Seemed that way. Heard good things about him."

Eric knew Bobby was right about their payables. The marina office and paperwork were a mess. And that was being charitable. They needed to find some help.

"I'm gonna hire somebody as soon as I get this situation taken care of. Gotta be some college kid home for the summer that has some computer or office skills." Eric would make some calls, maybe put a flyer in all the local haunts and post it by midweek when he got out from under the Ashley situation.

"Sounds like a plan," Bobby said. Eric knew his foreman was dying to hear the details of what happened last night. "Come on. You gonna give me a clue what's going on?"

"No time right now, but it'll blow you away. Talk

to you soon."

"All right. You got it." Bobby sounded disappointed as he hung up.

Eric had ignored the office for too long. It hadn't reached critical. Until now. He clicked off his cell, left the truck, and headed for the hospital's main entrance, trying to think of a strategy for approaching Ashley. Play the nice guy, be sympathetic. The poor girl had come 600 miles to find him and just suffered a miscarriage. He knew less than nothing about that, but it had to be traumatic. Or should he play bad cop and get in her face? She'd descended on him out of the dark, unexpected and uninvited. Picturing her standing in that downpour in her old navy slicker Eric decided on the former. He'd try nice guy as long as it worked.

He asked the woman at the information desk where to find her. She was on the second floor in the obstetrics ward. Room 234. He walked by the elevator and ran up the stairs two at a time. It was a game he played to challenge himself. Eric felt winded when he reached the landing. He knew he was in better shape than ninety-nine percent of the population but promised himself he'd begin working out again next week.

On the second floor, Eric turned right, following the signs. When he arrived at room 234 the door was closed. He looked in through the narrow window. Ashley lay on her bed, face in a pout, surrounded by men and women in white coats listening attentively to the doctor he'd met last night. Eric crossed the hall and sat down on one of the sterile plastic chairs. A nurse walked by. She was young, stunning, and had a smile that lit up the hallway. She nodded and raised her eyebrows. The nurse looked like Elaine. He closed his eyes.

It had been the Christmas before last. Seven months after their marriage. Josh Groban sang in the background. Elaine loved his voice. They lay on the floor wrapped in the thick quilt Louise had made as a Christmas present. The fire crackled as Eric searched for Elaine's liquid, pale-blue eyes. He found them. Eric was sure he could walk right into them and get lost. It would be fun to try. A smile crossed his face as he lay back on one of the small pillows they'd stolen from the couch.

Elaine smiled back and let out a long breath. "You think it'll still be this good?" she asked as she turned, looking satisfied and at peace. She propped herself on one elbow to face him. "Even when we're seventy-five?" Elaine laughed in the musical way Eric loved.

He stared at the ceiling. Sometimes his eyes hurt when he looked at Elaine. Her perfect, heart-shaped face, flawless skin, those eyes, that smile. It wasn't fair. She was just too damn beautiful!

"I guarantee it," he whispered and reached over to tickle her. She giggled. He found her soft, slender body with his eyes. It had grown fuller, richer in the last two months. He noticed she'd refused her favorite Cabernet at dinner. Eric tried to hide the smile. He couldn't. "Are you going to tell me?"

"Tell you? About what?" Elaine pretended.

Her eyes gave her away.

He turned toward her and raised his eyebrows.

Elaine pushed her full lips into a pout. She couldn't hold the expression. She turned and squeezed him so tightly he protested. "I was waiting for Christmas Day, Ricky!" she said, scolding him. Then she laughed out loud. "But since that'll be in"—she craned her neck to find the anniversary clock on the mantel—"ten minutes, I guess I can tell you now. Yes," she said beaming at him with a proud smile. "You're going to be a father!"

"Mr. Montgomery. Are you all right?" It was the obstetrician from last night. The one conducting rounds in Ashley's room.

Eric sat up abruptly and brought his hand to his eyes. "Yeah, Doc. I'm fine. How's Ashley?"

"Seems all right. Stronger. Fortunately, it was early in her pregnancy so there should be no complications. She's anxious and a little irritable," the doctor answered with a smile. "I think she wants to get out of here. And considering the circumstances that's understandable."

Eric raised his eyebrows. "And?"

"She should be fine by tomorrow. That scrape on her face has turned nasty, though. I can't send her home with an infection."

Eric nodded. "Makes sense. All right if I speak to her?"

"Sure." As the doctor started to walk away he turned toward Eric. "I may be overstepping my authority, but…" He paused. "I'd say that Ashley's been through some pretty hard times. Social work's not in my job description, but I care about my patients. We haven't heard from Rebecca. I hope Ashley's going to live with you. If not, Social Services has to call DCF and start the process of finding a place for her and her daughter to live." His face said it wasn't the alternative he'd choose.

"They'll be staying with me," Eric assured the doctor. Despite the mystery, he couldn't turn them out. Eric set his jaw and crossed the hall. He knocked on her door quietly. When he opened it, she looked away quickly, pulling her hands from moist eyes.

"Hi." She nodded.

"Ashley." He nodded back. "How're you feeling?"

"Better," she whispered, turning to face him. Her jaw squared. "Thanks for helpin'." Ashley smiled weakly and looked out the window again. "It's so pretty here." She looked at the harbor then back at Eric. "How's Kylie?"

"Fine. I can bring her by if you'd like."

Ashley shook her head. "I don't want her to see me here." She pushed her lips together. "She wouldn't understand why I had to come to the hospital, and she's been through a lot. Too much for a little girl," she said in an angry whisper. "She should be home playin' with dolls and ridin' her bike." Ashley paused. "I'm real sorry about what happened. Guess we've all been through a lot." She sighed deeply and shrugged. "How're you doing with all this?"

"Not really sure."

"I figured that." Her words sounded sincere, apologetic. Was she questioning the wisdom of making their long pilgrimage?

Eric found her eyes. She sniffled as they began to fill again.

"I've got some questions." Eric pulled up a chair and sat next to Ashley's bed. He felt compassion but needed some answers...especially after Ralph's call. "How did you manage to get here and why?"

For a moment Eric wasn't sure she'd heard him. She fidgeted with her hospital gown and twisted her lower lip. "'Cause Daddy—that's what I called your brother—always told us you were a good man. Said he wished he could have been more like you," she whispered. "When he said we should leave, I remembered meeting you. You were real nice when you visited us and so…here we are." Ashley's face flushed. The smooth drawl gave her words a hypnotic, almost sultry tone.

"Really." Her explanation caught Eric off guard. He hovered between confusion and doubt. If Ralph harbored such affection and respect for him, why no phone calls, letters, not a word in years, even when their father died.

"That's a surprise. I didn't know he thought that much of me." Eric tried to avoid sarcasm. He failed.

"Don't know about the 'like' part. But he respected you." Ashley shrugged and arched her eyebrows. The dimpled smile she offered had a cryptic quality. She was holding something back. "Always called you special. The good son—smart, athletic, war hero." Her voice held irony, almost amusement, but her face showed no humor.

Ashley studied him very closely. Eric's opinion of her had been off target—one hundred eighty degrees. This girl was no simple recluse. She used her words well. He wondered if Ashley was trying to manipulate him?

"So when he threw you out…" Eric began.

Ashley blew out a breath and held up her hand. "You weren't listening. You'd been drinking last night. I smelled it. I never said he *threw* us out." She fixed him, her enormous eyes narrowed in frustration. "He told us we *should* get out."

Eric played with the distinction. "So you agreed to leave? Just like that?"

Ashley looked at him with frustration. "Yes. I did."

"But you don't know why?"

She shook her head slowly. "Could have been a lot of things. You know what he was like."

Eric nodded. He knew exactly.

Ashley glanced at the doorway then offered, "Maybe it's best you don't know."

"But despite all the questions you expect me to take you in? To help you?" He watched her reactions closely.

"It's your call," she answered after another long pause. "I hope you do. Least till we can get our feet on the ground. It doesn't matter about me. I could get by. Always have. But for Kylie's sake—yes." Ashley played her trump card. She'd turned stubborn and prickly. But could he abandon Kylie—turn her over to the state? Ashley had him and she knew it.

Touché.

"I got a strange phone message from Ralph." He found her eyes again. They held his, giving no ground. "It sounded like he was afraid. Said he was in trouble and asked me to help you if you showed up."

Confusion crossed her face for a split second, followed by something he'd seen too many times in too many faces: Fear. "He called you? Ralph...called *you?*"

Eric nodded. "It was an old message. Don't know how old. Why?"

Her mouth fell open. Ashley looked out the window. "No...no reason."

She turned her face back to Eric, gave him an artificial smile, and shrugged again. The innocent expression that materialized would have done her seven-year-old proud. "Maybe he was worried 'bout us." She was trying to look casual. "You never know. Daddy—Ralph—had a lot of balls in the air."

Something he'd said hadn't fit with her. The comment about Ralph. But she'd done a good job covering it. Hadn't missed a beat. Ashley was playing him and stonewalling him at the same time. This was one clever girl. He *had* underestimated her. Badly. She'd read him and found his weakness easily. He wouldn't turn that sweet little girl out or over to DCF.

"All right. You can come home with me," he agreed, knowing he might be opening himself up to disaster. "I'll talk to the billing department and get that straightened out. The doctor says you'll be released tomorrow if your face is better."

Ashley touched the bruise. "Yeah." She winced. "Walked right into a street sign in all that rain. Did a number on my cheek."

Eric didn't believe her for a second.

"About the money." Ashley sounded frustrated. "I'll pay you back soon as I can," she promised.

Eric stood and approached her bed. He nodded and held out his hand. "All right. We'll talk about the details later. I'll be at work this afternoon. Call me when they give you a discharge time."

Ashley nodded and offered her hand. He shook hers firmly and let it go as he backed away. Eric watched her closely. Was she playing him? He thought so but…he couldn't be sure. And if she was, what was her game? She never explained how they got to the Cape. *Diversion and misdirection*, he thought in a mix of frustration and begrudging respect. Ashley was better than some Al Qaeda operatives he'd interrogated. The questions would have to wait. Eric couldn't spend the afternoon jousting with her.

As he studied her it occurred that she'd made a remarkable recovery since her arrival last night. She looked damn good for someone who'd been through a 600-mile pilgrimage, a monsoon, and a miscarriage. Ashley cleaned up well. She was pretty. Damn pretty. He'd give her that. But this Ashley showed none of the innocence and wonder he remembered from the teenager he'd met a decade earlier. Despite that, there was something—a subtle chemistry when she touched him or found his eyes. *But is she dangerous?* he asked himself again. Eric needed to find out. While he got a handle on what was going on he wasn't about to let her double-talk him.

"Here's my card." He put it on the nightstand. "Call my cell if you need anything." He turned the card over and took out a pen. "Here's my mother-in-law's number if you can't get me. She's taking care of Kylie."

"Thank you for everything…Eric," she whispered, showing him a soft smile. It had a shy, innocent quality. Ashley blushed as she found his eyes. Suddenly, the adorable fourteen-year-old reappeared.

He cleared his throat and swallowed, caught off-guard by the high-speed metamorphosis from surly to sweet, cunning to cuddly. Was this the real Ashley or was she using that pretty face and feigning vulnerability to win his sympathy?

"You *are* a good man," she added, looking thoughtfully at him.

Yes. This is one clever girl. She nodded, her eyes holding his as he headed toward the door. Eric wondered. Had Ashley somehow become involved with one of Ralph's crazy schemes? Did it backfire on both of them?

"One clever woman," he repeated aloud as he ran down the stairs. Maybe that was her problem. She was too clever for her own good.

He called Louise from the parking lot. She picked up on the second ring. "Hi, we're just about back to the house. How's Ashley?"

"She's all right," Eric offered, not wanting to burden his mother-in-law with his confusion and frustration. "What about you and Kylie? How'd you make out?"

"Great. Got some cute stuff for Kylie and a couple of things for Ashley so she doesn't have to wear those ratty old things home from the hospital. Had to guess at the sizes but they'll do until she has a chance to shop." She paused and lowered her voice. "Kylie's asleep in the back seat."

"Great. Look," he hesitated, knowing Louise would balk. "Could you bring Kylie to Becky's office?"

"I guess so. Why?"

"She told me that when there was some question about the circumstances surrounding abuse they like to talk to family members."

"*Circumstances surrounding abuse!*" Louise whispered loudly. "Jesus, Eric. She's a shy, frightened, seven-year-old kid. I'll give Becky a call. The last thing Kylie needs is to be cross-examined."

"Don't shoot the messenger. I'm just telling you what she asked."

A few minutes later, she called back. "Okay. Becky promised to go easy with Kylie, but I want to be the one to bring her. Said she had some papers for you to look over and sign."

Louise was right. She and Kylie had bonded. If Becky had any chance of getting the truth from Kylie, Lu was the one to take her. He'd stop by the marina and see how Bobby was doing.

"Great. When you get home we'll call in that order for Chinese food."

Chapter Eight

"So this girl just appeared at your door with her daughter and a dog?" Bobby's gray eyes sparkled. He wore a curious expression as he stifled a laugh. "Hell. That sounds like something on one of those woman's channels."

Eric sat across from him on one of the marina's picnic benches. "Hmmm. My buddy the decorated Ranger. Jeez, Bob, didn't know you were a fan. Is that Hallmark or Lifetime?" Eric asked. It was his turn to hide a smile.

Bobby flushed. "Honest to God. It's not me, it's Gwen." He shook his head and scowled. "That's how I spend my Saturday nights. The early part anyway."

Bobby broke into a grin. They both laughed.

Eric proceeded to give his best friend the abbreviated version of the last twenty-four hours. Ashley's arrival and the questions it raised, never mentioning Ralph's phone message, the miscarriage, or the calls to Buzz or Lip.

"You gonna take 'em in?"

Eric nodded. "At least until they get settled. Hell, I can't leave 'em on the street. The little girl's only seven and seems like a real sweet kid. I'll try and help Ashley find some work. Maybe get her a place. Must be good at something." He shrugged.

"Maybe she's a computer guru." Bobby laughed.

"Could help straighten the office out."

Eric shook his head and shrugged. "She wouldn't be on the top of my list." He stood and headed to the parking lot. "Look, I'll be in early tomorrow, but I've gotta pick Ashley up from the hospital and get her settled. Thanks for taking over today."

"No sweat, boss. I love it. Got these guys doing jumping jacks twice a day." His friend laughed and slapped Eric on the back as he got into his Jeep. "Hey. By the way, what's Ashley look like?" Bobby asked as he shut Eric's door.

Eric thought for a minute. "Last night—like a drowned cat." He pictured her at the hospital. "This afternoon. Cute. Thin. Short dark hair. Nice smile and…"

He caught Bobby hiding a grin.

Eric stopped and cleared his throat. "I don't know. I'll bring her by sometime. You can judge for yourself," he promised.

His young friend laughed. "Are you *blushing*, Lieutenant Montgomery? I think you like her."

Eric frowned at the thought. "Don't be ridiculous." He cleared his throat a second time, but Bobby held his smile. Eric ignored the thought that he might have any attraction to Ashley. It was ridiculous. He'd only known her for a couple of days, and she was a mystery wrapped in a riddle.

He looked at Bobby. Eric wasn't the only local hero. His friend was tall, good-looking, and athletic. And Eric had to admit, his pal's dark, curly hair, strong features, and cleft chin set him apart. The local girls loved him. He'd been a staff sergeant in the Rangers and had his share of hardware to show for his years in the Middle East. Bobby had an impressive combat résumé. They had been on a dozen missions together. There was no one Eric would rather have beside him when the shit hit the fan.

But Bobby was way off base. He had to be. Ashley was cute, had that to-die-for accent, nice smile, but…hell, she was spinning a tale at best, outright lying at the worst. Using her situation and her daughter to gain his favor. Eric shook his head as he started his Jeep, hit the accelerator, and left a trail of gravel as he took a right turn toward Route 28 and home. He wanted to hear about Rebecca's session with Kylie.

Like Ashley? He shook his head as a frown crossed his face. No way!

****

When Eric pulled into his crushed-stone driveway he expected to see Louise's blue Camry. No sign of it. He pulled out his cell phone and was about to call when he saw her buzzing down the street. She parked next to Eric's Jeep. He watched as she got out of the car. Kylie followed slowly. The little girl looked at the ground.

"Hi, Kylie," Eric offered.

"Hello, Uncle Eric," she whispered back, still staring at the ground.

"Can you go sit on the porch, honey? Then we'll go inside and put your new things away." Lu handed Kylie a bag. A pink teddy bear as large as Kylie stuck out of the top. "I'll be there in just a minute. Promise."

Kylie took the bag, eyes still studying the ground as she nodded and headed to the house. She sat motionless on the swing suspended under the window on the back porch, waiting for Louise.

"Well?" Eric shrugged.

"I got another bag in the back." She reached in and pulled the second bag out as she looked toward the back porch. "Talk to you later. I don't want the poor child to wait while we talk. I'll let her in." Kylie rocked in the swing. Her enormous eyes, a gift from her mother, were fixed on an invisible specter as she clung to her new teddy bear like a life buoy.

****

The three of them had devoured the Chinese food like a school of hungry sharks. Eric sat on the back porch smoking his nightly Marlboro. He allowed himself one cigarette a day. Elaine hated the habit. He'd picked it up in the army and could never quite shake it. Eric tried to limit his smoking to one after dinner. His small way of respecting Elaine's memory. The clatter of dish washing came through the open window. Louise had shooed him out of the kitchen, asking Kylie to help her.

During dinner Eric had told Kylie her mother would be coming home tomorrow. She brightened. It was the closest thing she'd shown to a smile. Eric still wanted to talk to Lu about the session with Rebecca. So far there'd been no chance.

The late spring sun worked its way below the distant treetops on the far side of the street as Eric crushed his cigarette in an empty flower pot. He moved the swing casually, inhaling the fragrance of the late spring flowers—the ones Elaine had worked so hard to grow. They needed work. He'd have to get to them himself or call a landscaper. As he scanned his long narrow side street something caught his attention. A utilitarian van he'd never seen before, parked behind a large maple, almost out of sight.

As he stood and squinted to see if anyone was inside he heard the screen door open and looked, expecting to see Louise. Instead, Kylie came out clinging to her new teddy bear. Rusty followed close behind.

"Hi, honey." Eric smiled.

"Hello, Uncle Eric," she said politely. Lips firmly posed in a pout, Kylie took a tentative step, surveying the large backyard. Eric and Elaine had bought the house three years ago because of it.

Elaine had run down the stairs after seeing the master bedroom with dormers facing Nantucket Sound. From the low hill the house stood on, the blue-gray waves were just visible above the trees. You could close your eyes and smell the ocean.

"Oh, Ricky. I love it. Just love it!" Elaine's voice echoed with excitement. "Don't you?" The house offered more than a view. "Look at this yard." She swooned. The PJM rhododendrons were in bloom, while the forsythia shed their yellow mantle. "Perfect for kids. Lots of kids." Elaine raised her eyebrows and giggled. The lot was an oversized acre of low, rolling grass dotted with red maples, oaks, and the Cape's traditional white pines. A pristine pond sat to the left, guarded by tall grass, separating the lot from their neighbors. Conservation land bordered the property to the right. The house was an estate sale at a bargain price. Eric had heard about it from one of his customers. The property was perfect.

"Do you think we can afford it?" Elaine took his hand and asked when the broker went to answer a call on her cell.

Eric had done the math. Despite the owner's need

to sell, it was still more than they wanted to pay. It would be tight for a few years. He was just getting the marina back in shape, and Elaine's salary as a music teacher was modest. But it was an incredible opportunity. As he watched his wife's eyes sparkle and the loving, reverent way she touched everything in the house, Eric knew there was no choice.

"Sure. It may mean postponing that European vacation for a couple of years," he told her. They'd both studied French and talked of spending a month touring Normandy, the Loire Region, and Provence. That was just a dream. This pristine home was a reality and she was right: it was everything a young couple could hope for. "Let's do it." He nodded.

She ran across the kitchen and hugged him so tightly he couldn't breathe. "We'll be so happy here. Just wait and see…"

"It's real nice here," Kylie said as she sat down on the step next to Eric's chair. Rusty joined her, wagging his stubby tail with enthusiasm. The little girl touched his curly head lovingly and studied the generous yard. "Just like she promised."

"Promised?" Eric asked. "Someone said it would be nice here, Kylie?"

She looked up and put her lips together, nodding, her large eyes fixed on him. "Yes, sir. Mommy promised. Just like heaven." A sudden look of regret crossed her tiny face. Had she said something she shouldn't have?

"Your mommy said that, Kylie?"

She shrugged. "I…I'm sorry. She made me promise. I'm not s'posed to tell," she whispered. Her eyes filled up as she studied the porch floor. Kylie looked toward the small pond. "Can I go look at the lake now?"

She looked as if she was about to break into tears. Eric didn't want to interrogate her. She'd had enough for today.

"Sure, honey. You and Rusty go check out the pond." He let it go. If anyone had explaining to do, it was Ashley. "Just be careful," he added.

Eric watched her scoot down the steps and run off to the small pond, Rusty at her heels. He was still thinking about what she'd said. Ashley had promised it would be like heaven. A bribe? An incentive to get Kylie's buy-in for the trip? Or…was it possible that Ashley believed what she'd told Kylie?

He heard the door open and smelled the pleasant scent of Lu's perfume. She saw Kylie and shouted a warning. "Stay back. Don't get too close."

"Don't worry. I won't. 'Sides, I can swim real good." For the first time since their arrival, Kylie smiled as she and Rusty explored the pond and the tall grass surrounding it.

Eric looked toward his mother-in-law, turning Kylie's words over in his mind.

He felt her eyes studying him. "You okay? You look confused."

Eric shook his head. "I'm not surprised."

Chapter Nine

"Nothing?" Eric asked, following Kylie and Rusty with his eyes. The giant pink teddy bear sat propped on the lawn, a spectator to his new owner's adventures. "Nothing about how they got here? No details about their life?"

"I wasn't there the whole time. Becky asked me to leave. But I was in the room when Becky asked Kylie how she and Ashley got here. Kylie looked frightened and whispered that she slept a lot. Said she didn't wake up till they got here in the rain. Just remembered being *so* cold and tired. The poor kid even shivered as she talked. If it was an act, this child deserves the Academy Award, Ricky." Louise shrugged.

"She must have said something else," Eric insisted. "Maybe when you left the room."

"Sure. It's possible. All I know is when I was there Becky asked her questions to help her feel comfortable. You know, break-the-ice kind of things. How old she was, where she'd lived. That kind of stuff. Her eyes began to fill up, so Becky stopped. She shook her head and let it go."

Lu continued looking toward the small pond. "Don't get too close, honey," she warned again.

"Promise I won't." Kylie took a step back and waved.

Eric watched her come back to retrieve her stuffed

friend. "She sure loves that stuffed animal." He thought of things that might have been. What their child might have looked like. Would she have grown into one as sweet and beautiful as Kylie, laughing with a magical smile as she chased her dog around their yard?

"She did say Ralph was a nice man."

The comment brought him back. "What?" He shook his head.

"Your brother. Kylie said he was a good guy. Did nice things for her and Ashley."

"Really?" If Ralph was such a good guy, why were they here? For protection? And what about his phone call? Was that for real or something his brother had scripted to create a sense of fear?

Eric jumped as his cell buzzed in the kitchen. He looked toward Kylie. "Let me see who that is. I'm expecting an important call."

By the time he got to his phone it had gone to voice mail. Eric looked at the number. It meant nothing, but he recognized the area code. The same as his brother's—Virginia.

"Can you keep an eye on Kylie?" he called through the open window. "This might be the call I was waiting for. I'd like to return it."

"Sure. Make your call."

Eric played the voice mail. "Eric, this is Lip. Call me back ASAP. We need to talk."

Eric hit re-dial and waited. The phone rang twice, then three times. "Hi," it was a woman's voice.

"Jen?"

"Oh my God. Ricky?"

"Yep."

"Ron said he'd talked to you."

"How are you?" Eric asked.

"More important, how are you, honey? We've been so worried about you..." Her words faded into awkward silence.

"I'm okay. Thanks. Keeping busy with the marina. Trying to put the pieces back together." He didn't want to blow Jennifer off, but he needed his friend. "Is Lip around?"

"Just ran in the shower. He's umpping one of Mattie's softball games in"—she paused—"about thirty-five minutes."

"Okay, don't bother him. Just tell him I called."

"Will do, Eric. Now you take care and promise to get down here real soon for a visit."

"Sounds good, Jen." Eric hung up. His friend called from home to avoid being monitored. He looked at his watch. Assuming Lip wouldn't call with his daughter in the car, it would be two to three hours before they could talk.

Eric walked through the kitchen to the back door. The sound of Kylie's laughter in the backyard was catching. He smiled. When he went onto the porch he saw Lu chasing Kylie and Rusty around the ancient maple that stood between the house and the garage. Kylie held the teddy bear away from her pursuer.

Eric ran down the stairs while Kylie looked back at Louise. Suddenly, the little girl ran into his arms. He hesitated, then picked her up. She stared at him, looking confused. When Eric swung her over his head, Kylie erupted, squealing with delight. Eric found himself facing her, bringing her close to him and squeezing her tightly as her tiny body rocked with the welcome sound of laughter.

As Eric hugged Kylie, something caught his eye. The hidden van came alive, did a U-turn, and sped off toward the main road.

When Kylie was upstairs in bed and Lu was watching a reality show, Eric got into his gym shorts and T-shirt and went to the basement. He unlocked the door that led to his private room. It had lain fallow for too long.

The dehumidifier hummed as he flipped on the light switch and went inside. Eric surveyed the walls covered with photos, memorabilia, medals, and the accompanying citations.

His arsenal rested on the opposite wall in locked cabinets. Eric had been a champion wrestler in college and a natural in several martial arts disciplines in the military. He kept his service issue .45, two 9mm automatics, an illicit M-16, and two 12-gauge shotguns locked away. A generous gun safe beneath his weapons held enough ammunition to start a small war. Outside the gun cabinet were two swords, throwing, commando, and assault knives with varying blade types in different lengths. Next to this deadly array hung his favorite weapon—his crossbow.

Elaine abhorred violence. She never visited his personal domain or asked about his experiences. His tours in Iraq and Afghanistan remained hidden behind a wall of silence. That suited Eric. He had no desire to relate the hellish years that trailed him like the cashboxes hanging from Marley's ghost. Besides, unless you'd been there you could never understand.

The room also served as his gym. An empty forty-five pound bar lay propped on the weight bench. Next to it sat a rack with tandem weights from ten to eighty pounds. After some stretching, Eric sighed and hit the heavy bag—lightly at first to make sure it was hanging properly. Within five minutes he'd worked up a good sweat as he thrust his hands and feet in tight circular arcs, landing blow after blow.

Eric lifted a few weights. He was on his way out of the room when he spotted the picture of his team next to the door. It had been taken the day they landed in Kuwait. Ten men, all strong, deadly, and superbly trained, yet forged into a team they were much more than the sum of their parts. Only five came home. So much loss and for what? Eric had a strange feeling about the last two days. Nothing he could put into words but still…something made the hairs on his neck stand up. It was why he'd decided to revisit his fortress of solitude.

****

He lay on his bed long after his steaming shower, his body tight and sore. It was a feeling he enjoyed. Eric never realized how much he'd missed it. The sheer curtains blew weakly, moved by a soft southerly breeze. The distant sounds of night on Nantucket Sound offered a pleasant counterpoint to the turmoil running through his mind. His TV was tuned to the Red Sox, but Eric was somewhere far away again.

So many questions: Ralph? The kind man from the girls' stories or the scam artist of Eric's memory? Ashley—frightened, innocent victim or first-class manipulator? And Kylie—sweet little girl or the youngest participant in one of Ralph's convoluted schemes?

Just as a dazzling triple riveted his attention on the game, Eric's cell rang. He grabbed it and looked at the number. It was local. Somewhere in Barnstable County. He didn't recognize the number. Maybe a boater desperate to find a slip. That was common this time of year.

He sighed and answered, "Hello, Eric Montgomery."

"Hi. Hope it's not too late?" asked Ashley in her soft drawl. Eric turned and sat at attention, picturing Ashley the way she'd looked that afternoon.

"No. It's...it's fine," he stammered as a warm feeling swept over him. A smile crossed his lips. "I'm glad you called." He couldn't explain it, but he was. Very glad. "Is everything okay? Are you okay?"

"Pretty good. Face is still a little tender, but the doctor said I can come home." She exhaled deeply. "Thank God. I couldn't stand another night in here. It's lonely."

"I'm glad you can come home. I know a little girl who'll be thrilled." His smile broadened as he pictured Kylie's reaction. "Did they say when I can pick you up?"

"'Bout one if it's okay. I know you're real busy and...."

"One's great," Eric interrupted. Why did he sound so anxious? He took a deep breath and cleared his throat. "I mean—I can work with that," he forced a neutral tone.

"Glad to hear it." Silence hung in the cool air. "How's Kylie?"

"Fine. Lu's taking care of her like she was her own." Eric recalled her laughter in the back yard earlier.

"I knew she'd be fine with you." Silence. "Eric,"

Ashley whispered. "I'm real sorry."

"Sorry?" he puzzled. "I don't…"

"'Bout dodging your questions," she broke in. "Not answering you today at the hospital. About how we got to your house. You been so nice. Things been kinda scary lately. You get to a place where you don't trust anybody." Ashley was silent. He could hear her breathing. "But, I…I should have told you." She paused a second time. Eric heard a deep breath, then a second. Gathering her courage? "We took a bus. From Norfolk to Boston. Then to Exit 6 on the Mid-Cape Highway. I had directions and enough to pay for our tickets but no cash left so when we got to the exit we had to walk. It was either that or sit at the bus station and…well, we just couldn't do that. But it was raining so bad. I was worried 'bout Kylie and Rusty."

"Thanks for telling me how you got here." He stopped. "But I still don't know why."

"All I know is Ralph wanted us to leave. He acted scared. So we did what he told us. He didn't want me to tell anyone. But I wanted you to know. I know I can trust you."

"Ralph was really scared?" Eric probed.

"Seemed that way."

"Thanks." It made sense. Fit with the phone call. "Look, I appreciate you calling me, but you should go to sleep," Eric whispered, trying to ignore the pleasant warmth he felt as he talked to her. He felt emotions stir that had lain dormant since that dark night a year ago. "You need your rest," he insisted. "I'll be by at one."

"Okay." He heard her breathing. "The things he said about you. About you being a good man. He was right. Goodnight, Eric," she whispered back and hung up.

He stared at the cell for a long time, replaying her soft, smooth words over and over. She'd given him something. Insights that fit with the cryptic call from Ralph. It wasn't an answer, but it was a beginning. Now, if Ron or Buzz could add flesh to this skeleton then maybe, just maybe, Eric could understand who and what he was dealing with. He lay back, exhaled deeply, and closed his eyes. But it wasn't mystery or danger that came to mind. It was her, Ashley, her grand, velvet eyes, the delicious drawl, and the intoxicating vulnerability that covered her like a cloak. The alien thing that gnawed at Eric, the sensation this enigmatic girl had awakened in him was caring.

Chapter Ten

Eric lay staring at the ceiling, still replaying Ashley's call. Was it possible? His brother the caring man the girls described? He wanted desperately to believe them. Was his dislike for Ralph coloring his judgment? Eric's stomach tightened and burned. A sour taste filled his mouth. He was no detective. This was above his pay grade.

Eric went to the window and looked out on the tranquil Atlantic. The night was calm and soft. So soft. He inhaled deeply. This had been Elaine's favorite time of year. A squirrel skittered down the porch roof as he put his hand on the screen. Transition was in the air, the time when spring blossoms into summer. Far out he could see the running lights of a ship heading southwest—something small heading to New York or the Jersey Shore.

Eric checked his watch. Ten forty-five. No chance he'd hear from Lip tonight. Eric was drained. Needed sleep. He turned off the ball game, throwing the remote on the bed. As he headed to the bathroom, Eric stopped to stare at the picture of Elaine on his dresser. A five-by-seven of the larger one in the living room. She looked up at him, innocent and exquisite, smiling from the garden on their wedding day.

Eric hated drugs. When his men succumbed to narcotics or alcohol abuse he took a hard line. Catching one of them meant an article fifteen and a thirty-day trip to the stockade. But tonight his mind was on overload. Eric pulled out a bottle from his dresser drawer and popped two five-milligram Valium into his mouth. Instead of swallowing the tablets, he chewed them, making for a quick and easy entry into the bloodstream. Returning to his bed, he left his clothes in a heap on the floor. Sleep overtook him in ten minutes.

****

Through a fog he heard the ringing. He was dreaming. Elaine was there. Eric wanted to stay with her—fought to. She was smiling deliciously at him, giggling, beckoning to him, but the ringing was unforgiving, relentless.

Eric gave in and opened his eyes. The morning sunlight streamed in through the sheer curtains, but he could tell by its angle it was early. The air had a damp feel. Last night's cool, fresh breeze was a memory. He rolled over and reached for his cell. It fell off the night table, landing on the floor. The digital clock said 6:22. As he tumbled off the bed Eric grabbed the phone and pressed Talk.

"Yeah," he whispered. "Eric Montgomery."

"Eric, it's Lip."

"Sorry. I was asleep."

"Wake up, buddy!" his friend commanded. "I wanted to call you from home."

"It's okay. I understand." Eric stopped his friend, needing to hear whatever Lip had found out. "What's up?"

"Well..."

"Let me have it. It can't be that bad."

"That's the problem," his friend said with a

tentative voice. "It isn't anything."

"What do you mean?"

"All I could find was name, rank, and serial number. When I tried to dig deeper, I drew a blank."

By this time Eric was up, sitting on the edge of his bed. "What are you talking about? Who could shut you out?" His friend was a senior Naval Intelligence officer in one of the East Coast's largest bases.

"I have no idea. All I know is that his records were pulled by someone a couple of weeks ago—first Friday in May to be exact. I couldn't get them. The computer said, 'File temporarily unavailable.' No hard copies, either. I figured the thing on the computer was a glitch, so I sent my chief over to records. Nothing. Next thing I know I'm getting a call from the ranking officer over there. Jesus, the guy's a rear admiral and he was on the horn before my chief even got back. He sounded tough and curious, too curious—asking me why I was interested. I gave him a BS answer. Told him that Ralph's name came up in a routine inquiry into a security breach. Guy didn't say shit. But I don't know if he bought it."

Eric sat on his bed trying to get his arms around what he was hearing, to put it together with what Ashley had told him. Ralph was frightened by something. And for him to put Ashley and Kylie on the street, to send them to him so suddenly with nothing meant it was no Saturday night barroom scuffle or an angry bookie. No, this was something heavy or dangerous. Maybe deadly.

And it was looking more and more like Ralph had sent them to find him. Eric didn't know who or what to believe. Suddenly, a sick feeling gnawed at his gut. Eric wanted to know what had happened to Ashley's mother.

"Lip, this is damn weird." Eric whispered into the cell. "Ashley told me that Ralph was scared. I hadn't talked to him in years, but the other day, just after they got here, I found a voice mail from him. Don't know how long it had been there. But he *was* scared. Scared shitless."

"*Je-sus*. You never told me that! He called *you?*" Eric heard his friend breathing heavily. "That's FUBAR, Rick." Lip was silent for a minute. "Sounds fucked up." Lip's interest seemed to ratchet up a notch. Like a bloodhound with a fresh hint of the scent.

"It surprised the hell out of me, too. Ralph was small time. Into nickel-and-dime shit. I told you about him." Eric shook his head. "And now, according to what you're telling me, as far as the Navy's concerned, he doesn't exist."

"Oh no. He exists. At least his footprint. Name, rank, and serial number. But his records—what you Army guys call a 201 file—are missing."

"Okay. Thanks." Eric didn't know what else to say. Maybe he could find out more from Ashley. Assuming she really did know anything more.

"Look, don't worry. I'm not giving up on this. I've got the bit in my teeth. I'm gonna find out what's going on."

"I appreciate it. I know I'm putting you on thin ice, especially if this really is bad business. But can you find out where he is—his current duty assignment? I may want to come down there and… and talk to him."

"You got it. I'll solve this if it kills me."

"Ron. You're an old friend, so do us both a favor."

"Okay. Shoot."

"Make sure that doesn't happen."

****

Eric showered, got dressed, and went down to eat breakfast with Lu and Kylie. As he was about to take a mouthful of eggs, Louise kicked him gently. When he looked up he saw Kylie with her hands together and eyes closed. She mouthed a silent prayer.

"I'll pick your mommy up and be back here before dinner, honey," he promised with a reassuring smile when she finished.

"Thanks, Uncle Eric." Kylie came around the table slowly and gave him a quick hug. Then she backed away and returned to her chair, attacking a big helping of scrambled eggs and English muffins heaped with a mammoth topping of orange marmalade.

Lu found Eric's hand and squeezed it. When he found her eyes, they glistened. "See you this afternoon."

He nodded and stood to leave.

Eric went to the marina and spent the next few hours, staring absently at the desktop. The QuickBooks software he'd called up stared back at him. His mind was on overload. He kept picturing Ashley on Friday night—wet, cold, and exhausted. Eric remembered their sparring at the hospital and her surprising phone call last night. They made him feel—what? He wanted her and Kylie to be safe, but what else? Hell, he'd only seen Ashley twice. What was he thinking...

"You okay, boss?"

Bobby stood in the doorway with a clipboard.

"Sure. I'm fine," Eric snapped. "Why?"

"'Cause you've been staring into space for five

minutes." Bobby shrugged and showed a grin. "Is it…her?"

"Her? Who the hell are you talking about?"

Bobby knitted his brows and grinned. "You know who, Eric." He paused. "Her. *Ashley the mystery woman!*" His attempt at a European accent left something to be desired.

He waved Bobby out and scowled, trying to focus on the laptop again. Eric thought about Bobby's question. He'd resigned his commission and come home for two things: Elaine and peace. He'd seen so much death and misery—enough for two lifetimes. Young guys on his team, street kids in rags, the staff sergeant who'd been his mentor and best friend...All dead. Torn in half by AK-47s, RPG rounds, or blown to bits by IEDs. No, he'd come home to find a better life. Or thought he had. First Elaine's death, now this—part jigsaw puzzle, part nightmare. Eric needed to find the truth.

"A penny for your thoughts," Josephine Murray said as she stood in the doorway.

"Hi, Joey."

"Had last night off. Thought you'd remember? I was hoping you'd call."

"Yeah, I remember. I'm real sorry. It's been a crazy weekend."

She shrugged and came inside. "So I heard." She raised her eyebrows. "I'm all ears if you want to share."

Eric exhaled slowly, trying to gather a smile. "Don't want to bore you." Joey was sweet, pretty, available, and interested in him. Eric enjoyed her company. They'd gone out for dinner and a movie once or twice. But Elaine's memory hung over him like a specter. Now this thing with Ralph and Ashley and Kylie.

"No, really, Joey. It's complicated and kinda personal."

Joey looked hurt but managed a smile. "I thought we were friends, Eric. Personal's okay." She stopped and watched him. "Talk to me." She was determined, but Joey was the last person he wanted to talk to right now.

Bobby came to the rescue. "Hey, Boss. Joey." He nodded in her direction. "Sorry to bother you. But I need a few minutes."

Joey looked frustrated. Hurt. "Catch you later. At the Café. See ya, Bobby." She returned his nod, did an about face, and left abruptly.

"Okay. Thanks. Catch you soon," Eric said to Joey. He turned to Bobby. "You needed me?"

"Yeah." Bobby followed Joey with his eyes. "I do." He turned back to Eric. "Nice girl. Cute. And it's no secret she likes you."

"Thanks for the advice." A frown crossed his face. "Look. I know she's trying to help. But I got no time right now."

Bobby held up his hands. "Okay, Boss." Bobby looked around then stepped into the office. His expression softened. "It's been a year, Eric. You know how I felt about Elaine. How everyone felt. But she wouldn't want you to go on like this forever."

Anger surged. Eric bristled momentarily but it passed quickly. He knew his friend didn't counsel the lovelorn. Bobby was trying to help.

"Got no time for this right now," Eric insisted as he stood. "What do you need? I've gotta go pick up

Ashley. I'll call later if I can't get back."

"What do you want me to do about the Jacksons' Sea Ray?" Bobby asked.

The Jackson family had been good customers for three generations. One of the marina's first. Allen had lost his job recently and they were having financial problems.

Eric shrugged, scratching his day-old beard. "What would you do?"

"Hell. You know I go back a long way with Al. He used to catch my touchdown passes in high school. I'd give 'em another month."

"Sounds good to me." Eric stood and patted Bobby on the back. He grabbed his jacket.

Bobby nodded. "See you later."

"Yeah. I'll try and get back." He slipped the windbreaker over his sweatshirt.

"Take your time. The place isn't going anywhere."

Chapter Eleven

"Ashley?" Eric called her as he drove to the hospital.

"Hi. I been waitin' for you. Can't wait to get home. I…I mean to get out of here." Her words tumbled out. A long silence followed. Eric had no regrets that Ashley thought of his house as home. He liked the idea.

"Louise picked up some new things you can wear home if you want. Your choice," Eric said, breaking the long stalemate. "I'll leave them at the nurse's station. Call me when you're ready."

"Thanks. Something new *would* be nice," she enthused in her soft drawl. "See ya in a few minutes."

As Eric was closing his cell, it rang. He opened it, seeing a familiar number. "Buzz?"

"Yep. Sorry it took me so long to get back to you."

His friend sounded tentative, non-committal. Not Buzz's style. Eric's throat tightened, wondering if the next shoe was about to drop.

"What'd you find out?" Eric asked, hoping the answer was something he wanted to hear.

"Ashley's clean. No wants, warrants, no record of any kind."

Thank God. Ashley wasn't a fugitive from justice. Eric slumped in his seat and breathed a sigh of relief. "Thanks, Buzz. Good to know since I'm about to pick her up."

"That's good," Buzz offered.

Eric knew his friend too well. He was holding something back. "You want to give me the rest?"

"Damn! I knew I couldn't fool you." Eric pictured his friend's ruddy face twisting into a frown.

"C'mon. Give. I need to know the whole picture. What's going on?"

"That's the problem. There's nothing but a driver's license on file."

That sounded familiar. Eerily familiar. Shades of Lip's report on Ralph. "What do you mean...nothing?"

"Nothing means nothing, my friend." Another silence followed. "Look, because it was you I called in a couple of favors," Buzz volunteered. "Checked with FBI, Homeland Security, even called a contact the chief had with the Norfolk PD."

"What are you saying?"

"That everyone has something on file somewhere with somebody. Everyone but Ashley Fitzhugh."

Eric pulled onto the shoulder, trying to comprehend this latest revelation. First Ralph, now Ashley. Two phantoms?

"What do you think?" he asked. Eric was no detective but his friend was. Buzz was a seasoned pro who knew his business.

He heard loud breathing on the other end. "Well, if I was to guess, I'd say that the girl who showed up at your place wanted to leave some evidence she existed but nothing else. No trail. Nothing anyone could follow."

"Could she erase her own records?" Eric asked as he stared at the three-foot swells drifting across Nantucket Sound. "Wouldn't that take someone who knew a lot about technology and computers?"

"Yeah. Lots of knowledge." Buzz cleared his throat. "Put it this way. I know computers and there's no way I could do it."

"She doesn't seem that...sophisticated." Eric whispered, more to himself than his friend. "And why would she do that? Why would anyone do it?"

"Can't say. And I can't swear that she did. I'm making a big assumption. If Ashley did it, maybe she wanted a casual inquiry to show she existed. You know. Leave a skeleton with no flesh on its bones. Remember, a driver's license is our primary source document today—the most important ID we carry. If someone wanted to hide in plain sight, it's the documentation they'd want to leave intact. But to be honest with you, Rick, I'm grasping at straws. I've never run across anything like this so I'm guessing."

"But you think there's something funky about it?"

"I can't say for sure. It's always possible she never got a traffic ticket, went to college, voted, or the half-dozen other things we all do. And it's damn hard to get a job without a Social Security card but there's no record she has one."

"You were able to search for all that information?" Eric asked, checking his watch. He was late.

"Look, I know you're a superb warrior but not a whiz with technology..."

"I really appreciate this, but I'm late, Buzz. Real late." Eric wanted to know more but he had to interrupt. "Are you gonna tell anybody about this?"

He heard Buzz's throaty chuckle. "Tell 'em what? That there's a girl living with you who's done nothing wrong and isn't wanted for anything? The chief would have me in a padded cell!"

"Got it. And thanks. You'll be hearing from me again if I find out anything more."

"Just for the record," Buzz asked. "What does Ashley look like? If I want to dig deeper a description might help."

Eric pulled the Jeep off the shoulder and back onto Route 28 as he headed toward the hospital. He drew a mental picture of Ashley as he drove. "About five-five, maybe five-six, 110 pounds. On the thin side but pretty. Very pretty. Short dark hair, big brown eyes, nice smile, large dimples…" Eric stopped and cleared his throat.

"Aha. I'm definitely beginning to get the picture." He could almost see his friend's smile through the phone.

"What…what do you mean?" Eric asked defensively. "What picture?"

"Why don't you save us both the trouble and just say she's hot and you like her."

"Well, she's kinda cute but…" Buzz was right. Only a couple of days and it was obvious his interest in Ashley went beyond kindness.

"Okay. She's cute and I like her. Satisfied, Sherlock Holmes?"

"Yeah, Rick, I am." His words weren't judgmental or sarcastic. "Glad you like her. And I'll keep digging to see what I can find. But Eric…"

"Yeah."

"Cute or not. Be careful. Looks like there may be more to her arrival than any of us understand. If things start getting strange or out of control, I want you to call me right away. Day or night. Understand?"

"I promise. Anytime I need help you're number one on the list." Eric promised, repeating his friend's cell phone from memory, adding, "Now…I gotta pick her up."

Eric closed his cell, pulled the Jeep into the hospital parking lot, and exhaled deeply. He felt a strange sense of ambivalence. Part excitement, part anxiety. Eric had to admit he was looking forward to seeing Ashley and bringing her home. Very much! Another part felt concern about who and what she might be and why she wanted to become his housemate.

He entered the hospital and ran up to the second floor, dropping the new clothes with the duty nurse as promised. He waited near her room, staring at his cell but not seeing it. Maybe if he stared long enough an answer to this riddle would miraculously appear. But Eric was a realist. That would never happen.

Twenty minutes later Ashley appeared, holding a plastic bag. Eric looked at her. She wore a timid smile. Everything about her cried innocence. The coy, flippant young woman of yesterday afternoon had morphed into a shy, pretty girl who stood, studying the floor and the walls. Was she as nervous about their arrangement as he was? What about the suspicious lack of info that Buzz had found? Everything about her and this situation cried "Foul!" But till he had something more than a lack of traffic tickets or a missing college transcript Eric would give Ashley the benefit of the doubt.

The new clothes looked great on her. And he couldn't deny Ashley had a world-class smile. The dimples carved into her cheeks were so big Eric thought he could get lost in them. She wore her thick, dark hair behind one ear. It reflected the afternoon sunlight beaming in through the long corridor windows. *Yeah, she was thin but cute. Very cute!* he confirmed as he watched her.

"Hi," she said meekly, breaking the silence, holding out a slender hand. "Thanks for pickin' me up."

"Hi." Eric returned the greeting, taking her hand, adding, "I couldn't leave you here."

An awkward silence followed as Ashley's face showed hurt while she studied the floor again. "Guess not," she whispered.

Brilliant! Eric wanted to kick himself. "I'm sorry, Ashley. I... I didn't mean it like that." He shook his head. His frustration went into overdrive as they headed to the elevator. This was not going smoothly.

They exited on the ground floor and followed the green line that promised to take them to the billing department. Eric and Ashley arrived at a small office with a door whose top half was open. A small shelf served as a platform.

A stout young woman appeared in the top half of the door, putting her elbows on the shelf as she surveyed Eric. She liked what she saw and gave him a delicious smile. "What can I do for you, *sir*," she offered.

"I'd like to settle the bill for my..." Eric stopped and looked at Ashley, not sure how to describe their relationship. "For Ashley Fitzhugh." The woman behind the desk lost her smile when she saw Ashley.

She disappeared, returning with the bill in a few minutes. "Here it is," she said, turning it toward him. Ashley's balance was $5,234.56. "How would you like to pay for that, sir?" she asked, eyes darting back and forth between Eric and Ashley. He pulled out his wallet. Ashley pushed closer, staring over his shoulder at the bill.

"Here." He turned to look at Ashley. Eric pushed his Visa across the counter. "Or I can write a check."

The woman took the card. "No, sir. Visa's fine. I just have to run it through." She stole a look at the girl on her right and raised her eyebrows.

As she was processing the transaction, Ashley grabbed his arm. "*Je-sus!* Did that paper say $5,200?" She shook her head vigorously. "I was only here two days." She frowned and gave the billing clerk a nasty look. "Hell, they didn't do brain surgery!"

Eric looked at the woman behind the counter who'd stopped and raised her eyebrows. "Sir, your card went through all right. Is there a *problem?*" She held the charge slip in her hand.

"Excuse us." Eric flashed a pleasant smile at the billing clerk and took Ashley's arm, guiding her away from the desk. "Hospitals are expensive. You were exhausted and sick. You didn't plan that or come looking for a handout did you?"

Ashley lifted her eyes to meet his. They were soft, sad, and moist. "No I didn't. Eric, I—" She shook her head slowly. "I've always paid my own way. But five thousand dollars? I can't pay you back or do anything to help with this. At least not now. I..." She pushed aside fresh tears. "I can't let you do this."

"I understand how you feel, Ashley." He took her arm gently. "We'll work something out, get you a job somewhere. But for now, unless you want to go to court, risk losing Kylie and a lot of other bad things, you're stuck with me," he said with conviction. "We'll figure it out." Eric smiled confidently and released her. "I promise." He gave her a nod.

Eric took the charge slip from the payment clerk's hand. She handed him a pen. "You need to sign here and your…and Ms. Fitzhugh needs to sign this release form." She pointed. "Here and here. And miss, the doctor would like to have a word with you before you go." She gestured toward a hallway to the right of the payment desk.

"Me?" Ashley asked.

The woman behind the desk nodded. "You can wait here, sir." She pointed to the row of plastic chairs across from the accounting window.

Ashley twisted her mouth into a timid frown as she shot a nervous look at Eric. He followed her with his eyes, giving her a reassuring nod. As he watched her he thought again that Lu had done a good job at guessing Ashley's sizes. The new clothes fit like they'd been tailored. He closed his eyes, imagining Ashley's pale, pretty face, the enormous brown eyes, framed by thick dark hair. This was the grown-up edition of the teenager he'd met a lifetime ago—before Afghanistan and Iraq, before the senseless deaths, and before the death of Elaine, their unborn daughter, and the nightmare that haunted him.

Ashley managed a cautious smile as she approached the large double doors leading to the doctor's private offices. Eric had no idea what the doctor wanted. He wanted to go with her in case she needed help. Just as he was about to she took a deep breath, gave him a tentative wave, and disappeared wearing the look of a prisoner heading to the gallows. Before he could call to her, Ashley was swallowed by the brightly lit corridor.

Eric fidgeted, annoyed with himself for watching and thinking about Ashley so much. He couldn't help it. No matter what mystery surrounded her there was an undeniable chemistry between them. He liked her. Too damn much for someone he'd only known for a few days.

Attempting to ignore what he was feeling, Eric picked up an outdated *Sports Illustrated*. He stared, thumbing through the pages absently. Dustin Pedroia, the Red Sox star second baseman was featured in the article. Eric checked his watch. Was she okay? What were they talking about?

"Eric?" her voice brought him back. She stood in front of him, wearing a smile. "Doc Murray says we can go."

"You're sure everything's all right? You're all right?" he asked with concern.

She touched his forearm and nodded with a smile. "He's so nice. Just wanted to make sure I felt okay. Gave me his card." She held it up proudly. The doctor appeared behind Ashley.

She withdrew her hand quickly and flushed crimson.

"Hi, Doc. Thanks for everything." Eric held out his hand.

"You're welcome, Mr. Montgomery." The doctor shook Eric's hand firmly. "I'm glad Ashley's feeling better. She told me about her daughter." He cleared his throat. "I suggested she could bring her by some Tuesday. We have a free clinic for children. You know. Just in case she needs help." He gave a her a slight nod and let it go. The doctor's smile grew as he spoke. "I think you're in good hands, Ashley." He nodded toward Eric. "If you need anyone, anytime...you know where to find me."

They returned his smile and headed for the parking lot. Part of Eric looked forward to the prospect of taking care of Ashley and Kylie. Someone to care for and worry about again. Another part of him was terrified.

She looked up at him and smiled with a quiet confidence, taking his arm. "I promise. I'll do my best to make sure everything turns out okay."

"I know you will, Ashley. We both will. Let's go...home."

Chapter Twelve

Ashley sat next to him in the cab of the truck, hugging the door handle. Eric hoped it was locked or she'd be roadkill on Route 28. Despite her upbeat comments as they left the hospital, she'd been silent ever since. It was no act. She stared absently at the landscape and fidgeted with her hair, eyes pensive and downcast.

"I have to find some work. I'm not a freeloader," she announced quietly again, breaking the thick silence.

"Never thought you were," he assured her.

She stared at him.

"Look, Ashley." Eric shrugged. "I've got to get used to your being here..." He pulled the truck onto the shoulder. "It's not bad, just different." Eric forced a smile, still struggling with his feelings.

She nodded. "I never owed anything to anyone. Ever!" she snapped at him, eyes red and angry. "I got a good head on my shoulders. Got good grades in school and had some decent jobs back home," she said. "I *will* find somethin' I can do. Some way to help pay you back."

"I want you to take a couple of days off. I insist. I don't know anything about...what you've been through, but you must be tired. Please. Rest till the weekend. Then we'll find something for you to do. If you've worked in an office, maybe you can help us at the marina. Believe me, we could sure use some help there. We'll figure out what to do with Kylie. Maybe my head mechanic can teach her to strip a diesel blindfolded." Eric grinned.

"You never know." Ashley leaned back in her seat, relaxing. She looked straight ahead but returned his grin. "Kylie's quite a girl. She may surprise you."

Eric watched Ashley, thinking again how much he enjoyed her smile and her smooth drawl. Eric was letting his guard down and enjoying that, too.

"We'll figure some way for you to repay some of the money. But you and Kylie are like family, so until you find your own place you can stay with me—if that's what you want."

Ashley nodded. "Eric. I told you, Daddy said you were a good man. I trust you. I just need to feel useful," she added.

"Sounds good to me. Next weekend's Memorial Day. It's our busiest time. You can spend a few days getting to know our operations, the systems—how things work and..." Eric hesitated, holding out his hand. "Let's just say when it comes to the office, anything you do will be an improvement." He paused. "Deal?"

They exchanged looks. She took his hand and shook it. Her shake warm and firm, sending electricity up his arm. "Deal," Ashley agreed.

****

Eric pulled the Jeep into his driveway, parked, turned off the engine, and got out. Lu's car sat on the crushed stone parking area next to the street. He looked at his passenger.

"We're home." A strange ambivalence crept over

Eric. Not sure why. Like the times he'd led his team into an empty building that looked safe. Too empty and too safe. Trouble was no matter how many times you scouted it, by the time you saw the danger it was too late.

Ashley sat, frozen, eyes searching from one side to the other. Eric walked around the truck and opened her door slowly, reluctant to invade wherever her mind had taken her. She flinched. Had he violated some private space? What had those soft eyes seen? Part of him wanted to know, to care. Another resisted. He had demons of his own. They consumed enough of his time. At least they had till Friday night.

"Sorry." She looked at him with a hesitant smile. He took her hand and helped her out, touching her arm lightly. "You go in. I'll get your things and the mail and be right there."

Ashley stared straight ahead, then looked around warily. Was she searching for something or someone? Taking one final glance, she headed slowly up the walk toward the back porch. He watched. She wore the look of a hunted animal. Eric pulled the plastic bag with her clothes and toiletries from behind the seat, then quick-timed it to the mailbox.

He thumbed through the envelopes. Couple of bills, a Pennysaver. Nothing important. When he turned around, Ashley stood frozen—head down, shoulders slumped. As Eric approached, he could see she was trembling. Drawing next to her, Eric saw tears covering her cheeks. Turning toward him, she whispered, "They been through so much. And I wasn't even here. I left them alone," she whispered, adding, "I feel so guilty." She shook her head, angrily pushing the tears aside.

"Don't know what to say—how to explain what happened."

Eric found her eyes and took her shoulders gently. "From what I've seen, you have nothing to feel guilty about." And she didn't. Kylie was an amazing little girl. After only two days, Eric liked her—very much. She was sweet, soft-spoken, caring, looking after Rusty like a little brother. Kylie never asked for anything without a "please" followed by an immediate "thank you." No matter what darkness Ashley had been through, she'd insulated her daughter. "Nothing," he repeated softly.

Suddenly, Ashley sobbed, falling into his chest and clutching his shirt as she pulled him close. "And now," she began in a tone of quiet regret, "I brought our problems on you." She pulled him tighter. "I didn't want to. I'm...I'm so sorry."

He should have pushed her away. Kept a safe distance. No question. Doubts and mystery surrounded her like a shroud. But Eric didn't care. He wanted her close—needed to feel her safe and warm. To protect her from whatever evil pursued her. Ashley belonged in his arms. The warmth and electricity surged between them as he held her. Eric shut his eyes, softly stroking her lush hair. He hadn't felt like this in such a long time. Slowly, hesitantly, he let his arms surround Ashley.

"Ahem..." Louise cleared her throat. She stood on the small porch next to the kitchen, wearing an apron and a curious expression.

"Come on, you two. Time for supper," she said, narrowing her eyes.

Eric backed away quickly, releasing Ashley. Her eyes were moist and downcast. Her cheeks flushed. He raised his eyebrows and shrugged as he went by Lu, expecting a cross look. To his surprise, she gave him a nod and squeezed his shoulder.

Just as he was about to introduce Ashley and Louise, his cell rang. When Eric looked at the number, he swallowed deeply. His BlackBerry's screen said Private Number. He held up one hand and pushed the talk button with the other. The connection was poor—a voice, very faint—hidden by static. "Be right back. This could be important," he ran outside, hoping to get a clear signal. Louise nodded. Maybe it was a telemarketer, but maybe it was Lip, even Ralph. His heart pounded in his chest and his throat felt coarse as sandpaper. Nothing. The line went dead.

He tried voice mail but there was no message. *Damn!* When he hit redial, a mechanical voice announced, "Your call cannot be completed as dialed." He repeated the exercise only to hear the same message.

Inside, the reunion between Ashley and Kylie was long and touching. When Eric returned to the kitchen they held each other, faces beaming, streaked with tears.

Ashley whispered soft assurances to her daughter. "I'm so sorry. I'll never leave you again, honey. I promise." Eric overheard. Even Rusty got into the act, yipping happily, dancing around and jumping onto their legs.

"Everything all right?" Louise found his eyes.

"Yeah, fine," Eric lied. Things had never been more mixed up, more confused. But he smiled and nodded at Ashley and Kylie, who still held each other as if their lives depended on it. Whatever sadness or misery life had dealt them, they had an amazing bond. Could what they said about Ralph be true?

"How can I help, ma'am?" Ashley broke their embrace and asked Louise as she sniffled and wiped her tears away.

"First, call me Lu." She held out her hand. Ashley took it with both of hers. "Then you can set the table." Louise gestured toward Kylie, who stood brushing her own tears aside with a huge smile fixed on her face. "Kylie knows the routine."

The little girl proceeded to show her mother where the plates, silverware, and glasses were kept. The two of them laughed and joked with each other, setting four places, every item in perfect alignment. Eric took it all in.

They were just about to sit down to dinner when the phone in the kitchen rang. Louise was the closest. She picked it up. "Hello…" She waited five seconds and repeated the greeting. "No one there." She shook her head and shrugged, then sat down to dig in to her homemade meatloaf and mashed potatoes. "Funny. That's the third time that's happened today." She shook her head. "Sounds like someone's there but they don't answer. Phone's been acting funny all afternoon."

"Probably telemarketers," Eric said casually. "This is the time they call." He was about to cut a slab of meatloaf, when he glanced at Ashley. She wore a curious expression. Eric couldn't read it. She stole a look at him as she fidgeted with her napkin. Then, clearing her throat, Ashley stood and crossed to the sink, pouring herself a drink of water. She scanned the yard and narrow road leading to the house.

He got up and followed her to the sink, looking out the window. The little girl next door was laughing and playing, and the man across the street cut his grass. He was about to turn away when he saw it. A nondescript white van. Could be nothing but it looked like the vehicle he'd seen the other night. The kind someone might use for shadow and surveillance. A few feet behind it stood another with lettering on the side. It was too small to read from the window, but two small antennae perched above the dark roof like misshapen ears. She saw the vehicles, stared for a few seconds, then smiled weakly, and began to walk back.

"Friends of yours?" he whispered so the others wouldn't hear. Ashley played with her lip and found his eyes.

She looked confused. "Don't know what you mean."

"I'd like to talk later," he suggested, watching her reaction. Nothing. No subtle body language or nervous ticks to indicate anything other than bashful innocence.

"Sure. Whatever you'd like." She shrugged and put on a pleasant smile as she headed back to the table, glancing over her shoulder toward the street. When they were all seated, Ashley orchestrated everyone grasping hands. Louise reached for Eric's. Ashley wore the stern look of his old Sunday school teacher. She nodded, closed her eyes, then began, "Lord, thank you for this food which we are about to receive…"

Eric glanced at Louise. She hid a grin. After finishing the blessing, Ashley crossed herself. Kylie followed her lead and looked up with a stern expression that mirrored her mother's. Ashley nodded at Eric.

After dinner everyone adjourned to the living room. Eric made an excuse and went back to the kitchen where he checked the street for anything unusual. As he watched, two workmen emerged from one of the houses on the opposite side of the street. One leaned slightly under the apparent weight of a massive tool box. The second carried a stack of small boxes. So much for intrigue!

"Ahem." Ashley cleared her throat loudly behind him. She approached and stood next to him, following his eyes. "Friends of *yours?*" she asked with obvious amusement.

Eric wanted to be angry. He wasn't sure whether to smile or frown. He chose the latter. Ashley had an interesting sense of humor. "Guess not." He turned and gestured toward the living room. "Mind if I check out the ball game?"

"No, Kylie and I can clean up," Ashley volunteered.

"Thanks, honey, but you should be resting," Louise said as she joined the growing crowd.

"I appreciate the kindness, ma'am, but I been cooped up for too long. I like being active," Ashley explained as she called to Kylie.

"Okay," Lu agreed. "I bought some groceries. Cold cuts, breakfast stuff, detergent, and soap. I'll show you where everything is."

Eric passed Kylie as he headed to the living room and found the remote. After ten minutes of quiet talk, soft laughter, and the sound of dishes being washed and dried, Lu rejoined him. She sat on the opposite end of the couch and watched Eric.

"I know it's not my business but…" she said hesitantly as he turned toward her.

"Go ahead. If anyone has a right to question what's going on, you do."

"Did you pay Ashley's hospital bill?" It was blunt

and to the point. Lu's style.

Eric nodded and raised his eyebrows. "Guess I feel responsible for her." He didn't mention Elaine's insurance settlement. She would have wanted him to do some good with it. He was sure Louise would feel the same.

"That's nice, son. But remember, there's no blood relationship." She continued watching him closely.

"I know." She had a point. Was his mother-in-law thinking about the unguarded moment he and Ashley had shared before dinner?

Eric followed Lu with his eyes as she stood and headed to the kitchen to check on the clean-up. He wondered how she felt about this strange turn of events. She was kind and compassionate to a fault but still this—a mysterious, attractive young woman and her daughter occupying the home Elaine had cherished—was quite a leap of faith.

He heard more chatter, punctuated by casual laughter. Part of Eric felt compassion, even affection for the little family he'd inherited. He closed his eyes, thinking of Ashley. She'd felt warm and safe in his arms. The loneliness and despair that had consumed him and been his constant companion since Elaine's death vanished for the few moments he held her.

Was it possible that Ashley and Kylie had given him something to connect with? More likely it was his need to be where the action was. Adrenaline junkie. That was Elaine's name for it and a cliché, Eric knew. But his wife had hit the target—dead center. Eric never met an action situation he didn't enjoy. And while no immediate threat had materialized, the girl's appearance on his doorstep seemed to fit that description.

But whatever the cause of this sudden and newfound state of mind, part of him wanted to stay in the sad, lonely isolation he'd grown to embrace. Self-pity fed on itself. It clung like a parasite, reluctant to abandon its host.

Louise, Ashley, and Kylie returned, full of conversation.

"Kylie needs a bath, if that's okay?" Ashley asked.

Eric nodded. "Of course. You live here now. Kylie knows where everything is."

"Oh. I left some things in the bathroom upstairs for you two." Louise called out. "Shampoo, toothbrush, a couple of other things. We can go shopping tomorrow after my shift if you need to exchange anything. Maybe we can pick you up some more clothes."

"Thank you, ma'am. I mean Lu." Ashley smiled. "You've been wonderful."

"Now, I need to get home. I've got an early shift and I have to get to bed," Louise crossed the room. When she reached the girls, she gave each a hug. "I'll be back tomorrow," she promised. She winked at Kylie and kissed her cheek.

Eric rose and walked his mother-in-law to the door as Ashley and Kylie laughed, heading up the stairs to the second floor bathroom. "See you tomorrow." He shook his head in gratitude. "I could not have made it through this without you."

She nodded, hugging him, then turned as she opened the door. "What are you going to do?"

He looked at her. "Do?"

"You know what I mean, Ricky. About them, your brother, this whole situation?"

Eric exhaled. "Take care of them. Give 'em a place

to live. Until I find out what's going on or they can get by on their own. I didn't ask for this but—" He found her eyes. "About Ralph. I'm not sure. It's still a work in progress. Has been since we were kids."

Louise shot him a hard look. "I've never known you to sit back and let the world pass you by. Was that what all those calls were about?"

He shrugged again. "I don't know any more than you do. Right now, this is a game I've gotta play fast, loose, and alone. When I figure it out, you'll be first on the list."

She studied him. "Good. You may not understand this. I'm not sure I do." She shook her head slowly. "It's hard to see someone else in my daughter's home. And you know I'm no mystic. Never been into fate, the cosmos, or karma but—" She touched his cheek gently. "In a way I can't explain, I think Ashley and Kylie are here for a reason."

"Yeah. Ashley told me they came here to…"

"No." Louise stopped him, holding her hand up. "I don't mean that kind of reason. I mean something bigger."

"Like a conspiracy?"

"No." She laughed softly. "I think they're here for a higher purpose." She fixed his eyes with hers and arched her eyebrows. "To help you live again, Eric."

While Ashley helped Kylie with her bath, Eric went into the living room and turned on the Red Sox as he replayed Lu's words.

A higher purpose. To help him live again. Eric shook his head. Sure. He believed. Or he had. After seeing innocent ten-year-old street kids split in two by a

Kalashnikov, even after three of his team were so badly scattered by an IED there wasn't enough left to bury. Eric stopped believing the night the woman he worshipped and their baby lay broken and dying by the side of the road.

Chapter Thirteen

"Please tell me *something* I want to hear, Major."
The Director sat behind the massive desk speaking
quietly to the man facing him. His tone had the
authoritative ring of command.

The major—a veteran Marine officer—stared back,
hands grasping the arms of the antique chair positioned
strategically in front of the desk. The Director led a
super-secret cell. He had crafted its covert operation
delicately, with the precision and loving care of a finely
honed work of art. But his exquisite design was in
jeopardy. Not from the FBI, NSA, CIA, or another
high-level intelligence group. The person who
possessed the knowledge to destroy seven years of his
work was a young woman—a girl. Who could have
guessed she was a world-class hacker? Someone with
skills sufficient to breach their network and download
highly guarded secrets. No small feat. The Director was
impressed.

The major watched him cautiously as the Director
tented his manicured fingertips thoughtfully. A scornful
smile crept across the man's face as he studied the
officer facing him. No one who had seen the Director in
this special, secretive role had ever lived to tell the tale.
Did the major suspect that?

"The operatives who failed to capture her in
Norfolk have been dealt with. I saw to it personally," he

informed the man.

The Marine nodded compliantly. The room stood quiet for a long minute, a brooding silence interrupted by the perfect rhythm of the priceless grandfather clock that stood next to the door.

"You let this happen?" He addressed the major casually, his words devoid of emotion. Like the operatives who failed him in Norfolk this officer had come highly recommended. His résumé assured that mistakes in judgment never happened. It was the second time the Director had been misinformed. There would not be a third.

"I have no idea how she got away, sir." The major shook his head in deference, still wearing the guarded look as the Director held his eyes.

"I'll tell you," the leader said evenly. "You were arrogant, made clumsy attempts to impress this young woman. Wanted to show what a clever and powerful man you were."

The Director studied the vaulted ceiling. "You befriended the petty officer—the one she lived with—having never vetted the young woman properly to determine whether she represented a threat to our mission." When he finished his eyes rested on the major's. "A long litany of inappropriate actions. In short, you failed us…failed me a second time."

The officer sat motionless as the man behind the desk stood. A trace of perspiration glistened at the major's closely-cropped hairline. "But, sir. At best she found pictures of our targets. With nothing more than that there's no way she could come to any conclusions about our plans. And it wasn't my oversight that allowed the pictures to remain in the encrypted file she hacked into."

"Yes, Major. I suppose one could argue that point." the Director nodded and showed a neutral smile as he proceeded around the oak desk. The Marine had ten years, twenty pounds, and two inches on his accuser. Yet despite the smaller man's apparent agreement, the Marine wore the look of prey not predator. He had good reason.

"We tried, sir," the major continued. "Made it clear to the girl and the petty officer. Arranged *accidents* to frighten them and force her to tell us what she may have found, to surrender the data. That should have been enough. The girl had more backbone and brains than we anticipated."

"On the other hand, Major, you had far less of both." The Director rubbed his forehead in frustration as he studied his quarry. "And now, you have no idea where they've gone?"

"No. Not...not yet," the major stammered. After long years of arduous combat duty, fear should be no stranger. But raw, physical courage, the ability to run blindly into an oncoming hail of enemy bullets, was different from mental toughness. And the latter was what this task demanded. "We have men searching, sir." The officer shook his head. "But it's almost impossible. She has no family except her daughter. The chief she lived with has gone missing, too. I have no idea how they escaped or where they've gone...but I will, sir. Give me a few..."

"Enough!" The Director held up a hand, crossed the room slowly and looked down at the major as he reached casually into his pocket, retrieving something with his right hand. In a quick motion the syringe was in the major's thick, muscled neck. He gasped and fell forward, the Director watching as his body hit the thick carpet.

"That's all right, Major." The words were even, without emotion as the major lay dead. "The penalty for treason is hanging. I simply eliminated the middle man."

Chapter Fourteen

Kylie slept peacefully in the small upstairs bedroom. The first two nights she'd slept in the small bedroom at the end of the hallway off the kitchen. But Eric's sixth sense, an intuition honed by years of combat experience, told him she should sleep upstairs. He wanted to believe that no one was following the girls or meant them harm. But after what Lip and Buzz has discovered and listening to Ashley's vague innuendos about what Ralph might be involved in it eased Eric's mind to know that Kylie's bedroom was at the far end of the upstairs hall.

She'd given Eric a kiss on the cheek and a giant bear hug before running off to bed. After only a few days Eric doted on Kylie. As he watched her bounce down the hallway, her tiny hand squeezing Ashley's, Eric marveled again at how happy and well-adjusted she seemed. He found himself reluctantly arriving at the only explanation that made sense. The one he'd stubbornly resisted. Life at Ralph's must have been the pleasant experience the girls described...at least until the crisis that precipitated their hasty departure.

Ashley returned, sitting on the couch and staring out the window as she fidgeted, trying to get her thick hair to behave. Eric lounged in the recliner Elaine had given him on their last Christmas together. The Red Sox glowed in flawless high-definition on Eric's forty-two-inch Fujitsu flat screen—sound on mute. Ashley turned and stared at him. As he watched, her large, luminous eyes shifted from chestnut brown to a dark green as the light changed.

"Do you mind?" He held up the remote and turned back toward the TV, angry with himself. Eric had no business contemplating the color of Ashley's eyes. But his forces were in retreat. Even Louise had recognized it. He was finding it impossible to ignore this shy, pretty young woman he found so attractive.

Others had tried to help—Joey, Bobby, even Lip— offering a shoulder or friendship to deal with the grief Elaine's death had left in its wake. Did this make any sense? Was it possible that after only a handful of days Ashley was the long-sought savior he'd awaited?

"No, I love baseball." She nodded, bringing him back with a curious smile.

Just as he turned the sound up, Jerry Remy, the Red Sox color analyst, dissected the double-play the Blue Jays shortstop had completed.

"Nice underhand toss. The shortstop led the second baseman just right." Ashley nodded again, animated as she turned to look at him. "But this guy on the mound—got nothing but a fastball. No off-speed or breaking stuff. We'll get to him in a few innings."

A smile crossed Eric's face. "You know your baseball."

Ashley shrugged. "Played softball in high school. My team, the Lady Wildcats, came in second in the state tournament," she added with pride. "And 'course Daddy used to take us to Triple A games in Tidewater whenever he was home."

"Really," Eric said. Not the Ralph he remembered.

But the evidence continued to mount. "You want something, a beer, soda—anything? Maybe some chips or pretzels?" Eric wasn't sure how to talk to Ashley. He wanted her to relax and open up. *Patience, LT.* He needed the truth, to find out what happened to bring them here. But she wasn't a prisoner to interrogate.

Eric's stomach churned as he played with the remote. Small talk, especially with women, had never been his strong suit. Shy wasn't exactly the right word, but Eric felt at home with Bobby, Buzz, Lip, and the guys on his team. With Ashley, a whole new dynamic was at work. One he found hard to accept.

"No, thanks. I'm fine." She tilted her head to the side. "Don't drink much. Not since—" She looked away as her words trailed off. He wondered if the reason was a sweet seven-year-old asleep in an upstairs bedroom.

"I have one now and then," he volunteered, twisting the truth, still trying to picture Ralph taking the girls to baseball games.

"Eric," she said in her quiet drawl, watching him. "I know you got questions about all this."

"Questions? That's an understatement." An ironic grin crossed his face.

"I...I can understand, believe me." Ashley looked away. Her words tumbled out erratically. She cleared her throat and swallowed. He wasn't the only one having trouble making conversation. "You think Ralph was a bad man. I know. Don't have to be Sherlock Holmes to figure that out." Her lips curled into a crooked smile. "I'm pretty good at judging people. I can see it in your eyes," she said softly. "They get dark and angry when I talk about him.

"I don't know what happened between you two, but something did. All I know is he was always good to Kylie and me." She stared straight ahead. "I got into some trouble when I was a teenager. I wanted to—to take care of it." She hung her head and shrugged again. She turned, eyes cloudy and full of regret. "He and Momma wouldn't let me. They told me I made a mistake and had to do the right thing." Her dark eyes filled as she stood and walked to the bay window. "I did what they said. They were right. I never regretted that decision. Maybe you can't understand what I'm sayin', but Kylie's like a, I don't know exactly how to put it— like a beacon. When I'm tired or sad or scared, I just look at her. She keeps me on track—'grounded' is the word people use." She turned, pausing and wiping her eyes. "Could we go out on the porch?"

"Sure," he agreed, flipping the game off. Ashley continued to amaze. Some of the insights into her life were disarming in their candor. Maybe she was ready to open up, to share the truth about why they arrived on Friday night.

"I got this nasty habit," she confessed, shaking her head as they sat down on the back-porch swing. Ashley on one side, Eric on the other.

Ashley pulled a crumpled cigarette out of her jeans and lit it. Taking a deep drag, she exhaled a long plume of smoke with obvious pleasure. "I know it's not good for me, but I can't help it. I never do it in front of Kylie," she rationalized. "But I've been dying for one the last few days."

He laughed softly. "I know the feeling." Eric hesitated. "Got another one?"

Her large eyes grew larger. "You…*smoke?*"

He chuckled. "Yep. Picked it up in the Army." He paused. "Combat's strange. You spend hours, sometimes days, bored out of your mind. Then suddenly you're sent on a mission. You're scared, terrified not for yourself but for your men," he confessed. Eric noticed that whenever he spoke she seemed to hang on every word. "When you're sitting alone in ambush or in your tent, a cigarette almost seems like a...friend. Strange, huh?"

"Not really. Guess I never thought about it like that." Her eyes narrowed as she slid closer. "So it was real bad over there?"

"Yeah," he told her, then shook his head. "It was sometimes, but let's talk about something else."

"Just so you know." Ashley touched the top of his hand lightly. "I'm a good listener."

"Thanks." He flushed at the intimate offer and the warmth of her touch. "My wife hated both—smoking and war stories. I'd sneak a cigarette at the marina, but only smoked one at home—every night after supper. I promised to quit after the..." He couldn't finish the thought.

Ashley smiled softly and stood, fishing in the pocket of her jeans. She sat down again as she passed him another crumpled cigarette and her worn plastic lighter. "Sorry about that," she giggled and shrugged as she stared. "It's nice to know that even Eric Montgomery isn't perfect. I figured you wore a halo." As Ashley giggled louder, he glimpsed the innocent teenager he remembered.

"No, Ashley. No halo." He chuckled softly as he lit up and inhaled deeply. Eric enjoyed the dizzying sensation adding, "You may be a bad influence on me."

Ashley turned as she moved the swing in a slow cadence with one foot. She let her tall, slender body relax easily as she blew smoke rings into the damp evening air.

"Give me time." She found his eyes. Hers twinkled with a mischief Eric hadn't seen before. He found it intoxicating.

They both laughed softly.

"Looks like our friends are gone," Eric nodded toward the street.

"Looks that way," she agreed.

"You didn't know who they were?"

Ashley shook her head. Her expression lost the playful look. "Don't think so. Why? Who do you think they were?"

"I have no idea. Most likely they were just workers installing a new cable system or phones." He watched her face closely. It wore an impassive expression. "Why? Would there be a reason someone would be looking for you?"

"Not sure, Eric. I told you. Daddy was into some things that…" She left the thought unfinished, shaking her head.

"You said he had a lot of balls in the air." Eric faced her. "Were some of them dangerous or illegal?"

Ashley stared, focusing on the dark street.

"Ashley." He took her shoulder and gently turned her to face him. "Was that why he was scared?"

She bit her lip and found the new moon. "Could be."

He had to ask. "But if Ralph was into some bad business why would they be following you and Kylie?"

She pulled away from him and stood, crossing the

porch, sighing as the peepers played backup to her breathing. "Can't be sure. It wasn't what I wanted for me or Kylie. But…" She exhaled deeply. "Sometimes things happen by accident. Things you don't expect." Ashley's words were soft, but her face wore a hard, anxious look as she crushed her cigarette in the empty flower pot.

"You're not exactly a font of knowledge."

She stared at him. The smile that appeared never reached her eyes. Suddenly, Ashley had morphed into the sad lonely girl he'd met on Friday night.

"Sorry, I meant…"

"I know what you meant, Eric." She looked hurt and angry, pushing her lips together in frustration. "I went to school, had good jobs. I'm not some dumb piece of trailer trash!"

"I didn't mean it like that." Her words made him feel small and guilty. Suddenly it struck him. "By the way, where'd the cigarettes come from?"

She continued to frown for a moment. Then her smile reappeared. Ashley was enjoying her little mystery. She twisted her face into a grin and held up a finger—like a child with a secret. "Be right back."

When she returned she carried a worn backpack over one shoulder.

Eric laughed out loud. "Where was that the night you arrived?"

She sat down and turned toward him, sitting closer. Her fragrance washed over him. "Under a tarp behind the garage. Just in case you didn't take us in."

"I could never have turned you away." He held the grin. "But I figured you had to have something with you. What else you got in there? A magic wand."

Eric enjoyed studying Ashley. Her moods changed as often as the color of her eyes. Being around this girl was like riding a runaway roller coaster. But Elaine had pegged him correctly—an adrenaline junkie. He loved riding roller coasters, the steeper the better. And for the time being he was enjoying being a passenger on this one.

It was Ashley's turn to laugh. "I wouldn't mind a magic wand. But you won't find one in here. Got an old toothbrush, a couple of clean T-shirts for Kylie, a leash for Rusty, and this."

She pulled out a wrinkled one-hundred dollar bill, snapping it open. "Daddy said to keep it for emergencies. Case everything else failed at least we'd have somethin'. It was all he had left."

Eric sighed. He faced Ashley, listening, drinking in her words—intoxicated by the melody of her voice, the soft cadence of her drawl, and the musky fragrance surrounding her.

"Everything okay?" Ashley caught him staring. She looked puzzled.

"Everything is just fine, Ashley. I promise." He held up three fingers in a Boy Scout salute.

She stood. It was her turn to study him. Suddenly, her eyes grew soft and moist again. Without warning Ashley leaned over and kissed his cheek softly, letting her lips linger.

"Thank you." She backed away quickly as her face flushed. "I...I hoped you'd take us in. After Momma died, Daddy kinda turned inside. Figured he was afraid something bad might happen to us."

"How'd your mother die?" Eric didn't want to dredge up bad memories, but maybe he could glean something from the information or pass it on to Lip or Buzz.

"It was a while back. Late winter. She was all alone on a back road. She and Daddy had a terrible fight—about Daddy's job, I think." Ashley's eyes grew hard and dark again. Her jaw stiffened. "They yelled a lot and Momma ran out. Daddy went frantic. Next day the State Police came to the house. They said she drove off the road and the impact broke her neck. There were no witnesses."

Eric felt the chill run down his spine. "Drove off the road...broken neck...no witnesses..." he repeated softly.

Ashley nodded. "Daddy went into his bedroom. Heard him talkin'...on his cell phone. He didn't come out for a while. Then *he* took off. Told us to stay at home, not go out, and lock all the doors. Even left a loaded shotgun. He used to take me shootin', so I knew how to use it."

She crossed and picked up the backpack. "When he came back he was...different." Her eyes looked distant and frightened, focused on a place far away. "After Momma's funeral he was never the same. Finally one day last week he just told us to leave. Never told us where to go. Said he didn't want to know where we went, but we needed to get as far away as we could real quick. I remembered you livin' up here, the way Daddy talked about you so I..." She broke off as she watched him. "Eric, what's the matter?"

"Nothing." Eric swallowed deeply, recalling the night of Elaine's accident.

The tension was broken by a sharp cry from Kylie's room. Ashley rushed inside, ran up the stairs, dropping the backpack in the upstairs hall. Eric heard her singing softly. He tiptoed upstairs and down the hall, peeking in to see Ashley holding Kylie, rubbing her back slowly. Ashley rocked her daughter, then eased her back onto the bed. Ashley saw him and put her finger to her lips, nodding as she stood.

"It happens sometimes." Ashley sighed deeply. "She gets real frightened. Didn't understand what was happenin'. I promised her that when we got here…"

"I know. She told us," Eric interrupted, putting a hand on her shoulder. He went downstairs and out to the porch, taking one last look around. Eric came inside, locking and bolting the back door, patting Rusty on the head on his way upstairs. Ashley's backpack lay on the hall floor. He picked it up to give it back to her and was struck by the weight. *Some clothes and a leash for Rusty?* Before he could do anything, Ashley snatched the backpack. Her eyes showed fear as her face flushed.

"Thanks. I'll…I'll take that," she stuttered.

He released it. She hugged the backpack like it held the crown jewels. "Wouldn't want you to see my…my secrets," she stammered with a nervous smile and turned, her face still crimson.

"'Course not." He nodded.

Ashley just stared at the floor and continued clutching the backpack.

"Goodnight," Eric said curtly as the roller coaster took another deep dip. Just when he thought she was opening up. She was still holding back. His own face heated with anger and frustration as he brushed by her toward his bedroom.

"'Night," she whispered with a nod and stood

planted to the floor.

****

Eric sat on his bed. Another cigarette hung from his fingers. He absently flicked the ashes in a coffee cup.

After the revelation about her mother's death and Ashley's secretive behavior with the backpack, Eric wanted to talk to Lip. Maybe he'd have some light to shed on the situation.

He crept down the hall and listened outside Ashley's door. She was asleep, snoring softly. He returned to his room and checked his watch: 10:30. He went into the master bathroom, washed up, and brushed his teeth. He pulled out the sleeping pills, thinking he might need them again.

Just as he sat on the edge of the bed, his cell rang. He pressed Talk.

"Ricky?"

"Yeah. I was afraid I might have lost you." Eric spoke softly. The interior walls were thin and sound carried easily.

"Lost me?"

"I got a call from a throwaway earlier. Figured it was you."

"Not me, bro."

"Really. Then who the hell…?" Eric stopped in mid-sentence, knowing his friend had no answer. "You get anything more?"

"I met an old friend today—a Norfolk Police lieutenant. We help each other once in a while," Lip explained. "Sometimes we bend the rules to help the good guys and keep the bad ones off the street."

"Sounds fine to me."

"Yeah. He owes me a couple of favors." Lip chuckled. "I had to coax him. He bobbed and weaved but finally coughed up something."

"Okay?" Eric said with anticipation.

"Well, he claimed he didn't know too much, but said there was something strange going on at the base."

"Wait a minute. You're at the base—in *Naval Intelligence*?"

"Hell. This isn't your usual Naval Intel kind of stuff. The unit I'm with now is more tactical. You know, boring, day-to-day shit. Not like the stuff you and I did in the Middle East. Some guy may break into his CO's safe, or a seaman steals a couple of documents to impress a girl working for the bad guys. Stuff like that. What he's talking about is big—strategic. He knows people. Got connections to all the heavyweights, FBI, Homeland Security, even CIA. Swore he didn't know much." Lip stopped. "Look, my career's all I got, but I'll keep digging. He said there's a lot of people involved."

"Okay. What'd you get? Your secret's safe with me."

"That's the problem. He couldn't or wouldn't tell me any details. Swore all he had was rumors and hearsay. But don't worry. I'll get it out of him."

"Okay. I know I'm pushing you, but I need one more thing."

"Shit, Eric. I know we go way back, but this is getting deeper all the time." His friend paused, adding a reluctant, "What now?"

"I need a copy of the accident report for Ralph's girlfriend, Melissa Fitzhugh. She was killed in a hit-and-run. Drove off the road, no witnesses. It was a little while after that the girls left to come up here."

"Okay. I'll see what I can do. But please, tell me you're not implying what I think you are? That there's a connection…"

"No. Yes. Hell, I don't know!" Eric interrupted. "I know it's probably a coincidence. But we've been getting strange phone calls and it looked like there might be surveillance on the street tonight. Shit, Lip! Surveillance for a couple down-and-out girls from Virginia? And get this. Ashley was hiding a backpack she brought. Told me it had some T-shirts and her dog's leash. I picked it up and the thing weighed ten pounds. There's something more going on here than I can figure out."

There was a long silence on his friend's end. "Really?" Lip whispered after a pause. "A backpack? Heavy? Like she was carrying something?" More silence. "You're right. That is strange."

"I know it makes no sense. But I'm begging you. Can you run down the accident report?"

"Sure. I'll give it a shot. But you could probably look it up yourself." His friend explained. "You know a lot of that stuff is public record now. It's online."

"Hell, you know I'm a total klutz when it comes to technology. I'm asking *you*," Eric pleaded. "I got no one else. Anything you can get would be great."

"All right. You got it! Maybe I can part the Red Sea in my spare time."

Eric couldn't read his friend. Was Lip backing away or just up to his eyeballs in day-to-day stuff?

"Okay, okay. I'm sorry, Lip. But please. For me. I've never asked you for anything before."

"I'll try. But I still have a day job. And I'm due for

a ten-day leave over Memorial Day. Jen and I and the kids are going down to the shore to visit her folks, so I won't be able to do much while I'm away. This may take a while."

"Anything you get is more than we've got now."

Chapter Fifteen

Eric stood, staring absently out of his bedroom into the mild night. The flat, dark expanse of Nantucket Sound reflected a sliver of moonlight. A faint breeze moved the sheer curtains. He glanced at the digital clock: 1:16. Exhaustion filled every fiber. Yet even after a prescription sleeping pill, he was wide awake. Sleep refused to come. *Overtired? Adrenaline high? Mind on overdrive? Take your pick, Eric.* More likely it was the confusion that had overtaken his life since Friday night. Was it only Monday? It seemed a lifetime since Ashley had arrived.

Eric's life dealt with the tangible. Facts, logic, reality. Things he could see, measure, and touch. In the world Eric knew, everything made sense. But someone had thrown him a curve in the dirt because none of this did. The brother he'd demonized since childhood was suddenly a stand-up guy. The perfect father.

Eric was being pulled into a vortex with a mysterious girl who seemed wedded to contradictions and mystery. Yet despite his attempts to keep her at arm's length, he felt more and more drawn to her. And tonight—the frightening revelation about her mother's death. Was it possible? Could there be some connection that...

Suddenly, something drew Eric's attention. He held his breath. His senses were sharp, alert to anything out of the ordinary. His life and that of his team had depended on it. Now, as he stood, looking out his bedroom window, Eric heard a noise. But not outside. It came from Ashley's room. Sound travelled easily through the thin walls. He closed his window carefully so he could hear more clearly. Ashley should have been sleeping. She had been. Eric crept to the wall and listened. There was a voice—barely audible but there was no doubt. It *was* Ashley. Her words sounded muffled at first, difficult to understand. Was she talking in her sleep? As he drew closer to the wall his question was answered. He caught a few words. "Going okay— all set—and good-bye." Unless she had a friend hiding under the bed, Ashley had a cell phone.

Eric tiptoed to the door and peered into the hallway. Ashley's door was closed. He waited, but there was nothing more from her room. Silence. A faint squeak signaled she was getting back under the covers. He walked to his own bed and lay down. Every time he thought this was a bad dream, that his imagination was playing tricks, something happened to snap him back to reality.

Thirty minutes later, he still lay wide awake. Knowing he needed to rest, to give his mind respite, Eric took a second sleeping pill from the bottle on the night table and pulled up the covers. His eyelids grew heavy and fell shut. His sleep was deep and dreamless again.

****

"Uncle Eric." It was Kylie at the door. Eric looked at the digital clock on his night table: 6:50 a.m.

"Yeah," he said, clearing his throat.

"Momma and me been fixin' breakfast."

"Huh?" He opened the door and caught the smell of bacon cooking. "Okay. Be right there."

Eric rushed through a shower, brushed his teeth, and combed his hair. He was down the stairs in ten minutes. Ashley moved around the kitchen like a veteran, humming while she scrambled some eggs. She looked completely innocent, even energetic, upbeat. No evidence of lost sleep. What was happening? Why would she be talking on a cell phone? And to who? Ralph? Someone else in this strange drama? But then, he rationalized, everyone he knew had a cell phone today. Was he overreacting? Did that make Ashley a criminal? Of course not, but why talk in the middle of the night? He thought about the back pack and Buzz's suspicions, wondering why she refused to simply tell him the truth. But watching the intoxicating smile she wore and following her lithe movements around the kitchen he decided to ignore his suspicions.

"Didn't know if you liked 'em scrambled, poached, or sunny side up so I took a chance." She blushed.

"Scrambled is fine." He watched her. No. Nothing out of the ordinary.

He heard her singing softly with the radio. She caught him staring and her blush grew. "Sorry, I found a country station. Just love this song. It's from a movie. Song's called 'Give in to Me.'"

As she spoke the title her eyes held his and a shy smile showed at the corners of her lips.

Eric cleared his throat and let his eyes drift.

"It sounded nice," he told her. And it did. As he watched he saw a pretty girl making him breakfast. Nothing sinister or suspicious. It was hard to reconcile this Ashley with the hard, gloomy person she became when pressed.

"Now, why don't you and Kylie sit down? Let's enjoy our breakfast."

Eric stood and pulled out Ashley's chair. He was about to reach for the toast when she cleared her throat and took his hand firmly, then Kylie's. "Thank you, Lord, for the food we are about to receive, this beautiful spring mornin', and the fine company." She stole a look at Eric, released his hand, and gave him a nod.

The conversation flowed easily. Eric felt surprisingly comfortable.

Ashley beamed, announcing she'd been right about the ball game. "Heard on the Cape radio station that the Red Sox won eleven to two," she said, wearing a superior look.

He nodded. Putting this casual table chatter together with last night was difficult. Who and what was Ashley? The sweet, almost naïve girl he wanted her to be, the one he liked and was attracted to, or the other Ashley—the girl who kept secrets and skulked around his house with a cell phone and who knows what else in that heavy backpack…

"Uncle Eric," Kylie interrupted. "The lady in the livin' room—in the picture. Was she your wife?"

"Kylie! Please." Ashley gave her daughter a stern look and shook her head.

"It's all right." Eric nodded. "Yes. Her name was Elaine."

"She was so-o-o pretty. Looked like an angel," Kylie exclaimed with wonder.

"Thanks, Kylie. Yes. She was very pretty." He sighed. "And very nice."

Ashley studied the table, cleared her throat, and

stood. "More coffee?"

"No, thanks. I'll grab some on the way to the marina."

Eric stood and left the table.

"That was too good. I hate to leave. You know, I was thinking." He found Ashley's eyes. "Since you girls will be here alone for a few days and the phones have been acting up, I could pick you up a cell phone. You know. Just in case." He studied her face—a mask of pleasant innocence.

She shrugged. "No need to bother. We'll get by. Always have." Ashley looked at Kylie and smiled. "Haven't we, honey?"

Kylie nodded. "Yes, Momma."

Ashley walked Eric to the door. "Will you be home for lunch? I'd love to fix you something."

"Probably not. I usually grab a sandwich or soup somewhere. Busy time of year." He shrugged.

"Oh." Ashley looked hurt. She exhaled. "All right, then. Call if you change your mind." She touched his shoulder gently. Her smile seemed different. It was soft but radiant. Something special he hadn't seen before. Shy with a hint of…temptation? "Please. Don't worry 'bout us. We'll be fine."

He headed to the Jeep, scanning the street. Empty.

"Remember…like I said, if you change your mind—'bout lunch," she repeated, calling after him.

"All right. And you call me if *you* need anything. If you have a problem with the phones you can go next door. The lady's name is Virginia. Just explain you're visiting for a while. She's very nice."

Ashley nodded.

Eric waved. As he watched her and Kylie wave

back, he hoped she could explain last night's conversation. Did it warrant an explanation? Would he ask her about it? It was hard to watch her—the pretty young woman with the tempting smile that stirred him in so many ways—and imagine she was part of some sinister conspiracy. But as Eric put the key in the Jeep's ignition, he couldn't shake his uneasiness. *Too little sleep and too many gangster movies, Eric.* His memory replayed flaming cars in *The Godfather* and *Casino. What the hell are you thinking?* He laughed at his foolishness, turned the key, and the engine fired up.

****

Bobby stopped by the office, grinning broadly. "Well, where is she—the mystery girl?" He looked skeptical. "You're not fooling me. She's a complete hottie, and you're keeping her to yourself."

Eric shook his head and smiled. "Not a chance." He shrugged and raised his eyebrows. "She seems to have a good head on her shoulders, so you may get to see her sooner than I thought."

Bobby gave him a sly look. "I still think she's hot, and you'll make up some excuse at the last minute so I"—he paused for effect—"do not get to meet this woman."

Eric was about to give it back to his friend when his cell rang. He checked the number and answered on the first ring. "You got it. Be there in ten minutes."

Bobby shrugged then gave him a smug expression. "It was her, wasn't it?"

"Nope. It was Joey. I'm taking your advice. Meeting her at the Kreme and Kone for a burger." Eric gave him a sarcastic smile, picked up his windbreaker and headed out the door. "Try not to break anything while I'm gone!"

Lunch was an inquisition. The Mid-Cape was an insular community and rumors spread like a fresh breeze across the Sound. Joey had heard rumors about Ashley and her surprise arrival. She wanted to know everything that had happened since Friday night.

"Ricky. Don't shut me out. Please...honey." She reached across the scratched Formica and squeezed his hand. "What happened over the weekend?"

"Okay." He nodded and gave her the sanitized version—referring to Ashley as a young girl who lived with his brother. Eric wanted to avoid jealousy. He neglected to tell Joey that Ashley was a pretty twenty-four-year-old that slept in the next bedroom.

The afternoon was quiet. No news, no calls, no more mystery. Thank God. Louise was coming over to take the girls out for another shopping spree. As he turned down his street he searched for signs of anything unusual. The long gravel road was empty. He pulled into his driveway and put the Jeep in park. As he headed toward the house, he could hear the faint sound of singing coming from inside. Sweet harmony. Pretty. Sounded like one of those Christian stations his dad used to listen to. "Amazing Grace" floated on the light breeze blowing through the house and out the kitchen window.

When he reached the porch the music stopped abruptly. He heard muffled voices as Ashley and Kylie appeared from the living room, faces flushed. Both looked down. Their lips were pushed tightly together.

"Did someone sew your mouths shut?" Eric asked, resisting a smile.

"I'm so sorry." Ashley began, hand fidgeting

through her thick hair as her eyes darted around. "I had no right to play that beautiful instrument. I was just cleaning it and got fiddling with it and playing a few notes and…and we got carried away."

Kylie stared at the floor peering up, wearing a guilty frown. She nodded.

Suddenly it dawned on Eric. "That was you two playing and singing?"

Ashley and Kylie both nodded, stealing looks at each other.

"Sorry," they whispered in unison.

"For what?" Eric approached them and grinned. "That was wonderful. Elaine would be happy that someone was using her piano. And your singing." Eric shook his head. "I thought it was the radio."

Kylie let a smile emerge. Ashley followed slowly.

"You mean it?" Ashley said curiously. "You don't mind us playin' and singin'?"

"Mind? Of course not." Eric pushed them down the hall and pointed. "I'd like to hear more."

Eric scanned the room and beamed. "Look at this place." The girls had straightened and cleaned everything in the house.

"Thanks." Ashley glowed when she saw his expression.

While they waited for Louise to arrive with more groceries, the two girls put on a concert any choir would have been proud of. Kylie had a sweet, shrill soprano. Ashley sang a pleasing alto harmony. She played Elaine's beautiful Baldwin with grace and ease.

Eric was so swept up in the tiny musicale that it took Lu's applause from the doorway to break the trance.

As they headed back to the kitchen to help prepare supper, Louise looked the place over and wore a smug expression that recalled her final words from last night. *I told you so* was written all over her face.

Chapter Sixteen

Despite the unanswered questions, Eric signed the documents necessary for Ashley and Kylie to live with him. The remainder of the week settled into a pattern. Eric was determined that he was going to get back into fighting shape.

They went to bed early every night. Eric rose at 5:45 each morning, stretched for ten minutes and then went for a run. By the end of the week, he was up to thirty minutes. And from the first morning he had a constant companion: Rusty. As soon as he opened the door the little spaniel would go out to "do his business" as Ashley called it. That first morning he sniffed around Eric's running shoes and licked his ankles. He refused to go back into the kitchen. So like it or not, Eric had a running partner. And despite his stubby legs the slender pup kept up like a champion.

When Eric and his furry little friend returned every morning Ashley was already up, singing her way around the kitchen, while she fixed him a large breakfast. She made dinner every night while Kylie assisted. Eric continued to marvel at how happy and well-adjusted they seemed.

Eric kept asking himself why Ashley and Kylie had made the long trek, trying to find some rational explanation for what Lip and Buzz had told him. Lip was away, but Eric had talked to Buzz again. His friend drew another blank—nothing more to offer. Eric knew he should do something, but he had no idea what. Were the heavy backpack, the hidden cell phone, and Ashley's apparent lack of a personal history worth raising a fuss over? Probably. Had there been anything else to raise a question or deepen the mystery, he might have confronted her. But the simple truth was that Eric enjoyed the girls too much. So, though it went against all his training, experience, and intuition he remained silent.

And with each passing day, Eric thought less and less about the girls' strange arrival and fell more and more under their spell. He loved Kylie's giggling and the cozy, familiar way she clung to him when something scared or upset her.

And though he tried to avoid the truth, after only a few days, Eric had become Ashley's willing captive. There was nothing about her that didn't attract him. Her accent was as warm and smooth as maple syrup. Eric could listen to the intoxicating drawl endlessly. And the new clothes she and Louise bought fit like they'd been tailored for her. He found it difficult to avoid following her lithe figure while she glided across the kitchen like a TV chef. He beamed as he sat at their kitchen table, watching her make breakfast. Each time she'd pass Ashley would tickle her daughter. And there was the way her eyes held his, the slight tilt to her head and the way she studied his face with a look of wonder when he talked…Eric thought she felt the same attraction he did.

Every evening Kylie and Rusty played in the spacious side yard, joined by Lola, the little girl next door. Eric sat on the porch swing enjoying a cigarette while Ashley weeded Elaine's precious flowers. On

Thursday, when a warm, spring rain dampened the grass, the girls put on another impromptu concert at Elaine's Baldwin. Ashley played from memory. "The Water is Wide" was his favorite. It was a hymn Eric remembered from his childhood. To a bystander they looked like a happy, well-adjusted family.

But the week followed another pattern. Each morning Ashley asked him to come home to lunch and each day he met Joey instead. When he and Joey parted company on Friday, she gave him a long kiss on the lips. But Eric wasn't fooling himself. His goal wasn't encouraging his relationship with Joey; it was an attempt to avoid one with Ashley. Despite the powerful chemistry and the obvious attraction they shared, Eric wasn't sure that a relationship with her was the way to claw his way back from months of grief and self-imposed exile.

Things appeared normal, almost routine. Perhaps too much so? No strange phone calls interrupted dinner, no anonymous vehicles hid behind the giant maple. No more mysterious cell calls in the middle of the night. Could it be? Were they who and what they seemed or was this just a charade? *Was it possible Ralph's fertile imagination fashioned this whole scenario for some reason yet to be revealed?*

Whatever doubts troubled him about Ashley, he felt no ambivalence toward Kylie. He couldn't wait to get home every night and spend time with her. He adored her. Loved running around in the tall grass with her and Rusty, teaching her horseshoes, how to tie a square knot or kick a soccer ball. And every signal Kylie sent said she cared just as much for him.

But on Friday night, when he pulled in, Lu's car sat

in the driveway. She was getting out. "Hi, Ricky. How goes the Memorial Day push? Got everybody in the water?"

"Almost," he answered, looking for his favorite playmate.

Kylie burst out the door in another new dress and sweater. "Hi, Auntie Louise. Are we going out for hot dogs, ice cream, and miniature golf?"

Lu continued to spoil both girls, but especially Kylie. But she refused to use any of Eric's money or his credit card. Eric was afraid she was spending her life savings on making them the best dressed runaways on Cape Cod.

Louise opened her arms as Kylie threw herself into them. "You better believe it." She picked Kylie up and twirled her around to squeals of laughter.

Eric felt a frown cross his face when Lu glanced in his direction. "That is, if Uncle Eric doesn't mind."

"No. No...of course not." He forced a smile. "You go out with Aunt Lu and have a great time."

Quite a pair, Eric thought as they headed for the car, laughing. He had an empty feeling gnawing at his stomach when he realized he'd be spending the evening alone with Ashley. Something he hadn't done since their soul-searching conversation on Tuesday night. Part of him felt excited, another surprisingly anxious.

He slowed as he walked up the stairs to the back porch. Entering the kitchen, Eric expected to see Ashley at the stove. The kitchen was spotless...but empty. Rusty stood, wrapping his slender body around his running pal's calves. Eric opened a cabinet and extracted a large doggy treat. The spaniel chewed on it, wagged his stubby tail, and returned lazily to the little bed Ashley had fashioned in the pantry. The living room and her bedroom were vacant, too. Like the kitchen, both were spotless and in perfect order. They had been since the girl's arrival. He passed Ashley's room, noticing his door was closed. Pinned to it was a neatly penned note:

Eric,

> *Checking out the beach. It's such a beautiful night. I made some sandwiches, potato salad, and cupcakes. Brought some beer…and a couple of cigarettes. Join me if you don't have plans. If you're busy we can catch up later,*

> > *Hope you can come,*
> > *Ashley*

Eric read the note. Ashley's scent clung to it. He knew nothing about perfumes. Elaine's taste in fragrances was high-end. Everything surrounding her said "elegance." Something expensive. He knew it was a Chanel brand. She always had to write it down for him when it was a special occasion and she needed more. But the scent that Ashley wore was different. It had a heady, almost musky quality that lingered long after her. Eric couldn't get enough of it.

He walked to the window and looked toward the water. The emerging foliage hid any sign of the beach. Nantucket Sound was in a sleepy mood tonight, the surf barely visible. Sitting on the bed, he exhaled deeply.

Eric had an uncomfortable feeling about being alone with Ashley. He swallowed and picked up his cell, dialing Bobby in hopes his buddy would be free and they could hang out. Joey was working at the Pub till after midnight. So she offered no alternative.

"Hey, man, what's happening?" Bobby answered on the fourth ring. "Sorry it took me so long. Just got out of the shower. Got a date, boss." There was a moment of silence. "What about you? Playing uncle again tonight?"

"Not exactly," Eric said. "I'm alone with Ashley. Lu and Kylie went out for junk food and ice cream."

"That's cool. You said Ashley was...nice. Can't wait to meet this hot mystery woman. Spending a little one on one time might be a good idea. You can find out all her deep dark secrets." Bobby chuckled, having no idea he'd come close to the truth.

Eric sat on his bed, silent, scratching the day-old stubble on his chin.

"Am I missing something?" Bobby paused, his voice hovering between curiosity and concern.

"No. It's okay, man. Have a good time," Eric whispered and hung up.

Having run out of options, Eric changed into a pair of Dockers and a clean sweatshirt. Putting his hand to his face again, he went back to the bathroom and stared into the mirror. Should he shave? Hell, no. He slapped a little Polo on. Good enough. This was a casual meal. *Nothing fancy, nothing serious, nothing else*, he told himself as he snatched a piece of gum from the draw. When he reached the kitchen he glanced out the window and froze. *Shit!* A large gray sedan and the van with the electronic ears were hiding behind the giant maple again. He couldn't have missed them on the way in. If this was handiwork on his neighbor's house why show up so late?

Instead of heading for the beach, Eric opened the back door and walked casually toward the mailbox, careful to avoid looking at the vehicles. If he could see inside maybe he could get an idea of what and who they were, but both vehicles had tinted windows. Not SOP for a common utility van.

As he headed to the mailbox, he stopped and made a show of picking weeds along the driveway. By the time he was halfway to the mailbox, the large sedan started, made a leisurely turn and headed away from him at high speed, throwing up a trail of dust.

He retrieved the mail, glancing at the van. From this distance he could read the lettering: Cape Cod Direct—Your New Approach to Satellite Television. Could be a coincidence. Despite the time, maybe the neighbors really needed something done ASAP.

He took the mail and walked leisurely back to the house, pretending to look over the flyers. Was someone watching them and if so, why? Eric shook his head. He went into the kitchen, put down the mail and took out his cell. *Damn it!* Eric wanted an answer! He called information and asked for Cape Cod Direct. When the computer sounded confused, an operator came on, asking which office he wanted: Hyannis, Dennis, Falmouth or…

"Thanks, I'm all set." He put down the phone. So much for intrigue…again. The mysterious strangers in the van must be part of the team hooking up a new TV setup for his neighbors. The gray sedan was probably nothing more than the car of one of the workmen. It still seemed odd that they'd be getting to the job at 5:30 but…

Enough! He shook his head, laughing at his fruitless attempt to play detective. Eric headed for the front door and the rambling dirt path that wound through the beach roses and assorted foliage to the rocky beach that fronted on Nantucket Sound.

He walked down a ten-foot wooden stairway that needed repair and arrived at the sandy strip that bordered the small, smooth stones filling the last twenty feet to the water. He scanned the hundred yards before the coastline took a sharp turn to the east. There was a mild southwest wind. It blew the cigarette smoke toward him before he saw her. Ashley sat on a small blanket with a bag and cooler.

"Ashley," he called and waved.

She didn't see him. Her eyes stared straight ahead, focused on the Sound.

He walked toward the blanket. "Ashley," he called louder as a light wind blew in his face.

"Hi," she said as she snapped out of her trance and waved. Her face wore a pleasant, glassy smile. When he got closer he saw an empty Sam Adams on the blanket and one in front of Ashley. A six-pack rested in the small cooler she'd borrowed from the garage.

Eric sat down on the blanket. She slid toward the edge and patted the place she'd vacated. "Wasn't sure you'd show." Her smile broadened. "Sit down. I won't bite. Least till we're better acquainted."

She threw her head back and giggled like a little girl.

She was dressed in a fitted pair of running pants. Her Red Sox team jersey had a silky look. The front was tied in a precise knot, leaving a hint of midriff exposed. She looked nice. *No, she looks downright spectacular!*

Ashley pointed to the South Side Marina hat on her head. Wisps of thick brown hair escaped from underneath it.

"Found it hanging in the back hall," she explained. "My hair's always such a mess. Figured this would help."

"Glad to see you're advertising. Nothing like a pretty girl to help promote the place. And I love the way your hair looks." Eric's face flushed. Had he really said that?

Ashley's face turned crimson at his compliment. She found his eyes, showing him the shy version of her dimpled smile. "Thanks. Anything I can do to help," she agreed, looking back toward the Sound. "Glad you found my note." She turned toward him again. "Figured maybe you had somethin' better to do."

Eric shook his head. "'Fraid you're stuck with me." He pointed to the empty beer as she put out her cigarette. "I thought you didn't…"

"Met your neighbor, Ginny Allen, this afternoon," she shrugged, interrupting, and avoiding his eyes. "She told me about you. She came over and tried to pump me, figure out who I really was, and why I was here. But I turned the tables on her." Ashley looked back at him, lips curling up. She was pleased with herself. "Hard living in the same house with a local legend. Hell, you're a damn superhero. Didn't know if I could handle it. Decided I needed a couple of these to loosen up." She held up the empty Sam Adams.

"You're of age." Eric shrugged as he reached over and pulled one out of the cooler. "I don't know what Ginny said. She gets carried away."

Ashley nodded and broke in again. "I like her. Brought her daughter over, too. She and Kylie had a ball. Played all afternoon. Hide and seek, climbing trees, exploring 'round your pond." Ashley beamed. "It's nice Kylie's got a real playmate. Your neighbor told me about..." Ashley stopped suddenly. When she turned, Eric read regret on her face. "About your wife." Her large eyes glistened. She looked down at the blanket. "Quite a lady—smart, beautiful, everybody loved her from what Ginny said. The perfect couple." Ashley's words sounded sad, almost ironic. She raised her eyebrows and studied the water again. Pulling out another cigarette, she offered Eric the pack and lighter.

He nodded. "Thanks." He shook a Marlboro out of the wrinkled soft pack and handed it back. "She's right. Elaine was something special."

He lit up and joined her in studying the Sound.

Ashley exhaled deeply. She opened her mouth to speak. "Do you want to..."

"No, but thanks." Eric anticipated her question and shook his head. He'd spent too many Friday nights mourning Elaine. "Not tonight."

"Sorry if I stepped on sensitive ground." Ashley looked down at the beach.

"It's not a problem," Eric said. "Just something I'd rather not talk about tonight."

She turned toward him again, wiping her cheeks of some stray tears. She worked to put on her best smile.

Ashley reached over the blanket and found his hand with hers. "Remember what I told you? If you ever want to talk I can listen real good."

"I appreciate it," he told her and gently pulled his hand away.

Ashley put her lips together. Her look could have been regret or embarrassment.

"You hungry?" she asked as she exhaled and

opened the paper bag, pulling out two seafood salad sandwiches.

"Sure. They look good. Smell great, too." He rubbed his hands together.

"That's me. Five star chef." She laughed. "Maybe I could go on TV."

"You've done a great job cooking this week, and the house looks like new. But don't go running off to TV. I need you around the marina."

She flushed and shrugged, obviously pleased by another compliment.

"Well, how 'bout it? You ready for work tomorrow?" he wanted to bring the subject back to the mundane.

"Damn straight. Been feeling like a freeloader all week. I'm primed." She pulled a wrinkled piece of paper out of her pocket. "Here."

"What's this?"

"My plan to pay you back." She said with conviction. Written in the same fine script as the note he'd found, the page was detailed, based on her assumptions about salaries. "I figure I could get around $12.50 an hour for an office job. Googled it today. Well, at forty hours a week…"

She'd spelled it out meticulously. "I figure if you don't charge us room and board, in a few months I'll be paid up, depending on taxes."

Eric raised his eyebrows. "Well, taxes shouldn't be too bad. Besides, you may be running the payroll." He gave her a mock scowl and then winked.

"Okay." She sounded anxious. "That should leave us some spending money. Can save up a little and maybe find our own place." The thought of Ashley and

Kylie leaving sent a wave of regret through him. It must have shown on his face. Ashley looked confused, then hurt. She snatched the paper back and studied it. "Did I mess up? Are my numbers wrong?"

"No, they're perfect, Ashley."

A strong gust blew in from the Sound. She shivered.

"You're cold. I'll go back and get a jacket."

"No, I'm fine. Eat your sandwich and here." She threw him another beer and took one for herself. "That'll warm you up."

"Be careful. They can sneak up on you."

She laughed. It had a cold, bitter sound. "No, Eric. Nothin's ever gonna sneak up on me again."

Her eyes grew dark and sad. Eric could only guess at her meaning.

They ate the sandwiches and potato salad and polished off the six-pack of Sam Adams. The food tasted as good as it smelled and the beer went down easily. Too easily. Ashley pulled out some black-and-white cupcakes she'd whipped up. They were wrapped in cellophane.

Eric felt himself relaxing. He was tired of intrigue, suspicion, and playing detective. He wanted to enjoy her. As the conversation moved from one subject to another, the tension melted. After the third beer he was lying on the blanket, laughing and teasing Ashley like he'd known her for years. She asked about the marina, his time in the Special Forces and Williams College.

But when Eric turned the tables, Ashley played defense. Played it well. Any questions about her childhood, their life in Norfolk, her education, or Ralph brought on heavy doses of misdirection. She'd dodge a question, answering it with another.

Maybe it was the third beer after a long day, maybe just curiosity when Eric found himself asking, "At the hospital they said it looked like you'd been"—he hesitated, not sure how to put it—"as if someone had hurt you."

Ashley had been propped on one arm watching him. She pulled herself upright at the question.

"And you want to know who did it?"

She was perceptive, Eric had to admit that.

"Yeah, I probably have no right to ask but I would."

"I did have someone in my life. Someone who wasn't nice to me." She put her lips together and looked at the gentle surf again. "But it wasn't your brother if that's what you're thinkin'. I keep telling you he was nice to us."

Her words were loud and clipped. She sat playing with the sand as she turned toward him. "And that's all I'll say about *that*. I have my secrets, too."

Eric nodded, knowing he may have gone too far, too soon. He sat up and found the Sound himself as he put his arms around his knees.

"It's okay, Eric," she assured him as she touched his shoulder. "The neighbor lady says you got a girl?" Ashley changed the subject. She flushed as she stood and began whipping small stones into the light surf.

"*Joey?*" He shook his head and smiled. Eric didn't think of her that way, though he was sure Joey did. "She's nice. Trying to help I guess, but Joey's not my girl." Adding, "Hey. You got a good arm there."

"Told you I played softball in high school. All-League shortstop," she answered through clenched teeth as she threw harder. Ashley looked angry and frustrated.

What did I do? he wondered.

As dusk descended over the shore he felt Ashley watching him. She pouted, playing with her jaw. She brushed off her hands, then put them in her pockets as she found Eric's eyes.

"That's too bad. I can understand why any girl would want…want to be with you. You're special. Real special," she whispered, letting the wind steal her words. Ashley bent. Reaching out, she brought her hand to his face. Her touch felt so light. For just a moment Eric thought she was going to kiss him. Eric stared into her magnificent eyes. Instead, she backed away. "When you came to visit that time I…I never forgot you." Her face grew red and her words sounded slurred. True confession time. "We all need someone, Eric. I hope you find a special person again. I only wish…" Ashley's words died again. She shivered as her eyes dropped and her touch fell away.

"You *are* cold." Eric stood and swallowed deeply. Their conversation was getting intimate. Too intimate and too much on target. "Be right back." Heading to the edge of the scrub foliage, he found a handful of dry twigs. He looked back at Ashley as she lay on the blanket, wrapping herself in her arms. He'd build a small fire to keep her warm. To take care of her. Ashley was funny, pretty, and showed every sign of caring for him. A lot. A dangerous combination? Maybe, but for the first time in months he felt good about something.

"But how about you?" he asked as he approached the blanket. "Don't you…?" He stopped in mid-sentence. Through the twilight he saw her, tightly curled up with a pleasant look on her face. Her eyes were closed. Ashley lay asleep, purring softly.

Eric knelt, watching her. He smiled, touching the scar on her cheek. It was almost healed. As he touched it, she curled up tighter and made a gentle sound. A soft murmuring like she felt happy and safe. Her hand moved, finding Eric's, squeezing it in her sleep.

She looked so sweet, so innocent, so content. As he stared at Ashley, Eric knew why he avoided being alone with her, spending too much time with her. He knew it was happening. He'd done everything he could to avoid it.

Eric lifted her slender body and walked, cradling her tenderly in his arms. When they reached the path leading to his house, she put her arms around his neck in her sleep and nestled closer to his chest. He followed her lead and pulled her tighter. He liked the feeling. Safe. Warm. At home. He stopped, watching her, wanting to pull her lips to his.

Eric shook his head, angry with himself. Very angry. Because he knew why he'd felt so uncomfortable about being alone with her. Since that first day at the hospital he'd been falling in love with Ashley.

Chapter Seventeen

Eric was glad that Kylie was out with Louise. He didn't want her to see him carrying Ashley into the house. After taking her upstairs, Eric laid her gently on the bed and covered her with the thick quilt at the foot. Ashley turned on her side, pulling her legs into a crouch and wearing a pleasant smile as she reached out in her sleep. Eric sat down, studying her face as he found her hand.

Love? No. It made no sense. He'd known Ashley for a week. But as her hand rested tightly in his, it felt so warm, so right. As if it belonged there. His gaze washed over every feature, realizing he'd already committed them to memory. Pleasant warmth crept over him.

Eric had the urge to kiss Ashley again. He resisted a second time, gently touching her cheek, letting his hand follow the curve of her neck to her collarbone. She sighed softly and showed a sleepy grin. He closed his eyes and let his hand fall away. Doing his best to control his desire, Eric stood, and tiptoed to the door. As he glanced toward her closet, the door was slightly ajar. Inside rested Ashley's backpack. The one that weighed too much.

Had Ashley twisted the truth? Had she lied? He couldn't be sure. Even if she had, did that give Eric the right to violate her privacy? He considered it as he took a half-step toward the closet. The decision was taken out of his hands as he heard the kitchen door fly open and Louise and Kylie burst in laughing. Eric walked to the closet, pulled the door closed quietly, and went downstairs to meet them, closing Ashley's bedroom door on the way out.

"Well. Sounds like you two had fun," Eric said as crossed the kitchen and ran his hand through Kylie's hair while she yawned. He gestured in the direction of the Sound. "Be right back, ladies. Gotta grab some things Ashley and I left on the beach."

"Okay," Lu agreed. "I'll get this sleepy head ready for bed."

He bent down, made a silly face, and tickled Kylie as he walked by. She twisted her face into a grin and giggled.

Grabbing a flashlight out of the utility drawer, Eric headed to the beach. The moon lit the sand and bleached the gray stones that bordered the water. After making his way down the rickety steps, he collected the empty beer bottles and papers in a trash bag. He shook the sand from the blanket, folded it, and grabbed the picnic basket as he surveyed the picnic area. Perfect.

He headed toward the steps. Stopping, Eric put everything down. Opening the basket, he retrieved the remains of Ashley's sandwiches, tore them into tiny wedges and threw them across the beach. The seagulls would have a banquet. By the time he'd mounted the steps the birds were broadcasting the signal, telling their companions that good food was free for the taking. Eric mounted the rickety steps, feeling better than he had in months.

Approaching the door that opened on the Sound, he

heard Louise and Kylie still laughing as they re-lived their adventure.

"How'd it go? You know—with Ashley?" Lu asked while Kylie shrugged into her pajamas.

Eric never had a chance. Before he could answer, Kylie exploded, describing their litany of activities. "Uncle Eric, I ate so many hot dogs my tummy aches. I had a chocolate shake and fries, then played miniature golf!"

When Eric glanced at Lu, she winked.

"Then we rode go carts," Kylie continued.

Louise groaned good-naturedly as she rubbed her back. "Our young friend put me through the ringer." She crossed to the table and sat down heavily. "Next time I'm sending someone in better shape—like you."

"It was so much fun. Like when Granddaddy used to take us to the county fair."

Eric's smile froze as Kylie referenced Ralph's amazing metamorphosis again.

"Is Mommy asleep?" Kylie asked, looking up the stairs.

Eric nodded.

"Can I give her a hug and a kiss goodnight?" Kylie asked. *"Please?"*

"Let's let her sleep," Eric whispered. "She's really tired."

"Where is Ashley?" Lu asked, looking around.

"Asleep. She made us a picnic supper and we ate on the beach. Then she went up to bed. Now, you and your mommy have to be up early for work." He gave Kylie a mock frown.

She nodded. "Mommy told me all about it." Her lips took on a determined expression.

"You finish getting ready for bed, honey," Eric pointed toward the bathroom.

"Okay," she said and ran back, giving Louise a long kiss. "I'll wash my hands and face and brush my teeth." She looked pleased at having recited her tasks, adding, "Will you come up with me and tuck me in, Uncle Eric?"

Kylie crossed the kitchen and gave Eric a hug.

He bent down and kissed her cheek. "I'll be there in just a minute. We'll read you a story and say your prayers," he promised. Kylie made a silly face and ran to the bathroom.

"Is Ashley okay?" Lu asked with concern.

"Sure. She's fine. She doesn't drink much. Had a couple of beers and fell asleep." He grinned as he gestured to the stairs. "She's in her room purring like a kitten."

She found his eyes. "You give Kylie so much attention. I'm glad you spent some one-on-one time with Ashley. She...she looks up to you so much, Ricky."

Eric's face flushed as he turned to throw away the trash.

The words sounded strange coming from his mother-in-law.

"Thanks. What about you?" Eric asked. "You doing okay with this whole thing?"

"So far, so good..." Louise exhaled and rubbed her back again, leaving the thought unfinished. She rose, crossed the room, and gave him a peck on the cheek. "Now, I have got to get home to bed. I am pooped!"

"Night, Kylie," she called from the kitchen door.

Eric watched his mother-in-law, wondering what

she'd left unsaid. She cared so much for Ashley and Kylie. There was no doubt about that. But it must be taking its toll on Lu, watching another woman and child come into her daughter's house and fill it with affection and love.

He walked to the screen door and waved. She got into her Camry, started it, and turned, heading to the street. As he began to turn away he saw something under the giant maple—a faint reflection. The same place he'd seen the vehicles parked earlier. Eric heard an engine start. Tires spun and headed up the street without headlights.

Damn! Possibilities raced through Eric's mind. None of them good. He ran to the landline and picked it up, dialing Lu's cell. *Voice mail!* He hit redial. Same answer.

"Uncle Eric. I'm ready for bed," Kylie called from across the kitchen.

"Okay, honey." His heart pounded. "Give me a minute."

He followed Kylie up to her room. Should he call the police? Go after Louise in his Jeep?

The land line rang. He ran into his room and picked it up.

"Hi." It was Lu. "Did I forget something?" she asked.

"Is everything okay?"

"Sure. Why wouldn't it be?"

He looked at Kylie and exhaled. "No special reason."

"What's going on?" she asked. "I saw you called twice, but I dropped the cell on the floor. Some nut drove by me on High Bank Road at fifty." Louise sounded annoyed.

"You're sure you're okay. Maybe I should come over," he said.

"*For what?*" she asked in a curious voice. "Are you crazy? I'm going home, bolt the door, and pour a Skinny Girl margarita. Then me and all six-foot six inches of Jack Reacher are gonna snuggle under the covers." She chuckled. "I've got a forty-two ounce bat next to my bed, a hunting knife under my pillow, and my cell. You keep your butt over there where you're needed."

"You're sure you're okay?"

"Jesus. Yes, Ricky. How many times are you gonna ask me? Relax! Take a night off," she said softly. "Put the ball game on and go to bed. Busy day tomorrow."

"Yeah. Okay," he said and hung up the phone.

He directed Kylie, who'd been standing with her face twisted into an impatient frown back to her bedroom. "Can we *go* now?" she demanded.

Eric wasn't sure what to say. She was adorable but...seven-year-olds were not his specialty.

"Patience is a virtue, Kylie," he said sternly.

"Huh?" She looked confused. He burst into laughter. This was his second false alarm of the evening. He was too damn jumpy—swinging at shadows.

"Nothing. Just something us old folks say," he said as she hopped under the covers and made room for him on the bed.

"Uncle Eric." Kylie said thoughtfully after considering his words. "You're not *that* old."

"Thanks, Kylie." He chuckled under his breath as

he picked out a book and headed to her bed.

They said her prayers and read her favorite book, a story called *Naughtily Natalie* that Lu and the girls had bought at the store.

"Good night, sweetheart." He kissed the top of her head. "Sweet dreams." He was almost out of the room when the patter of tiny feet caused him to turn.

Kylie grabbed him tightly around the legs. "I love you so much, Uncle Eric."

Eric turned, holding her tightly and swallowing hard as he felt the lump in his throat. "I love you too, honey," he whispered. "Very much."

Eric turned on the teddy-bear night light and blew Kylie a kiss as she wrapped the covers around her shoulders. He did his nightly check while Rusty found a convenient tree. The street was empty. Eric closed, locked, and bolted the door, then stood against it, exhaling deeply. He looked at the alarm system and activated it.

He stopped at the foot of the stairs, looking up. Eric mounted the steps quietly and knocked softly as he turned the knob, opening Ashley's door.

She lay, eyes closed, facing him, her breathing rhythmic. The faint odor of beer hung in the room. He crossed the room and cracked the window. A lazy breeze blew in from Nantucket Sound.

Suddenly Eric knew why he felt so strongly about Ashley. Her vulnerability. She was hurt, lonely, and needed someone desperately. He needed her, too, maybe more so. It occurred to Eric that he wasn't alone anymore.

He thought about the last week and everything that had happened. Cars that had suddenly appeared on the street. The strange phone calls. Were Ashley and Kylie in danger? Was he? Or was this a product of an overactive imagination? It appeared that way tonight. He stood frozen, watching her, knowing what it meant if he stayed in her room.

She stirred and opened her eyes. "Hi," Ashley whispered, closing her eyes and dozing off again after a sleepy smile.

Eric pulled the quilt up wrapping it tightly around her. He tiptoed to the chair across from her bed and sat down, unable to take his eyes from her face. Eric wanted to forget the secrets, the half-truths, the questions that nagged him. He wanted to trust her. He'd fallen under her spell. Eric never believed in witchcraft, but Ashley had certainly bewitched him.

****

The early sun filtered in, making random designs on the throw rugs as it peeked through her sheer curtains. Eric awoke slowly, looking around as he remembered falling asleep in Ashley's room. His tight muscles cried for help after spending the night in the overstuffed easy chair next to her dresser. He caught sight of the digital clock on her night table: 6:04 a.m. It occurred to Eric that this was the first time he'd slept through the night in weeks.

He could hear her rhythmic breathing as she turned in her sleep. Eric raised himself and watched as she lay snug and cozy under the thick quilt. She looked so peaceful, so content. Eric closed his eyes for a minute, knowing he should get up, stretch out the stiffness and head to the bathroom, but…

"Time to get up, sleepy head." She stood over him, whispering. Her early-morning drawl sounded deep and sexy. Very sexy. And he loved it. Her eyes found his as she kissed his cheek softly, letting her lips drift across his face. "We have a big day ahead of us. I am goin' to fix *you* a special breakfast." She began to walk away, then turned and showed him her best smile. "Thanks for always takin' care of us…" She paused, adding, "…of me."

His eyes followed her as he swallowed deeply. For the first time in months, Eric was glad to wake up.

Chapter Eighteen

Eric glanced at his watch: 6:52. He heard the commotion downstairs. Stiffness filled his limbs. Stretching would have been great, a run to loosen up even better, but there was no time.

"Uncle Eric. Come on. Mama's got breakfast ready," Kylie called from the foot of the stairs.

After leaving Ashley's room, he showered and shaved at warp-speed, pulled on clean jeans and a dark-blue polo shirt with South Side Marina stitched over the pocket. As he rushed downstairs, the smell of food and coffee brewing drifted up the stairway. Mouthwatering. Ashley was spoiling him. He stumbled over Rusty hovering on the bottom step.

"Hey, buddy," he complained, giving the little spaniel a cross look as he stumbled. "No time for a run this morning," Eric told his canine companion, wondering if Rusty understood his explanation.

"Sorry. Rusty, get off those stairs," Ashley scolded the little spaniel as she gave him a gentle nudge with her sneaker. "He likes you," she said, grinning as she nodded toward Rusty. She shrugged and put down a plate of bacon and eggs for him. The dog wagged his stubby tail like a pendulum and followed his mistress as she guided him toward the back door.

Ashley wore a pair of khakis and a polo shirt. She looked downright professional.

"Made you something special this morning," Ashley said softly, licking thick batter off her fingers. "Blueberry pancakes," she announced proudly. "Think you'll like 'em."

"Sounds great," Eric said, remembering how he'd felt as he carried her into the house and later, when he'd sat watching her. Love was the word he'd used. He wanted to deny it. But in only a few days Ashley had stirred emotions that had lain dormant for a long time. Could he be wrong about Ashley? Were all his suspicions and the things that had happened just coincidence? When she spoke, Eric sensed sincerity. There was something so open and caring about her. She was different than any woman he'd ever known.

"Do the pancakes look okay?" Ashley asked.

"Out of this world," Eric enthused, realizing that he'd begun to compare Ashley with Elaine. Being such polar opposites made it difficult. It was so soon and he knew so little about Ashley. Besides, he rationalized, one enjoyable evening fueled by too many beers did not a relationship make!

Ashley looked at the clock on the kitchen wall. "Don't want to be late on our first day," she said, concern on her face as they joined hands and quickly blessed the meal. Eric caught her smile as her hand tightened around his. Ashley finished the prayer and they dug in. The food tasted as good as it smelled. Better.

He watched the two faces staring back at him as they gulped their eggs. "Slow down, everyone. Slow down. Don't worry about the clock," he assured them. "I'm the boss."

After cleaning up at warp speed, the three of them

piled into Eric's Jeep, pulling into the marina parking lot at 7:50. In the three years since his return to the Cape, it had been transformed. Once a tired, ramshackle assemblage of shacks, it had emerged as a thriving, vibrant business. The buildings and grounds showed attention and pride. Driving through the gate, Eric enjoyed watching Ashley and Kylie stare, eyes wide as saucers.

"All this is yours?" Ashley whispered, looking at him. She wore the look of a child in a toy store. Eric loved her ability to find pleasure in the simplest, most mundane things. He watched as she studied the marina property, turning toward him with an excited smile. He reveled in her admiration.

He parked in front of the office and boat store he'd opened two years ago. The three of them walked slowly up the gravel path, bordered by a freshly painted white picket fence. An expensive, hand-carved sign hung from a lamppost with the words South Side Marina in four-inch gold letters. The hours of operation and his name were listed underneath. Rusty jumped out of the back where he'd made the trip in obedient silence next to Kylie. He followed, taking it all in, barking enthusiastically as Eric opened the door.

"Hey, boss," Bobby greeted him. "Can I help you folks?" he asked, not realizing Ashley and Kylie were with Eric.

"It's okay, Bob. They're with me."

A grin crossed Bobby's face. "Oh my God. You must be Ashley." He walked toward her and extended his hand, pumping hers. "Eric's told me so much about you. Says you may be able to help us in the office."

"I'll try." She released Bobby's hand, giving him a

shy smile. "And you must be Bobby. Eric says you can make an engine stand on its hind legs and dance."

They all laughed, even Kylie, though Eric was sure she had no idea what they were talking about.

"If you can show me the office and your computer, I'd like to get started."

****

Administration and technology had never been Eric's strong suit. After Elaine's death he'd given in to grief and self-pity, letting the paperwork pile up. Eric hoped that part of his life was over. He'd spent too many nights thinking about things that might have been. But in the short time since the girls had arrived Eric discovered what it felt like to live again. He shot a glance in Ashley's direction.

"Well?" She interrupted his thoughts, arching her brows. "I can't help just standin' here, *Mr. Montgomery*. Are you gonna show me what's goin' on?"

"Absolutely. Follow me." He gestured toward the office.

For the next two hours, Eric showed Ashley the piles of papers, invoices, and folders he'd let accumulate. He gave Ashley a brief profile of their business: they rented slips by the foot, forty-two in all. All but the six they kept for transients were rented for the entire season at $36 a foot—the best price for the most complete service on the river.

"Got it." She nodded.

Eric and his staff did everything from fueling their customers' boats to doing complex repairs on the Cummins Diesels that powered half the fleet. A skilled diesel mechanic was a rare commodity. So Eric had stolen his friend Bobby from Hyannis Marina, a high-profile operation four miles away in the Cape's only city. Eric's marina served as the primary fueling stop for most of the river's hundred resident boaters. They'd even begun to show a profit from the boat store he'd opened two years ago.

He wasn't sure what to expect, but rather than sit by passively and bewildered as they proceeded through the files and papers Ashley paid close attention, studying every form and outlining each process. She carried a pad and asked intelligent questions, making notes while following Eric around, sporting a pair of worn, horn-rimmed glasses she'd retrieved from her bag.

Within minutes Ashley shooed him out of the office. "Let me spend a little time getting to know your systems and playing with your laptop." She nodded at the HP Pavilion on Eric's desk.

"Of course," he agreed, leaving her in his private domain—a small eight-by-ten-foot space with no windows and the funky smell of stale take-out and beer. As she powered up the computer Eric went into the store to watch. After a few minutes, Ashley crinkled her nose and came out of the office wearing a frown.

"You got a fan 'round somewhere?" she asked.

"Sure." He went to the storage room, pulled out a pedestal fan, and put it in the office door.

"Thanks." Ashley turned it on and went back to work.

Eric watched her, trying to look casual. Ashley's fingers ran across the keyboard with fluid expertise. She knew her way around computers. No doubt about that. Eric watched in amazement. He recalled Buzz suggesting the possibility of someone erasing Ashley's personal history. While it seemed like a long shot when his friend had mentioned it, as Eric watched Ashley using the laptop like a seasoned pro he found himself wondering.

Eric returned to the small office on the pretext of looking for something in the file cabinet. He glanced as Ashley manipulated the icons on the laptop's fifteen-inch screen. She'd open one, search it quickly and go on to the next. He found himself staring. Ashley stopped and turned.

"Something wrong?" Her lips worked into her familiar pout.

"No." Eric shook his head. "You just seem to know an awful lot about computers and software. More than..."

"Still think I'm a dumb girl from Dixie, Eric?" she interrupted through drawn lips, her face drawn.

Eric's face flushed. "No. I didn't mean that," he said. This was the second time he'd underestimated her. He'd never do it again.

She looked back at the screen. "We have computers in Virginia. I went to school and worked a lot. Coming from the South doesn't mean I spent my life chained up in the woods with an axe and overalls." Ashley shook her head, adding, "And growin' up with your brother doesn't make me stupid."

He held up his hands. "Sorry. I didn't mean that." Eric knew he'd screwed up.

Ashley turned away and resumed her research of the icons. "Is there some way we could get some ventilation in here?" she yelled after him. "It doesn't smell very good."

He paused and shrugged. "We can try."

"If I'm going to be working in here, I'd like some fresh air, better light, and a view of the water."

"Sure," he agreed, as he walked out feeling like a fool...again.

****

Most of the boats were launched or ready to be, so Eric asked Bobby to take Kylie and Rusty with him while he was showing Ashley the operation. Lu worked till one, so he didn't have a lot of choices. When he left the office, Eric found Bobby and his new helpers on dock four, working on a thirty-two-foot Sea Ray cruiser. Eric stood behind a cradle and watched as Kylie gave Bobby a tool while Rusty supervised, tail wagging, and giving them a bark for encouragement.

Kylie was such a quick study that by the time she left, Bobby nicknamed her "Data" referring to the infallible Star Trek android. As Eric watched them it was obvious Kylie was the latest female to fall under Bobby's spell. She beamed when he spoke or smiled at her.

Eric avoided the office for the next ninety minutes, still angry with himself for hurting Ashley's feelings again. But Ashley's performance continued to raise more questions. Buzz told him that Ashley had no work or school history. She told him just the opposite? Someone was lying or mistaken.

When Louise stopped by to pick Kylie up at one he took her to say goodbye to her mother. After Kylie gave Ashley a big kiss and hug, he stuck his head into the office. He had to admit she was right. It smelled pretty funky.

"Want some lunch?" he asked. "I usually pick up a

sandwich for myself and Bobby."

She nodded, her eyes dark and moody, avoiding his. "Okay. How 'bout a BLT?"

He drove to the corner sandwich shop, bringing her back a BLT and a Pepsi.

"Thanks," she whispered as she took the bag.

"C'mon and eat at the picnic table with Bobby and me. It's a beautiful day."

Ashley shook her head. "Thanks. I'll take a few minutes off, but I'm just startin' to get somewhere with your stuff."

"Okay." Eric sighed and headed out to eat with his friend, sneaking a look back at her. Half of him wanted to kick himself for hurting her. The other half was still trying to reconcile her astounding job performance with her non-existent personal history.

"Everything all right, boss? You look confused." Bobby asked as they ate.

Eric exhaled deeply and shook his head. "Think I screwed up big time. Insulted Ashley."

"What happened?"

"She's so good with the computer it took me by surprise. I said something stupid that sounded like I was putting her down."

"Maybe that's why she's standing over there looking like she lost her best friend." Bobby gestured toward the office as he took the last bite of his ham and swiss. Ashley walked behind the building.

"Thanks." Eric nodded at Bobby and walked to find her. *Best friend?* Was that how she thought of him? Was that really what he wanted? To be her best friend or something else...something much more?

Ashley stood behind the building that housed the

office and ship's store, head hanging as she lit a cigarette.

"How's it going?" Eric asked as he came up next to her.

"All right." She sighed deeply.

He was about to offer an apology when Ashley pushed the cigarettes toward him.

He pulled one out of the pack and lit it.

"Guess I'm still a bad influence," she whispered, looking away as she put the pack back in her pocket. She turned and studied the river.

He studied it with her. "I don't think so." He added softly, "I'm glad you found me."

"You mean it?" Ashley turned toward him and put out her cigarette. "'Bout before. I'm real sorry I went off on you like that. I had no right. Here we arrive out a nowhere and you been nothing but kind." She let her head drop. "I had no right," she repeated.

"We both overreacted," Eric whispered and gently lifted her chin, finding her eyes. "Like I said, I'm glad you're here."

Ashley found his hand and squeezed it, taking a deep breath. The electricity flashed up his arm.

"Me, too." Her face grew a smile that could melt steel. "Real glad," she repeated, touching his face softly, like she had on the beach last night.

Ashley cleared her throat as she took a deep breath. Her face grew crimson. "Guess we should get back to work."

She let his hand go as her smile turned shy. "Now, if you've got a few minutes, I got some questions."

"Okay. Shoot," Eric said as they walked inside. Ashley spent the next hour asking him about several things she'd come across on QuickBooks. She'd printed an Excel spreadsheet to help him follow her. Eric sat, still amazed.

The afternoon passed quickly. Almost too quickly. Eric enjoyed working with Ashley. By four they were laughing and teasing each other the way they had on the beach. He could never get enough of her seductive drawl or the dimples that seemed carved into her cheeks.

After answering Ashley's questions, Eric went outside to see what his crew was up to. Before they left for the day, Bobby grabbed Eric's arm. "So that's the poor little girl whose been taking up so much of your time?"

Eric nodded. "Yep. Thanks for babysitting, by the way."

"Kylie? My pleasure. What a great kid." Bobby chuckled and shook his head.

"Yeah." Eric smiled as he thought of her. He knew Louise had taken Kylie to lunch when she got off-shift. His mother-in-law's affection for her was extraordinary. Eric wondered, if like him, Lu's mind wandered to things that might have been.

"Damn smart and a lot of fun," Bobby added. "Oh, and tell you what, boss," Bobby said as he watched Ashley approaching the Jeep. "If you ever have any more sad down-and-out young women you want to help, give 'em my number. In case you're blind, that young lady is so hot, she is smoking!"

Eric blushed. He smiled and nodded in agreement. "If I find another one lying around, I'll send her your way."

****

When they pulled into the driveway at five Louise was already inside, fixing spaghetti and meatballs. "I hope you guys like it. It's simple, and I've had a long day."

"We love pasta. Thanks so much." Ashley gave her a gentle smile and took Kylie to the living room where they watched Blue's Clues, then set the table.

"How'd it go?" Lu asked when she and Eric were alone. "Tough day?"

"Tough." Eric chuckled. "Ashley's amazing. Give her two weeks and I can retire."

"Would you mind if I took the girls over to the mall to do more shopping after they're done with the dishes?"

Louise was spoiling the girls, the way she had Elaine.

"'Course not. That'd be great, but you must be exhausted."

"No, I enjoy being around them." Eric thought he saw a tear.

"Take my Visa."

"Well, let's see how extravagant they get. I'll take it in case of emergencies."

"Don't be silly. I think of them like family," he told her.

She blushed and began to protest.

"Enough." He shook his head. "Now. Go get them some more new clothes."

When they left, Eric sat with the ball game on again. He ignored the TV and the score. Instead he stared out the window at the gathering dusk. Eric tousled Rusty's orange coat as the little spaniel lay next to him, softly snoring and wagging his stubby tail. Eric replayed the events of the last week. He had the urge to visit the Sam Adams but let the temptation pass. He wasn't about to bother his buddy Buzz on the weekend, but he made a mental note to call first thing Monday morning and try to figure out what was going on with Ashley's missing records. There was no doubt she hadn't spent her days eating candy and watching reality TV. She was intelligent, in great shape, and damn it, Bobby was right. She was very, very hot!

Eric changed, donned his sweats, and took out his frustrations on his weights and the heavy bag in the basement. Eric remembered again how good it felt to work out. He was glad he could still bench press 225 pounds and move the bag with authority. He hadn't lost too much despite his long sabbatical.

After an hour, he toweled down and headed up the stairs two at a time, pleased that his morning runs had brought back his wind, despite smoking more. He headed outside, accompanied by his running buddy Rusty, opened a bottle of water, and flopped down on the porch swing. Scanning the street, Eric noted it was absent any anonymous visitors.

His mind still swam with the images, contradictions, and mystery. Despite his fears that the face she showed him was just a facade, a cover to mask her real purpose for being with him, Eric couldn't help grinning. He thought about Kylie. She was the most adorable little girl he'd ever known. And with every passing hour Eric felt more and more drawn to Ashley, her natural beauty, wonderful sense of humor, and the awe she displayed at everything around her.

He returned to her immediate mastery of his office systems and paperwork. As if she'd run an office for years. She was obviously very intelligent and her skills cried "experience." More questions. More mystery. Still no answers. What was she holding back and why?

But when he closed his eyes, another thought came to mind. Something less logical but more pleasant and far more visceral: the way Ashley looked at him with those enormous eyes, the intoxicating fragrance that surrounded her, and heaven help him, the way she'd felt in his arms last night.

Chapter Nineteen

On Monday morning Eric stood on the fuel dock and called Buzz. "Hey, buddy, I got a question for you."

"Okay, shoot."

"Have you been able to find out anything more about Ashley?"

"Funny you should ask, 'cause I asked our specialist on computer forensics to give it a shot."

"All right, Jesus, Buzz. Don't keep me hanging. Did you find anything out?"

"Eric, my old friend. If I had I would have called you pronto." Eric thought his friend sounded hurt. "He couldn't figure it out either. All I know is he agreed that it was pretty strange and if her records were erased, as we all assume, it would have taken someone who knew what they were doing just to breach the firewalls in questions."

"Sorry, Buzz. I know you would have called. I'm getting frustrated."

"Why don't you just ask her?"

"I could and if she doesn't give me something more I may have to. Thanks."

"I'm here if you need me."

So much for expert help. Eric shook his head and hung up.

****

The rest of the week flew by. Despite the questions that hung in the air between them, there were moments when it seemed like Ashley and Kylie had been in Eric's life forever. He waited anxiously to hear more about Ralph, but Lip was on vacation. His ally in the quest for the truth had gone dark and silent. The mysterious vehicles—if they really were mysterious— had disappeared as well. His conversation with Buzz hung in the back of his mind as he waited patiently, hoping Ashley would lower her defenses and confide in him.

The days were full of last-minute details and loose ends at the marina. It was the time of year when the days sped by in a whirlwind of activity. Most began too early and it was often dark when Eric and Bobby locked the gas dock and the office and headed home for a late supper.

Ashley became the third leg on the stool. She pitched in with a dedication that was unexpected, but very welcome. When she had some free time in the office she had no problem donning a sweatshirt and jeans and helping out with cleaning and fueling the thirty-six boats that made up the complement of customer vessels.

Late one afternoon as she was helping them rinse off a new cruiser, Ashley stopped and stood, staring out at the river, shaking her head slowly.

Eric came up beside her. "Is everything all right?" he asked with concern.

She showed him her dimples and laughed like a child. "I…I just can't believe I'm so lucky. To be here in this beautiful place, workin'…with you. It's like a dream come true."

Eric flushed. He felt the same way.

He continued to be amazed by her intuitive grasp of what needed to be done and when. As promised, he had a generous window installed in the stuffy little office. The opening brought light and fresh air to Ashley's tiny kingdom. Where empty Sam Adams bottles had lain hidden behind the laptop, a fragrant spring bouquet picked lovingly from Elaine's garden now decorated her neatly organized desk.

"How's the new window working out?" he asked.

"Just great." She turned to study the yard and the river. "I love it."

"Do you want an air conditioner?" he asked.

"Not right now. I want to hear the sounds of the water. And it would block my view. It's so peaceful here. Just like heaven." Eric recalled Kylie saying that Ashley had promised her heaven right after they'd arrived. He was happy they'd found it. "I love it, Eric." she repeated, giving him a long glance. Ashley blushed and turned toward her work. "Can I ask you something?"

Eric nodded. "Sure."

"You're always so busy running around managing everything. Do you ever find the time to just sit down and take in this amazing place? It's so special, Eric." She touched his shoulder gently. "'Take some time to smell the roses,' Ralph used to say."

"I try," he said, finding her eyes. The positive references to Ralph no longer troubled Eric. He hoped that someday he'd get the chance to talk to his brother. Eric no longer held any anger toward Ralph. It was obvious that he'd taken care of the girls lovingly, like they were his own. But it would still take more than the occasional compliments the girls offered before Eric jumped on a plane, found him, and gave Ralph a big hug.

"Tell you what. Next time you see me rushing by without so much as a look at the river, you have my permission to come out and grab me. We'll spend a few minutes watching it together."

"I'd like that," she said and offered her hand.

Eric took it and walked out wondering how he'd ever gotten along without her.

****

Late that week Ashley called him into the office, beaming like a proud child at show and tell as she showed Eric her handiwork. "Check *this* out."

She showed him the two new file cabinets she'd ordered. Everything was organized and in perfect order. "I think I've got things under control." She pointed with pride to the reorganized icons on the desktop, opening a couple to show what she'd done. "What do you think?" she asked quietly.

"It looks great," he said. And it did.

"Here are the calls I've made." She handed him a list of vendors and customers who had some issues when she arrived only days before. "The checkmarks indicate that we're okay. We've paid them or they've paid us. There are a couple we have to talk about." She handed him a balance sheet and P&L. Eric studied the list and the financial reports.

"OK." Eric sat down and they went over her list item by item. "Whew," he whistled when she'd finished. "Where do I sign up for retirement?"

They both laughed.

Ashley watched him as her smile faded. "If you

ever go anywhere, Eric. I...I want to go with you." Her face reddened.

"Why...sure, Ashley," he managed after an uncertain silence.

She found the new window and stood, perhaps worried she'd said too much.

Eric wanted to take her in his arms, tell her she'd never lose him, but instead he cleared his throat, patted her shoulder, and headed back to the yard.

****

Kylie assumed the role of marina mascot. But having a seven-year-old underfoot wasn't the best thing for Kylie or the staff. On days off, Louise would babysit or come by and pick Kylie up. Since there were no other children on his street, their neighbor Ginny, Lola's mother, offered to watch Kylie when it fit her schedule. On the days when neither option was available, she tagged along and they made the best of it, finding little chores she could help with and not get in the way.

Every day Ashley packed a lunch. They ate at the picnic table, talking, laughing, or watching the river. They often talked about the spectacular rebuilt homes that populated both banks.

After the long days that drained Eric and his staff, he looked forward to their evenings together. They were special. Ashley would make dinner or if it was too late, they'd get take out. She and Eric would sit on the porch swing afterward, enjoying an evening cigarette and sipping coffee while Kylie, Lola, and Rusty chased fireflies across the generous backyard. Whenever she could, Louise would join them.

They constantly showed small, unmistakable signs

of their affection for one another, but neither spoke openly about their feelings. Eric's wounds were healing. The scars had started to fall away. He suspected Ashley had similar reminders of more painful, bitter times.

Every night when he went to bed Eric was all too aware that this special young woman who'd come to fill the emptiness lay close by. He hoped that Ashley felt the same longing.

****

It was early on the Saturday afternoon of Memorial Day weekend. Eric walked by the boat store and saw Jarrod McAllister, one of the newest boat owners, standing in the door of what everyone referred to as Ashley's office.

Jarrod was in his late twenties, tall, successful, and damn good-looking. Too good-looking. Eric stopped and stood where he could watch. He'd seen Jarrod hanging around the boat store and the office more than once since Ashley's arrival as office manager.

As Eric stood silently watching, someone tapped on his shoulder.

"What's going on?"

It was Bobby.

"Nothing," Eric explained, feeling self-conscious about being caught spying on Ashley.

Bobby followed his eyes. "You sneaky son of a gun. You're not fooling me." He broke into a smile. "You're checking up on Ashley."

Eric cleared his throat and started to walk away.

Bobby caught his arm. His smile softened as he found his friend's eyes. "It's okay. Your big secret's safe with me, LT. Not that it's much of a secret."

Eric stood, silently, not sure how to answer.

"You've got nothing to worry about, boss," Bobby assured him.

"I don't know what..." Eric began.

Bobby arched his eyebrows, interrupting his friend. "I only hope that someday someone like that looks at me the way Ashley looks at you."

Eric's shoulders relaxed as he exhaled deeply. A smile worked across his lips. He slapped Bobby on the side of his arm.

"Thanks," Eric said with a nod.

"What are friends for?" Bobby showed his broad grin and headed away.

It was late that afternoon. Closing time. They'd had an incredibly busy day. Jarrod had left the office uneventfully, looking discouraged. A perverse satisfaction speared Eric at his customer's frustration.

As he headed back to get Ashley after locking the pumps on the gas dock he spotted Joey's Volkswagen Jetta in the parking lot. It was empty. Joey was already inside and had probably seen Ashley. He was in for an earful. Since Ashley had been working at the Marina, Joey had barely crossed Eric's mind. She must be hopping mad.

Eric took a deep breath and set his jaw, resigned to the tongue lashing he knew was coming. The wait was short. When he was still a few yards from the door, Joey emerged, looking flushed and furious. She spotted him and stopped in her tracks.

"Just met your little friend. Ashley? That is her name, right?"

"Hi, Joey, and yes, her name is Ashley," Eric answered quietly.

"Real cute, pleasant, and don't tell me—I'll bet she's smart as a whip, too."

"Yes. She's been a big help around the marina," He began as he nodded. "Look…"

"No, Eric. You look! Take your pick." Joey held up her hand and looked back at the door, giving Eric an ultimatum. "You haven't called me in a week. I got tonight off. Meet me later or we're through."

Ashley appeared in the doorway behind Joey, looking pale and anxious. She shrugged and mouthed *Sorry*.

Eric sighed and looked at Ashley for a long moment, then back at Joey. "I'm sorry, Joey." He shrugged. "I've got other plans tonight."

"Damn you, Eric Montgomery!" Joey fixed his eyes with hers, turned around, and saw Ashley behind her. "Have fun with your little friend." She walked away, tears streaming down her cheeks.

Ashley stood fixed in the doorway mute, looking as if she wanted to say something.

Eric walked to her and put his hand on her shoulder. "Time to go home."

She swallowed deeply and found his eyes as she pushed her lips together.

"Okay," she said and disappeared into the building. When she came back she had her shoulder bag and Eric's jacket.

They locked the door and walked silently to the Jeep. As soon as they were both inside, Ashley sat staring straight ahead. "Do you…" She hesitated as if not sure she should continue. "Do you really have plans tonight?"

He looked at her. Was it possible that she didn't

understand the meaning of what had just happened?

She continued staring straight ahead, lips pursed in her classic pout.

Eric reached over and took her chin gently, turning her face toward him.

"No. Of course not," he whispered.

Her large eyes filled as she found his. They overflowed when she closed them, sighing deeply. Ashley took his hand from her face, weaving her fingers into his and squeezing them tightly.

"Let's go home," she said quietly as she smiled broadly.

The usual routine changed that night. Ashley made sandwiches for everyone, including Louise, who'd dropped by.

"Sorry. I'm just too tired to cook tonight." She looked at their faces and offered an apology.

"You've had a long, hard week," Eric said enthusiastically. "I don't know how we could have got through it without you."

"Thanks," she said quietly, her face impassive.

Ashley ate quickly, speaking politely only when spoken to. Eric would catch her glancing at him, but her eyes would snap away when he looked at her.

When dinner was over, instead of taking her nightly cigarette on the porch with Eric or playing with Kylie, she excused herself and headed out front toward the beach. Lu raised her eyebrows at Eric. He shrugged.

"What's going on?" Louise whispered when the screen door closed. "Did you two have a fight?"

Eric stood staring at the screen door. "No," he answered, mystified by this new behavior. "Kind of— the opposite."

His mother-in-law studied him. "What?" Her face looked vague and confused.

"I feel funny talking to you about this."

"For God sakes." She scowled. "I care about that girl, too. What the hell happened?" She raised her voice, wincing as she looked around to make sure Kylie was out of earshot.

"Something...nice happened between us." He avoided being too explicit.

Lu sighed as a faint smile crept across her lips. "That's good. What do you think?" She scolded him gently as her eyes narrowed. "I've been watching you two watch each other for two weeks, Eric. I'm not blind or dead. Not yet."

"Thanks." Eric squeezed her shoulder and turned toward the door leading to the beach. Louise took his arm gently and held him.

"We both knew that Ashley had some baggage, right?"

Eric stopped and nodded. "Right."

"Then let her go, son." Lu looked toward the door. "Ashley may have some things she needs to work out. Give her a little time."

Eric shrugged and gave his mother-in-law a hug.

Ashley returned in half an hour. Her face showed strain and confusion. She put Kylie to bed and came back downstairs to say goodnight to Louise, smiling weakly but avoiding Eric's eyes as she walked by him up to her room.

He did his best to follow Lu's advice: let her be, give her some space. But it was tearing him apart. His heart had begun to thaw. Ashley was the reason. Now, just when it seemed they'd found each other, she retreated again, becoming the Ashley of those first days—the sad, enigmatic girl he couldn't find.

Eric studied the clear night sky. He smoked his last cigarette after letting Rusty out for his "business." After surveying the street, Eric closed and locked the door. Turning, he found Ashley sitting on the third step watching him. Her eyes found his as she stood. Her lips turned upward, growing into an inviting smile as she approached. When she was a foot away she stopped, letting her head fall for a moment. She closed the small distance that separated them, raising her face toward his.

"Please, Eric. Don't be mad at me," she whispered. "You must know how I feel about you." Her arms circled him tightly as she leaned her face into his chest. Her fragrance surrounded them as she pressed closer. Ashley clutched his shirt, nestling her head against him.

Eric bent, kissing the top of her head as he ran his fingers through her thick, dark hair. His hands fell to her cheeks as he cupped her face in his hands. "I'm not mad at you. I don't think I ever could be. I only wish I knew how to make you understand how much…"

"Shhh." Ashley put her fingers to his lips. "I do understand. It was a nightmare and now that we're here with you…it really does seem like heaven."

She pulled his face to hers and found his lips, kissing him, softly at first, pressing harder into him. Her lips were soft and sweet, melting into his as their mouths joined. Her tongue found his, playing over and around his in ways he'd only dreamt of. Suddenly, there was only Ashley, her firm, supple body pressing against his, her delicious mouth. Eric was lost, blinded by a fever of passion and desire. His hands found her back, pulling up her T-shirt. The silk of her skin glided against his fingertips. He began gently, but in a matter of seconds he pressed into her. Pulling her lower back closer while he pushed against her thighs. Eric wanted all of her. Reaching into the waistband of her shorts…

"Mommy!" Kylie cried desperately, sounding wounded.

Ashley pulled away, breaths coming in short gasps as she leaned against him, holding his shoulders to brace herself.

"Mommy's…coming, honey," she panted weakly as she pulled free of Eric's embrace. He let his hand fall slowly downward, following the line of her jaw to her collarbone as they held each other's eyes. She took his hand, caressing, kissing it jealously.

"Sorry," she managed in a throaty whisper. She turned, took a deep breath, and ran up to her daughter.

Eric stood, exhaled deeply, and turned to find a cigarette in the nearby drawer. He went out to the front porch and lit it, sitting on the stairs, eyes fixed on the Sound as his arousal slowly disappeared. Halfway through the cigarette, he heard soft footsteps behind him.

Ashley appeared, still flushed. "I'm sorry. That was my fault. I…I shouldn't have let that happen." She swallowed deeply. Shook her head. "Kylie had a bad dream," Ashley said apologetically, looking back toward her daughter's room. "I need to sit with her."

Eric nodded. He'd almost lost control. The chemistry between them was so strong, but… "Maybe we both need more time," he whispered, not quite believing the words he let slip out. He put out the cigarette, kissed Ashley on the cheek quickly, and headed up the stairs.

"Goodnight," she called after him.

Eric reached the top of the stairs without looking back.

Chapter Twenty

Eric lay in his bed, sleeping in short fits as he wrestled with the throes of confusion and guilt. Was any of this real? Could he trust the emotions that consumed him? What about Elaine? Did his feelings for Ashley violate his vows to her? Always more questions, never any answers.

Despite his restless night, when the alarm went off at 5:45 Eric tumbled out of bed, pulled on clean sweats, and went downstairs to find his running buddy. Experience told him that a good run cleared his mind. Eric and Rusty did the five-mile route in thirty-five minutes. When they returned Eric brought a dish of cool water for Rusty onto the porch. The two sat as the early sun lit the eastern sky. Eric's mind drifted back to his passionate few minutes with Ashley.

The clatter of dishes brought Eric out of his reverie. He went inside to find her dressed, moving around the kitchen, making breakfast. The radio sat silent. No singing this morning. A sleepy Kylie sat moping at the table.

"Good morning," Ashley said when she saw him. Her words sounded brittle. They held a formality Eric didn't recognize.

"Morning," he answered with equal coolness. He looked toward Ashley as he crossed the kitchen, putting his hand on Kylie's shoulder. "You okay, honey?"

She leaned into him. "Guess so, Uncle Eric," she answered with a yawn.

"My little girl had a bad night." Ashley bent and kissed Kylie's cheek as she put a bowl of sugar-coated cereal in front of her daughter. "Here, honey. It's your favorite."

"Thanks, Momma." She spooned a tiny amount into her mouth.

Eric turned to Ashley. "You must be exhausted." He touched her hand. She looked at him with a courteous smile that never reached her eyes.

"I'm okay. Why don't you get cleaned up?" she suggested without looking at him.

Eric stared for a minute in silence, then nodded and ran up the stairs. This was a new Ashley—personality number three—the cool, aloof Ashley. Eric considered making a catalogue of her moods.

Frustrated by her behavior, Eric came to a decision. He cared for Kylie. There was no doubt. And he knew he was in love with Ashley. There were times during his restless dreams when her image teased and haunted him in ways that no one else ever had. But he couldn't keep up with her personality shifts and the mystery that enveloped her. He'd follow Louise's counsel: be polite but keep his hands off.

Though the activity level was less than Saturday, the day dragged. Kylie had come with them that morning since Lu had worked the night shift and needed her beauty sleep. The poor child had trudged listlessly after Bobby, then taken a long nap on the hide-a-bed in the storeroom. Louise came by and picked her up about two.

"How's it going?" she asked.

He ran his hands through Kylie's rich hair. "Let's say I think giving Ashley her space will be no problem." He hadn't intended the words to sound so cold but they did. Lu saw through him immediately.

She bent and put her arms around Kylie's chest. "Could you go out and wait in the car, honey? For just a minute," Louise asked in the pleasing way. Words of wisdom were in the offing.

She watched Eric then found his hand, squeezing it tightly. "Close your eyes for a minute."

"What?"

"Close your eyes," she repeated. It was an order.

"All right," Eric followed with an impatient sigh.

"You've been abused by someone you love and have a child when you're a teenager," Louise began.

"What?" Eric asked in confusion.

"Keep your eyes closed and use your imagination," she instructed.

"Okay." Eric exhaled and frowned.

"Your mother's been killed in an auto accident," she continued. "The man you thought of like a father tells you to leave because something bad may happen to you and your little girl. You trudge through the rain and the cold with a frail child and a puppy and arrive at the home of the one person you think might give you shelter, then you faint from exhaustion and awake to find you've had a miscarriage. After two days in the hospital you go to a strange house where you know no one and try to pick up the pieces of your life and your child's, still not sure if somebody or something is out there in the dark to harm you. Finally, after being there for a few days, you discover that you've fallen head over heels in love with your protector, the person you sleep next to every night. How would you handle that, Ricky?"

Eric slowly opened his eyes as he held Lu's hand. He swallowed. The lump in his throat felt as big as a basketball. "I get it. How'd you figure all that out?"

She laughed softly. "Read too many mystery novels. And your body language. It seemed to fit." She paused. "I've known you for twenty years, Ricky."

"Not bad. You should work for the CIA." He squeezed her hand tighter. "Thanks for the dope-slap." Eric was still reluctant to discuss his feelings for Ashley with Louise. "I guess I've been self-centered."

"No, you've been kind and wonderful to the girls. The problem is that you feel as much for Ashley as she does for you." She released his hand. "You're torn. You're worried about Elaine's memory and the commitment it might mean if you give yourself to them, to her."

Eric nodded slowly, staring in amazement. His mother-in-law had some psychic blood in her. "But what if…"

"You're the finest man I've ever known, Eric. Whatever you do is all right with me. And for what it's worth…"

He nodded.

"… I love them, too."

Chapter Twenty-One

Of course Louise was right. Nothing new there. He needed a swift kick and she'd accommodated. Eric tried to imagine what Ashley must have gone through— confusion, fear, the terrible loneliness. He knew them all too well, especially the last. He'd been there not long ago.

Eric bumped around the rest of the afternoon doing his best not to punish himself for overreacting to Ashley's moods. At 5:30 he put his ego in his pocket and headed to her office. Ashley stood bent over the open window sill, watching the boats coming in from their afternoon on the Sound.

"Anybody home?" he asked quietly with a knock.

Ashley straightened and turned slowly, her face smudged with tears. She walked to him and took his right hand, playing with the fingers as she raised her eyes to his. "Just me," she whispered.

Eric found her left hand and took it in his, caressing it while she did the same with the right. "Good enough for me."

Ashley sighed and shook her head. "Why do you put up with me?"

He gave her a scowl, studying her with mock concern. "'Cause you're such a good cook."

She let his hands go, wiped her cheeks, and sniffled as a smile crossed her face. It morphed into a grin.

Eric stood, taking in her large brown eyes, thick, dark hair, her smile. He checked his watch. "Come on." He took her arm. "We're going home and get cleaned up. I'm taking you out to dinner."

She opened her mouth as if to protest.

Eric put his fingers to her lips. "No argument. You're my date for the evening."

She put her lips together and took his hand as they got their things and locked up.

They showered, got dressed, and left a revitalized Kylie playing in the backyard with Lola and Louise as they headed out for the evening. Eric told Ashley it was a thank you for all the work she'd put in over what seemed an endless and exhausting week.

He tried but found it impossible not to stare. Ashley was very pretty and had a wonderful figure. That was a given. She looked great in jeans and a T-shirt. But Eric had never seen this Ashley—the dressed-up, spectacular version with makeup, lipstick, eye shadow, and a knit dress that looked form-fitted.

"Will you please watch the road before you get us both killed?" she whispered as her face grew red.

"Sorry," he mumbled in embarrassment. "I just…" He shook his head.

They pulled into the parking lot of the Scargo Café, a popular restaurant on Route 6A on the Cape's north side.

"Looks very busy," Ashley said as she surveyed the parking lot filled to overflowing. Her mood was cheerful but subdued. "Must be great food," she added as she turned toward Eric.

"Yep, this was—" He stopped as he caught himself in mid-sentence, realizing he'd been about to tell her this was Elaine's favorite eating spot. "I used to come here a lot," he said, attempting a course change.

"It's okay," she said quietly. "We both had lives before I knocked on your door."

Her lips pushed into her signature pout.

Eric pulled in behind a large SUV.

"Are you sure this is okay?" Ashley asked.

"Sure. The Tahoe belongs to the owner," Eric explained, finding her hand when he'd parked the Jeep.

"I don't mean that, Eric." She looked straight ahead. "I mean you and me bein' here like this. Like we were, you know. A couple?"

It took him a minute. Eric had always been a quick study in all things intellectual and physical but when it came to social issues, well...

"I should have thought of this earlier, but you know a lot of these people. I'm living in your house, sleepin' in the room next to you with my daughter down the hall. Don't you think some folks are already talking about it? And seein' us together, like this, will just cause more gossip?"

Eric pushed back in his seat and put his lips together tightly. She was right. Whatever their feelings for each other they'd done nothing wrong. Kissed a few times and held hands. Not the stuff steamy romance novels were made of. But...

"Eric?" She took his hand tightly. "I'll do whatever you want, but I just got here and I think, hope, that maybe, there's somethin' special here for us—you and me and Kylie. Something real *special.*"

"But we've done nothing wrong," he argued, raising his voice. After a year of grieving Eric had found something, someone he cared about very much.

He wanted to take her out, show her a good time and yes, even show her off. Was that wrong?

He knew the answer. She was right. "Okay," he gave in reluctantly.

Ashley's eyes glistened as she squeezed his hand. She sighed deeply. "We can still go home and I can fix us something."

Eric held up his hand. "I promised you a night out. And a night out we're gonna have."

Chapter Twenty-Two

Half an hour later, they sat on the hood of Eric's Jeep. A lazy southwest wind blew in from Nantucket Sound while they devoured two mammoth burgers from a local fast-food place. The sun slowly worked its way below the elegant collection of homes at the mouth of the river.

They parked near the end of the seawall at West Dennis Public Beach. The perfect vantage point to watch the sun's rapid descent, tardy boaters making a hasty retreat from the Sound before dark, and the modest waves breaking on the beach.

Ashley giggled, using a paper napkin to wipe her mouth as she turned to face him. "Well, I must say when you promise a girl a night out, you don't fool around, Mr. Montgomery."

"Shhh!" he whispered in mock secrecy. "Don't let the word get out. I'll have to beat the women off with a club."

He joined her laughter.

Ashley's expression turned soft and serious. She put her food on the large paper bag and found his hand, letting her slender fingers work into his. "It'll be our secret," she whispered so gently and with such emotion Eric wanted to grab her, take her in his arms, and kiss her till she was breathless.

He inhaled deeply and looked at her. "Miss

Fitzhugh, I still have questions." He paused, squeezing her hand. "But I hope this fantasy never ends."

He could see her blush in the rapidly descending twilight. "Oh, Eric," she said in a throaty whisper. "You know I feel the same way about you, about us, but…"

She never finished. Letting go of his hand, Ashley left her food on the hood. Taking off her sandals, she held out her hand.

He followed her lead as she walked along the seawall. Ashley took a seat. Eric joined her, still holding her hand loosely.

Ashley scanned the parking lot. Apparently satisfied they were completely alone, she took a deep breath, swallowed, and began. "I studied computers. I specialized in technology at college."

That answers one question, Eric thought, nodding.

"I got good at it. Better than good. Seemed to have a knack for it. I could do pretty much whatever I wanted with computers." She took out a cigarette and offered him one. He lit Ashley's then his own. She inhaled deeply and blew a plume of smoke into the light, pleasant breeze.

"Okay? I'm hoping that's not the end of the story." He turned toward her.

"It's not." She took another long drag. "Ralph worked at the Officers' Club. It was the perfect job for him and for us. He kept regular hours and you know him, always smooth and friendly. Everyone loved him. A real charmer." Ashley shook her head. "Then late last year something happened. He never talked about what he was doing. But he began keeping strange hours. Some nights he'd get home way past midnight. And then, after New Year's he started acting really different."

"Different how, Ashley?" Eric asked.

"Ralph was always funny, full of life. He'd play with Kylie and take us to ball games and movies and down to the shore." Her words were slow, well-thought-out. Like something she'd been planning for a long time.

"You know it's still hard for me to…"

She held up her hand and shook her head. "I know you didn't like him, Eric. And he wasn't perfect." Her lips curled up in a half-smile. "But Ralph was like the class clown that everyone laughs at. He never hurt anyone till—"

Ashley stopped suddenly. She looked beyond him toward the long asphalt parking lot. Even in the twilight he could see her face grow ashen. She swallowed and licked her lips.

Eric twisted and saw what had caused her metamorphosis. Parked, side by side, stood two vehicles. They sat two hundred yards away on the asphalt. Their position blocked the way out. He looked back at Ashley. This was no act. She was terrified.

Eric took her by the arm, positioning himself between her and his Jeep. "Stay behind me."

She nodded and stood, following his lead back to the Jeep. Ashley was shivering. And not from the soft, evening breeze.

They walked the twenty-five yards to the temporary safety of his vehicle. "Duck down here behind the Jeep," he told her calmly, giving her a confident smile as he reached across her onto the console to retrieve his cell.

Just as he was about to make a call, the two

vehicles honked loudly and took off down the asphalt strip bordering the beach at high speed. They sped by Eric's Jeep yelling and laughing.

Eric smiled and threw the phone on the seat as they did a loud U-turn and headed back toward the main road at high speed laughing and tossing out empty beer bottles as they disappeared into the dark.

Ashley exhaled deeply as her shoulders slumped. She stared straight ahead.

"What's the matter? Who did you think they were?"

The suspicion and mystery were making a comeback, a major-league comeback.

She shrugged.

"Are you going to tell me why you left and what made your face go pale when you thought someone was watching you?"

She fidgeted with the hem of her dress and made a sour face. "Guess after Momma and Beau I got spooked."

"I know about your mother. Who's Beau?" he asked in a neutral tone.

She sighed and moved away from the Jeep, heading along the seawall again. After twenty feet she looked at him and sat on it. "I…I wanted to tell you about him."

"Okay. You've got my attention." Tension crept over Eric. He worked hard to control his emotions. Was this going to be the infamous other shoe—the revelation that brought them both back to unpleasant reality? He was in love with Ashley. Thought she was in love with him. Was that about to go up in smoke?

Ashley studied the small swells closing on the

shore. It was near high tide. "After last night I thought maybe you'd think I was just…" Her words hung in the soft breeze.

"Was just what, Ashley?"

"I know the kind of man you are—good, strong. I arrived here with nothing, had a miscarriage the first night, then next thing you know we're kissin' and huggin' like Romeo and Juliet. I was afraid you'd think I was using you."

"You were afraid I'd think you were trying to take advantage of me?" he asked. Eric listened but couldn't believe her words.

She nodded, twisting her mouth into a frown.

"You could have thought that," she whispered, turning toward him. "But it would break my heart if you did."

He put his arm around her shoulder and gently pulled her toward him. She rested her head on his arm.

"Ashley, there may be a lot of unanswered questions between us but in my wildest dreams I never imagined you were trying to take advantage of me."

Her slender arms snaked around his waist. "Really?" she asked, using one of her hands to push the tears from her tanned cheeks.

"Really," he told her.

They sat in satisfied silence for a long minute before she spoke again.

"Beau was the daddy of the baby I lost that first night," she whispered.

"You don't have to…"

"Yes, I do. Please," she interrupted. "You know how I feel about you. I want to tell you about it."

"All right." Eric nodded reluctantly.

"First thing you have to know is it didn't mean anything. I know that probably sounds terrible, but it's true. *He* didn't mean anything to me." She paused and took a deep breath. "Not like that. He was a friend. I guess you'd call him my mentor. Taught me things about computers not many folks know."

"Okay. Is that it?"

"No. We'd been hacking into government Web sites. Just seeing how far we could get. Breaching their firewalls, that kind of stuff. We were just fooling around. It was a game we'd play. Least it had been. We downloaded some reports and a few pictures. Didn't seem like anything at the time.

"I told you that Ralph had been acting really strange. He was out a lot, especially at night. And when he was home, he kept to himself—stopped taking us to places. Well, when Momma or I'd ask him if everything was okay he'd snap at us. I heard him talking one night on his cell when I was coming home. Heard the name 'Firestorm.' He didn't see me. Then I heard the name again when I went to pick him up at the base one day. Same thing. I found him talking on a cell. Funny thing is that when he finished talking he threw the phone into a trash bin. Like he was…"

"Destroying evidence," Eric interrupted.

She gave him a half-smile and nodded slowly. "Yeah." The smile disappeared. "Just like that."

"So Beau hacked into this database. It was real tough, but he was the best. We tried searching everything, trying to access files for Firestorm. It took a lot of work and they had that stuff well-protected. I told you, I was good. But Beau was incredible. There wasn't very much. Least it didn't seem that way. A few pictures and reports we didn't understand. I fell asleep on the couch in his office in the middle of the night. When I woke up he…he was kneeling next to me. I knew he liked me, but we were never more than friends. Next thing I knew we were kissing. He didn't force me. I was lonely and confused—going nowhere with no one else in my life so I…I just let it happen."

"I believe you." Eric nodded again, knowing he'd believe anything she told him.

"But I want you to know," Ashley continued. "There was no love in what I did. We never spoke about it again. The very next day he started getting strange phone calls. We used his system 'cause all I had was a cheap laptop. Someone on the line warned him to stay away. Never said what they meant but we knew. He said he thought people were watchin' him. Two weeks later Momma had the accident. That's when Ralph got really weird. Then Beau fell out his window. Police said it was an accident. But I knew for sure we'd been someplace we shouldn't have."

"What about the police?" Eric asked.

"I wanted to go to them. I told Ralph and he got angry—downright crazy. Said I'd get us all killed. And when I thought about it I realized that Beau and I were doing something illegal. They don't give out medals for hackin' into top-secret government Web sites."

So she'd finally told him the truth or at least the truth as she saw it. The question was what to do about it.

"Why are you telling me this, Ashley?" Eric thought he knew, but he needed to hear the words.

"I wasn't going to at first but, now I want you to know everything. 'Cause of what's happening between us. What happened last night was real. I know you think about your wife and you probably think I'm a..."

"Shhh." Eric put his fingers to her lips, pulling her close. Her arms tightened around his chest. She'd confided in him, trusted him with her life. "What I think, what I've thought since that first day at the hospital is that you're one of the most special people I've ever met. I don't understand you, but that's part of what attracts me. I don't care what happened before you arrived on my doorstep." He smiled down at her. "You said earlier that we both had lives before you knocked on my door."

"You really mean that?" Her words rang with disbelief.

He turned her face toward him and smiled. "Lu thinks you and Kylie were sent here for a purpose. To help me live again. She's right. All I want is to help you and protect you and..." He hesitated, knowing the impact his words would have and the commitment he was making to this sweet, frightened girl. "I want to rebuild my life with you."

Ashley slipped off the seawall and stood in front of him. She took both his hands in hers and kissed each one. "You know, when you came to visit Ralph I had a terrible crush on you." She blushed. "I thought I'd never seen anyone as kind and strong and handsome as you." Ashley swallowed deeply and continued. "I knew when you married your sweetheart and I prayed you'd be happy. When I heard about her accident I cried for a week knowing how much it would hurt you."

Eric stood and surrounded her with his arms, gently pulling her to him.

"When I knew we had to leave, there was never a

question about where to go." She chuckled softly as she nestled her head on his chest. "I wanted to find someplace we could feel safe and get a new start. A sanctuary. I knew we'd find that with you." Ashley pulled him closer. "But in all my silly schoolgirl dreams I never thought you'd end up caring for me. I never want to leave here, to leave you."

Eric pulled her face to his and found her lips. They tasted as soft and inviting as they had the night before. Her arms closed around him tightly, pulling him into her as the sweetness of her tongue tempted and teased his.

As it had last night, the fever building between them erupted into a passionate fog of touch and taste and scent. Her nails clawed into his back. He loved the feel of it. What passed between them was more than passion or love. It was desire filled with such primal energy, so erotic in nature that nothing else existed. No beach, no moon, nothing in the universe save the two of them.

His lips left hers, drawn to the soft fragrant skin of her cheeks. They worked their way down to her neck, following her collarbone toward her chest. His hand found the supple material of her dress as he touched her nipples, hard with excitement. He cupped her small, firm breast, squeezing it, caressing it gently at first, closing his hand over it as her delighted moaning celebrated her ecstasy.

"Oh, yes, please," she begged him as she raised her lips to find his again. Her hands fell from his back onto his buttocks as she pulled him closer to her.

Suddenly their reverie was broken as a light flashed in his face.

"Excuse me folks," the voice was resonant and commanding.

Eric let go of Ashley. He focused on the police car that stood in back of his Jeep.

"Yes…Officer," Eric managed, still breathing heavily as he held Ashley at arm's length.

She turned, facing away from the light.

"We got a call about some joyriding down here." The policeman cleared his throat. "Would you folks mind moving along?"

"Sure. Sorry." Eric nodded and turned, taking Ashley by the arm and closing the small distance to the Jeep.

He helped her into the seat. She looked flushed and embarrassed. Eric squeezed her hand and gave her a wink. A smile crossed her lips.

Hopping into the driver's side, Eric started the Jeep and backed out. He turned toward the exit. As he did, he picked up his cell and saw the red message light flashing.

He saw it was Louise and hit re-dial.

"Eric," she answered breathlessly.

"Hi, what's up?"

"I think you better get home." Her voice had a different sound. The usual upbeat Lu had gone missing, replaced by someone sounding tentative and frightened.

"What's the matter? Are you all right? Is Kylie?" he demanded.

"Just get back as soon as you can. We went out for ice cream. We were only gone for forty-five minutes."

"Okay, calm down. What is the matter?"

"While we were gone, I think someone was in the house!"

Chapter Twenty-Three

"That was Lu," he explained to Ashley as he punched the accelerator on the way out of the beach parking lot. "She thinks someone's been in the house."

Ashley put her hand to her mouth. "Oh, God," she whispered, her voice cracking.

"Are they all right?"

"Sounds like it." He nodded.

"I don't understand this. This shouldn't happen," she said as a confused expression crossed her face. "We have to get there. I need to check something." Ashley found his hand, squeezing it. "Please, hurry!"

Eric looked at her. Ashley's face was dimly illuminated by the lights from the dashboard. It had an ashen appearance again. What had she meant? It made no sense. Her large eyes were the size of saucers as she scanned the roadside, searching for some imaginary threat.

"Is it in the backpack?" Eric asked.

She nodded and looked at him with questioning eyes. "Yes. Was it that obvious?"

"'Fraid so," he said while negotiating the turn onto Route 28 and Memorial Day traffic.

Ashley let go of his hand, chewing her bottom lip as she looked at her watch.

Eric managed his way around the stagnant holiday traffic and took the corner of his street on two wheels.

He sped down the narrow gravel road and pulled into his driveway, coming to an abrupt stop.

Louise stood with her arm wrapped tightly around Kylie.

Eric and Ashley jumped out of the Jeep and ran the twenty feet to the porch steps.

"What happened?" Eric asked breathlessly as Ashley knelt and hugged Kylie.

Louise directed them into the kitchen.

When they went inside, Eric surveyed it. He looked at Lu.

"Everything looks okay. What makes you think someone was in here?"

"Hard to explain. I know this sounds paranoid but I have a photographic memory about where things are. They were moved around. Nothing big you'd notice but moved. I'd swear to it, Eric."

"I believe you." Eric swallowed deeply and nodded. He looked at Ashley. She was breathing rapidly. Her face wore the look of a hunted animal again. The look he'd seen the day he brought her home from the hospital.

"Are you okay?" Eric asked, taking her hand tightly and smiling reassuringly.

Ashley nodded, whispering, "I'm not sure." She said, holding his eyes.

"We went for ice cream. We were only gone about forty-five minutes, probably less." Louise looked around the kitchen. "When we got back, things just looked different. Not pulled out or messy just…different." She shook her head.

"What about the rest of the house?" Eric asked, heading toward the stairway.

"I called you and went out to wait on the porch. I had no idea what was going on or if someone was still inside, so I didn't go beyond the kitchen."

"What about the police?"

"Why call them? Since there's nothing out of place, they'd think I was crazy."

Eric smiled and squeezed her shoulder.

Without a word, Ashley ran up the stairs and into her room.

"Be right back," Eric threw back at Louise and followed her.

When he reached the top of the stairs Eric saw Ashley had her backpack, looking inside while Eric watched her tear her shoulder bag open and extract a knife. This was no ordinary kitchen knife. This was a smaller version of the commando knives locked away in his gun cabinet. She exhaled deeply as she took the weapon and made a precise cut, pulling the label off. When she did something fell into her hand. It was tiny—two inches long, half an inch wide. A small, shiny rectangle protruded from one side. Ashley sighed deeply, closed her eyes, and squeezed it.

Eric stood in the doorway. As she threw the backpack onto the bed, she gave Eric a glance as he entered the room.

"A flash drive?" he asked as he examined the backpack. He saw a small automatic inside...and a cell phone. He stared and held the weapon up by the handle.

She nodded. "I'll explain later. Now I need to use your computer." She ran by him, eyes narrowed, mouth set in a pensive cast.

"Sure," he agreed placing the pistol on a high shelf in the closet. Ashley was already halfway down the stairs. She patted Kylie on the head and headed toward his tiny office with a purpose.

Eric followed her, giving Louise a shrug as he passed.

Ashley was already at the laptop, waiting for it to boot up as she tapped her fingers impatiently on the small desk.

She looked up at him, eyes anxious and frightened.

The screen jumped to life and Ashley immediately thrust the tiny drive into the data port on the right. Ashley's hand shook as she directed the arrow to the computer icon and opened it. When the icon for a removable drive appeared she brought the cursor over it, swallowed deeply, and looked up at Eric. He had no idea what was happening but he knelt by her side and closed his hand around hers. Ashley took a deep breath and tapped on the icon.

Nothing happened for a long time. Suddenly, half a dozen files and PDFs appeared. The files bore the initials FS, followed by four digit numeric codes. Ashley exhaled deeply, raising her eyes to heaven. She turned toward Eric and smiled.

"What's so important about this?" Eric asked nodding toward the computer.

Ashley laughed coldly as her hands closed over her eyes. "It's what's keeping me alive."

Chapter Twenty-Four

"What's going on? Are *you* going to call the police?" Louise asked in confusion as Ashley and Eric came into the kitchen. She wore a puzzled look.

"No, you were right. What would we tell them?" Eric agreed with her. He turned toward Ashley. Her face looked pale and drawn. Ashley trusted him. She'd confided in him…partially. But had left out the part about the automatic, cell phone, and commando knife in her backpack?

"Do you want me to stay?" Louise interrupted.

Eric looked at Ashley. She shrugged.

"Go home and get some rest," he told her. "We've been working you too hard." Eric managed a smile. But his mind was on overload. In the field he'd expected this kind of mind-numbing tension. He'd left that behind three years ago—or so he thought. Now he was desperately in love with a young woman who was caught in the middle of some deadly conspiracy. This bore all the earmarks of the Tom Clancy or Michael Crichton novels he used to devour. Except he couldn't put this on the night table and go to sleep.

Lu opened her mouth in protest. "I know that someone was here, Ricky. I'm not crazy," she told Eric once more at the door.

"I know you're not." He gave her a peck on the cheek as she looked around the kitchen once more shaking her head.

"Time for bed, honey," Ashley told Kylie. She'd rallied, putting on a passable smile as she talked to her daughter about her day and her ice-cream treat.

Eric watched them and smiled.

Kylie ran up to her bedroom. She appeared with her giant pink teddy bear and a story.

"Goodnight." Eric gave Kylie a kiss on the head and a hug as they headed back up the stairs. He didn't follow but stood in the kitchen. That's where the keypad for the alarm system was located. He armed the system. All the doors and windows were included. When he went upstairs he would arm the motion detectors. It was a high-quality professional-grade system. Living at the end of an out-of-the-way back road, Elaine had insisted. Problem was, if Lu's instincts were right and this situation was going to get tense, even this alarm system was poor at best. If some high-level operatives were after Ashley, which seemed to fit what she'd told him, his alarm system would be child's play.

Had his mother-in-law's imagination run wild? After what Ashley had told him, he couldn't be sure. Better safe and all that. Eric was taking no chances. While Ashley read Kylie her story, Eric ran downstairs and opened the gun cabinet, extracting his favorite, a Glock 9mm and a box of hollow point ammunition. A round in the hand would blow it off. A round to the chest would mean instant death. He loaded the weapon, snapped on the safety, and stuck it into the back of his belt, pulling his shirt out to conceal it. He hefted a Remington shotgun that held five rounds, loaded that, and took an extra box of ammunition for each weapon.

Before closing and locking the cabinet he took his eight-inch commando knife and stuffed it in his belt.

When he came back into the kitchen Eric heard Ashley and Kylie upstairs. The sound of a lullaby drifted down the hallway. He walked around the house methodically flipping on all the outside lights. When he flipped off the kitchen lights he could see the halogen spotlights lighting up the entire yard. Perfect. The last thing he wanted was a fire fight with the girls in the house, but if it came to that he'd be ready.

But whatever his preparations, Eric was certain that if someone came they wouldn't come alone. Most likely in twos, threes, or fours. And they'd be heavily armed.

He listened to the last line of the lullaby and heard Ashley say goodnight to Kylie as she shut the door. He saw her outline at the top of the stairs. She took a tentative step toward the kitchen. Suddenly, Eric's throat tightened as he realized for the first time how terrifying their lives must have been. Hell, he felt the cold fingers of fear and he was a damn deadly weapon! No wonder Ashley blanched whenever she thought someone was watching her.

"Eric," she called softly. "You…you down there?"

"I'm here, Ashley. Why don't you go in my room and try to relax. I have a couple of calls to make."

"If it's okay, I'd rather be with you," she whispered as she reached the bottom step. She stared at the shotgun as he placed it and the two boxes of ammunition on the table.

"Sounds good to me." He nodded and opened his arms.

Ashley ran to him, encircling him with a tight

embrace.

He put his arms around her. "Everything's gonna be all right. I promise," he assured her.

"When you hold me like this, I can believe it." Her deep rhythmic breathing warmed him as she tightened her embrace. "I should have told you about all of it. The gun, the cell phone Ralph gave me but…"

"Shhh," he whispered and put his arms around her as he found her lips, kissing them softly. She kissed him back. Her mouth was so sweet and inviting. He could never get enough. She leaned into him and found his tongue. He could stay like this forever. Her lips on his, her body pressed into his. Reason won out.

He gently pulled her away. She looked up at him, putting her hand to her mouth. "Is there something wrong?" she asked as tears formed in her eyes.

"There's nothing wrong. But after what you told me tonight and on the chance that someone was here, I want to talk to some people." He kissed her lips lightly and took her by the shoulders.

They walked into the living room. "Pull down all the shades. Try to stay out of sight and turn off the lights." She understood his reasoning and left to do what he asked.

While she was gone he pulled out his cell and dialed Lip's number. No answer. Just voice mail. Eric tried a second time. Same result. He was sure this was the day his friend was returning from the shore.

Frustrated, he speed dialed Bobby.

"Hey, boss," his friend answered on the second ring.

"Hi, Bobby." Eric played with telling him a fairy tale. Instead he opted for the truth. "I got a problem,

Bob. Could be a big one."

"You know I'm your man. Shoot."

"Ashley's in trouble. Big trouble. May have some bad guys after her. Real bad."

"I'm still your man," Bobby said evenly. "Hell, we took everything the bastards could dish out over there and gave it back in kind."

"So you understand, I'm talking major-league bad guys." Eric wanted his friend to know everything. "She stumbled onto something these guys are into and they want to…to do her harm. Maybe worse."

Ashley walked back into the room and sat down next to him in the darkness. He took her hand tightly.

"Just so you know what you're getting yourself into. And we can't call the cops 'cause we've got no proof of any of this."

"If you're trying to scare me off, boss, you're doing a piss-poor job of it."

"Okay, here's the deal." He looked at Ashley as she snuggled close in the shadows. "Stay put for now. But keep your cell next to you. If I call, get your ass over here with your twelve-gauge and whatever other firepower you've got stashed away. And if I call and you don't hear me call Buzz and our friends at the Dennis PD and tell them to get their asses over here pronto."

"Sounds like a plan to me. On it right now. Be careful. Take care of those little ladies." He paused. "I've grown pretty fond of them myself."

****

Eric armed the motion detectors when they reached the second floor. Ashley went back to her room and changed into some gym shorts and a T-shirt, then joined him.

"How's Kylie?"

"Sleeping like a baby." Ashley managed a smile.

Eric sat in the overstuffed easy chair that sat near the window facing the sound. Only the upstairs hallway light was on. If anyone did get in, the well-lit, narrow stairway was as good a kill zone as you could want.

As she approached the chair, Eric watched her wiping streaks of tears from her cheeks. "I'm so sorry I got you into this." Her head hung as she shook it slowly. She knelt next to him and found his hand.

"So…you've got a weapon." Eric said focused on the doorway. "And a cell."

"A Walther PPK." She bit her lip. "And Ralph gave me the cell to check in. Only used it twice. Things seemed okay." Ashley shook her head.

"Wow. That's heavy firepower." She never ceased to surprise. "And you can use it?"

Ashley nodded as she continued brushing away stray tears. "I can hit a bull's-eye at fifty feet if that's what you mean. I know I should have told you," she repeated.

"It's all right," he reassured her, took her hand, and smiled. "Kinda sexy. You know, when your girl can do that. I'll never worry about you again."

She sighed and studied him, tilting her head the way he loved. "Your girl? Is that what I am?" she asked in her soft sensual drawl. Eric grew aroused as he listened. "Thanks for the promotion," she added with a giggle.

"Hope it's okay. That's how I think of you." He knew how much she cared for him but had he made a leap she wasn't ready for?

"I…I hoped you'd feel that way about me. But never thought it would really happen." She looked away. "You're such a good man. So smart, so strong, so…"

"Ashley." He held his fingers to her lips. She kissed them gently. "You must know that since you and Kylie came, I felt like I could live again, that my life had purpose beyond the nightmares and guilt."

"Guilt?" she whispered, eyebrows raised.

He nodded.

"What do *you* have to feel guilty about?" She tilted her head again and watched him, adding, "I've never known a better man."

He took a deep breath. She'd told him her secrets. It was true confession time for him.

"The night Elaine had her accident, I…" He hesitated and swallowed deeply. "I was supposed to be with her. If I had she might be alive today."

Ashley looked up at him with a puzzled expression.

"She begged me to go to that baby shower. All that day. Said she wanted to show me off. But I'd gone to two others that spring, and I had work to do so I asked her to go alone. Elaine was never a good driver and that night the roads were slick. If I'd been there…" The words stuck in his throat.

Ashley stood and took his hands, gently pulling him to his feet

She took him in her arms and held him, putting her head on his chest.

"Things happen, Eric. Things we can never understand," she whispered. "Your beautiful wife, the woman in the picture, is dead." She nodded toward the photograph on his dresser. "Most people search for someone or something to blame when tragedy strikes. But it was an accident."

He stroked her thick hair and kissed it. "Thanks for saying that, but…"

Ashley put her fingers to his lips. "A wise man once told me, 'The hardest person to forgive is yourself.'" She backed away and found his eyes in the dark. "I know you loved her, Eric, but it's time to stop blaming yourself."

Chapter Twenty-Five

"Thank you, Commander, for telling me the whole story," the Director said quietly. "I'm glad you understand how important this situation is."

"Yes, sir. I had no idea what this was all about."

"And you also understand you can't tell your friend you've spoken to me about this. It could jeopardize an operation at the highest level."

The man on the other end of the telephone line hesitated. "I do, sir, but…"

"Commander. There can be no equivocation," the Director said evenly in an authoritative voice. "If word were to get back to his brother or the girl we're looking for, it could destroy years of planning."

"Yes, sir. I do have to get back to him…"

He interrupted again. "I'm telling you that is not possible. I know you have a history with this man but further communication is impossible."

Silence.

"Is that clear, Commander?"

"Yes, sir. Clear as a bell."

"Goodnight."

The Director placed the secure handset in its cradle.

"He understands?" the man on speaker phone asked quietly.

"He understands," the Director assured the

General.

"When it's over he must be dealt with."

The Director agreed. "Him, the chief, the brother, and the girls. There may be more now. This has gotten too far out of control. Our people in the field will have to evaluate the threat now that we've located the girl and her daughter."

"Fortunate that we have an extraordinary network. Now we know where she is."

"Yes, but the man she's living with is something special. I've read his 201 file. He's a one-man wrecking crew. It would have been easier if she'd found a spinster aunt in Iowa," the General commented wryly over the phone.

"We got a stroke of luck in finding her." The Director shook his head.

"Yes. We know where she is and who she's with. This Montgomery may be good, but he's not fucking Superman," the third man on the line spoke for the first time. "We'll deliver a message tomorrow. Either she surrenders to us or people she loves will die."

Chapter Twenty-Six

Ashley lay in Eric's bed, quilt pulled up tightly around her neck, snoring softly. He'd insisted she take a pill to help her sleep. He told her it was a mild tranquilizer knowing she'd resist the idea of going to sleep and leaving him alone on watch. He promised to wake her in a couple of hours.

He sat stoically facing the open door, wondering and waiting with the Glock in his right hand and the twelve-gauge by his side. It wasn't the first time he'd waited for an assault. But that had been war and the men with him were soldiers. They knew there job was kill or be killed. Had signed up to serve their country. Death was part of the contract. Ashley and Kylie lay nearby, just people trying to live their lives. They didn't deserve to die.

As he fingered the automatic, he thought about the weapon in her backpack and the cell phone. Was all this cloak-and-dagger really necessary? Had she read too many thrillers? As Eric stared into the hallway he began to question Lu's instincts. She knew there was some intrigue associated with Ashley. Had her imagination leapt into overdrive?

As the display on the digital clock read 1:55 a.m. he yawned. Eric's eyelids drooped. No matter how he tried to stay awake he would doze and snap back to attention. Should he wake Ashley? She'd been asleep for more than three hours. If he could just get a couple hours of...

Ten on the damp May evening when the police called. Who could have known the evening would turn so ugly? Elaine had begged him to go. Said she wanted to show him off to her co-workers. The back roads had turned slick in the early spring drizzle. There'd been an accident. Elaine was at Cape Cod hospital. Could he come at once? He'd only been home for a few minutes, having worked late getting the books in shape for the year end audit. He ran down the driveway, jumped in his Jeep, and was at the hospital in ten minutes.

When he arrived at the emergency room Louise stood in front of him. He pushed her aside. She grabbed his arm. "Don't," she pleaded. Her eyes were red with the tears that traced their way down her cheeks. "I don't want you to see her like that."

He ignored her and ran toward the room she'd come from. Doctors and nurses called him to stop. They called security, but Eric brushed them aside like so many twigs. He pushed open the door. Elaine lay there—under a sheet. He walked slowly to the table and gently pulled it back. She looked perfect and pristine. His princess. The woman he worshipped. Unlike the casualties in combat, her face wasn't scarred or disfigured. She looked...serene. Wore the appearance of being asleep. He lifted the sheet. His eyes drifted downward. He felt sick. Her body was broken and torn, covered by dressings soaked in blood.

Nausea overcame Eric and he turned, vomiting in the nearby scrub sink. He'd seen so much death. So many lives lost for vague, nameless causes. But not her, not his Elaine. She'd fought no battle. No lives were at stake. She was the reason he'd come home. He straightened as the door swung open and Lu came in with two men. She cradled him like a little boy, putting her arm around him gently. He turned into her, sobbing like a child.

Their baby survived for six endless hours. Hovering between life and death. Then she joined her mother. Perhaps it was best, Eric thought. Elaine had been strong, kept them together. He would have failed as a single father.

I should have been there...with her. This would never have happened... wouldn't have happened... wouldn't have happened. The thought consumed and held him prisoner until...

Eric was awake. The intoxicating fragrance of Ashley's body mingled with the musky scent of sleep.

"You never woke me," she whispered.

He rubbed his hand across his face and sat up straight. "I was about to. Guess I must have dozed off."

She bent over and found his lips. Her kiss was soft, welcome and tempting, but he pulled away gently. She stood, looking hurt.

"Do I need mouthwash?" she asked in a husky voice. She put her hand to her mouth. "Every time we kiss you pull away from me."

A smile crossed his face. "Just the opposite," he assured her as he stood and pulled her close so she could feel his arousal. "I'm afraid that once we start we won't be able to stop."

She looked up at him, returning his smile. Hers was delicious, inviting. She took his buttocks in her hand and pressed against him. "Glad to hear that," she said, as she found his mouth again. "I was getting worried."

She began using her tongue, teasing him in ways that should have been outlawed.

He gave in to desire and walked her to the bed, pushing the door shut with his foot as they passed. They fell onto the soft mattress clinging to each other. His hands were underneath her T-shirt caressing her breasts and erect nipples as their legs intertwined, wrapping around each other.

His hands worked feverishly across every delightful curve and angle. He pulled her T-shirt up and over her head and saw her small, firm breasts poised upward. In an instant his mouth was on her large nipples, gently biting each one as she moaned in exquisite delight.

Her hand reached inside his shorts and found his erection throbbing as her supple fingers caressed and stroked it.

He wanted to spend all day exploring every subtle place on her tempting body but he knew there was no time. He found her eyes and started to ask. She groaned and put her fingers to his lips as she closed her eyes and nodded, whispering, "Yes…yes, please…now!"

With swiftness borne of desire each shed their remaining clothing. In an instant he was inside her. Her quiet groans of ecstasy set the pace for their love-making. He slowed his thrusts to bring them both every ounce of arousal and excitement. But the chemistry was too overpowering and their need to fulfill their passion so intense, it was over too soon. But it was exquisite.

Slowly, he withdrew and lay next to her, listening to her deep breaths while she held his hand tightly.

"I've only done that a few times in my life," she confessed as she turned toward him, her face a mask of sensuous pleasure. "But I never knew it could be like that."

"When you…love someone it makes all the difference," he sighed deeply, returning her smile.

"Are you saying that you…"

"Yes." He nodded. "I'm saying that I love you."

"I knew that you wanted me, but I never would have guessed you loved me."

He found her eyes and she blushed as she whispered the words, "I love you, too. More than I ever thought I could love anyone."

"Now that's settled, we've got to figure out what to do about your situation."

Ashley nodded. "I hoped that when I woke up it would all be a bad dream but then…if it had been, I never would have found you."

He ran his hand across her thick, lustrous hair. "I will never let anyone hurt you or Kylie—ever." He crossed his heart and held up three fingers like a Boy Scout.

She giggled. "You know. I believe you."

Their sweet intimacy, the short-lived respite from the dangers the outside world held was fleeting. Just as they turned to hold each other, the phone on the night table rang.

Chapter Twenty-Seven

Ashley stopped breathing for a full second as the landline rang. She looked at Eric and swallowed deeply.

"Who could that be at 6:20 in the morning?" she whispered.

Eric managed a smile and picked up the receiver. When he read the caller ID his heart stopped. The display read *number not available.*

"Hello," he said and pushed speakerphone still hoping it was Bobby or an overzealous telemarketer from Mumbai.

"Hello," the artificial voice said. The call was being scrambled so no one could identify the speaker. "I believe Ashley is there."

"Who is this?" Eric said evenly.

"Someone who wants to speak with Ashley." The shrill voice continued level and conversational.

"She's not here."

"I know better. I know from the echo that she's listening on speakerphone right now."

Ashley turned on the bed and stood facing the phone. "Just leave me alone!" she said angrily. "Leave us alone."

"I really wish I could, my dear. But I wasn't the one who violated a strict protocol and invaded a top-secret government data base."

Ashley pursed her lips and closed her eyes tightly.

"What do you want from me?"

"I think you know," the mechanical voice continued.

Eric stood next to Ashley and put his arms around her. "Shhh," he whispered. "Be strong. Don't let them get to you."

She sighed deeply and nodded, giving him a squeeze. "I'll try." She turned toward the phone. "I don't know who you are or what you want," Ashley said in a surprisingly confidant voice, adding, "You have to tell me."

Silence. Endless silence. Eric looked at her, unsure if the party on the other end had hung up in anger or frustration.

Suddenly the phone came to life. "What we want is every file, piece of data, any backup devices and of course, we'll have to meet you. Just to make sure you've been honest with us."

Eric stood, shaking his head vigorously. Did they really believe he would let them take her? He knew what they wanted and it wasn't to check her memory, it was to eliminate it.

"Even if Ashley was willing, those terms are unacceptable to me."

Ashley took his hand and squeezed it.

"Eric, I assume. Hello. I commend you on your…exemplary service to our nation," the voice said casually. "But I don't believe you were part of this discussion."

"Your mistake," Eric replied.

"No, I'm afraid it's yours, Mr. Montgomery."

The line went dead.

Ashley looked at Eric. She was shaking and

grabbed him tightly.

"What's all the noise?" Kylie asked, sleep still in her eyes as she stood in the doorway.

****

Buzz's boss, the head of detectives from the Dennis Police Department, sat at their kitchen table. Eric looked at his watch: 7:35.

Ashley was pale and frightened but she did a good job relating her story. Eric felt reassured that she'd recounted it in the exact way she had to him last night. It was accurate and had the ring of truth. The only alteration came when she told the policeman that she and her friend had stumbled onto the top-secret material.

Eric knew the detective wasn't buying it, but he was the father of Bobby's best friend and knew Eric by reputation. Maybe that bought Ashley some latitude. At least for the moment.

"Look, I'm not pulling any punches. Sounds like you may have stumbled into something serious, miss. And whatever you found may be part of some larger operation. I hate to use the word 'conspiracy' but contrary to all the popular movies this isn't the way the Feds handle someone who breach their security. They'd be here in force and you'd be in a holding cell." The man closed his notebook and put his pen away. "I'm gonna call my buddy at the FBI field office in Boston and see if the name you gave us—Firestorm—means anything to his people."

The man stood and headed toward the back door. "We'll get to the bottom of this." He shook Ashley's hand and smiled at Kylie who was finishing her cereal.

Eric walked him to the back porch.

"Look, Mr. Montgomery," the detective began. "I think she's in danger. And I won't sugarcoat it. From what you've both told me, this is no small group of low-level thrill seekers. These guys are after blood." He rubbed his chin and sighed. "I may catch hell from the chief but I'll put a car on her."

"Thanks, Lieutenant." Eric nodded.

"Seems like a real nice young lady and she looks scared. Really scared." He stopped and looked back toward the kitchen. Concern crossed his face. "I have a daughter her age. I wouldn't want anything to happen to her or that sweet little girl. Not on my watch."

Eric hesitated. "What do you think about her going to work?"

"Wait till the patrol car gets here and don't worry, they won't be too obvious. No black-and-white with flashing lights." He showed a half-smile. "We want to catch the bad guys, not scare them off. But yeah. She may be safer at your place than out here. If these jokers are that concerned about staying underground, they're less likely to try something in a public place. Plus, it may take her mind off this for a while."

"Okay. Thanks." Eric shook his hand.

"I'll call as soon as I hear something from the FBI." The man nodded and headed to his vehicle.

Eric walked back inside and explained what the man had said. Ashley looked thoughtful then managed a smile.

"C'mon honey," she told Kylie. "I'll help you get dressed so we can go to Uncle Eric's marina."

Chapter Twenty-Eight

The ride to the marina was punctuated by endless questions from Kylie about the yelling in Eric's room, why Ashley hadn't slept in the bed with her, and the visit from the policeman. The poor little girl had been dragged on a dark, frightening pilgrimage with nothing but a vague promise of heaven. Her face showed confusion. Despite the giggling, affectionate façade she often showed, Eric thought that Kylie had demons of her own. He and Ashley did their best to give her the child-friendly version, avoiding anything that could frighten her.

Eric hit Lip's number twice on speed dial. Nothing! It wasn't like his friend to go dark without some response. He wanted to believe that Lip hadn't abandoned him but his sixth sense was in operational mode. It was sending Eric a warning. He threw the cell on the dashboard in frustration.

Eric turned toward Ashley, pleased to see that she looked more thoughtful than frightened.

"Anything you want to talk about?" he asked.

She shook her head. "I was trying to imagine what would have happened if I'd gone to Momma's spinster sister in Kansas City."

"I thought you had no relatives."

She grinned and squeezed his hand. "I fibbed. And there was never a doubt. You were my first and only

217

destination of choice."

"I'm glad," Eric managed a smile. He tried to calculate how many hours of sleep he'd had in the last week. His mind had been out of combat mode for years, so fatigue was taking its toll.

"Me, too," she agreed, showing him an adoring smile.

"We've got a guardian angel." Eric gestured behind them as he spotted the unmarked police car a hundred yards behind. But he had no illusions about what one local cop could do if they were jumped by three or four well-armed mercenaries or black-ops types. He hoped their police shadow gave Ashley a sense of security.

The morning—the last of the long holiday weekend—passed more quickly than Eric expected. The sun was bright, the temperature pleasant, and the lazy northwest wind blowing south across Cape Cod kept the swells on the Sound light. Eric's customers and the other boaters on the river seemed determined to get in every last hour of cruising or fishing.

Ashley looked busy in her small office. She put on a bright smile, showing a good front for the customers and staff. No one could have guessed that someone might be lurking just beyond the shadows to do her harm. Eric met with his staff and made sure she was never without a watchful eye. When he ventured from the vicinity of the boat store, Eric made sure that Bobby or another person watched her closely. Eric's cover story was that she'd been threatened by an old boyfriend—a thug who'd come looking for her from Norfolk. Ashley was already a marina favorite with everyone. Add that most of Eric's employees had significant combat pedigrees and Eric allowed himself to attend the details of running the marina without constantly hovering over her. The unmarked police car and its occupant remained secreted behind the Dumpster and a stand of trees.

Kylie was always with one of them or in the small store room in the back. Eric had outfitted it with a small TV, aero bed, table where she could draw, and a generous assortment of toys. There was no outside access except through the main entrance. All this was far from a foolproof answer to the threat to Ashley, but it was all Eric could do till some word came from the detective or Lip. Preferably both.

Eric was buoyed by the thought that these people had gone to great lengths, including murder, to insure their anonymity. That made some Wild-West-style daylight assault on the marina very unlikely. Even an attack on the open road seemed a low probability. Too many people around on the last day of a holiday weekend.

What he worried about was at night in the house. Their pristine, isolated location lent itself to a nighttime assault. But they couldn't just hit the house with an RPG. That wouldn't get them the backup media he was sure Ashley had used. She was savvy *and* street-smart. Ashley hadn't shared it, probably to protect him, but Eric guessed she had a backup storage device in a safe place. If anything happened to her she must have done something, had some backup plan so it would fall into the right hands. No, they needed her alive and Eric didn't want to think about what they might do to get her cooperation. Frightening thoughts brought a picture of Kylie to mind as a nightmare from his last year in

Afghanistan came to mind.

A serene, tiny village thirty clicks northwest of Kabul. A peaceful, friendly place whose only crime was providing sustenance for a Ranger company the week before. Word of sudden and brutal Taliban activity had brought Eric's team and another from their base camp. They surrounded, then entered the village from two sides...a double envelopment. Eerily silent. Huts deserted. Twenty families, their livelihood nothing more sinister than raising a few dozen sheep. In the ancient village square, surrounding the well that had provided water for centuries were the bodies of the townspeople, hanging grotesquely. All dead. Their deaths had not been quick. The village elder hung above the rest, spread eagled, on the cross beam that held the pulley for the well. But the final sight, the one that never left Eric's memory, the one that drove him to question everything he'd ever learned or been taught about God and humanity was that of the chieftain's youngest daughter. Only eight or ten. Not much older than Kylie. Her unspoiled face wore a smile as if resting in a state of peaceful repose as it stood, severed from its frail young body. Impaled on the end of a crooked stake...

"Boss. Hey boss." Bobby stood over him. "You okay?"

"Yeah." Eric sat at attention, cleared his throat as he looked up at his friend. "I'm fine," he managed as he stalked off. The vision remained. Despite the terror of combat, Eric always believed he'd survive, that right would prevail. Or he had. He'd learned better. But suddenly he desperately wanted to believe again. Not just for his sake but for Ashley and Kylie.

Instead of his usual sandwich run, Eric sent Rocco,

the college kid who was helping with the gas dock for the summer. He sat down in one of the deck chairs on display. Ashley looked out of her office and gave him a half-smile just as Bobby came in.

"You want to tell me what's really going on here?" He sat down next to Eric. Bobby was a quick study. Eric knew he wanted the whole story...the rest of what he told him last night.

Eric scanned their surroundings. Seeing they were alone he began, "She's in big trouble." He nodded toward Ashley. "Turns out she's a computer whiz who happened across some top-secret files."

"No shit." Bobby's jaw dropped. He whistled as he looked toward Ashley.

Eric nodded. "It's looking like she stumbled into some deep-cover operation. Must have seen something she shouldn't have and they want to..." He couldn't finish the thought.

"Who's they? The government?" Bobby asked.

"No." Eric shook his head. "Trust me. This is definitely a rogue operation. They called this morning."

"They had the balls to call your *house?*"

Eric looked around then leaned closer. "It was something out of a bad thriller novel," he said quietly. "Ashley was really spooked."

Bobby stood and gave Eric a slap on the back. "I'm here for you, and for her." He nodded toward the yard. "We all are."

"Thanks." Eric held out his hand and took his friends. "But for now let's stick to the boyfriend story."

"Okay," Bobby agreed. "What about that sea trial with the guy from New York?"

Eric looked toward Ashley. "I'll see how she's

doing. If she's really spooked, I was hoping you'd take it for me."

As Bobby headed back to the yard, Eric crossed the boat store and knocked on Ashley's door.

"Hi," she said. Her usually fluid accent trembled. "Come in."

He stepped inside, closed the door behind him, and walked the few feet to her desk. She stood, took two steps, and fell into him. Eric pulled her tightly to him and kissed her hair.

She shook as her arms surrounded him. "I'm frightened."

"Ashley, I won't let anything happen to you or Kylie."

Eric turned her face up gently and kissed her lips softly.

"I promise." He summoned his best smile.

Ashley clung to him.

There was a knock on the door. Rocco announced he had their sandwiches.

"Do you want to eat in here today?" Eric asked.

"No." Ashley shook her head. "Let's get Kylie. I want to eat by the water. I'm sick of running."

As they ate Eric explained he had a potential buyer coming for a sea trial on the thirty-seven-foot Bertram cruiser. A sale could mean a $20,000 commission. But that meant nothing if something happened to the girls while he was away. He'd never repeat that mistake.

"I want you to go," Ashley said without hesitation. "We have to live our lives. I spent weeks thinking someone would find us, hurt us. Now that we're together, things will be all right. I know it." Ashley leaned her head on his shoulder, giving him the same adoring look she had in the Jeep.

Eric felt his throat tighten. "You're sure?"

Bobby reached across and took his friend's hand. "Nothing's gonna happen to this young lady while I'm around."

"Thanks." Eric nodded at his friend.

Ashley was right. Suppose the police drew a blank and Lip had gone dark on him. They had to deal with this as if they were completely alone. It was possible they were. Eric knew he had to find a solution. They couldn't spend the rest of their lives hiding in the shadows or running away. No. That wasn't why he'd spent five endless years fighting in the desert.

"Okay," he said. Leaning over he kissed Ashley on the cheek. "Be careful. I got the impression from the phone call that these people may be desperate."

Bobby stood and pointed toward three men who were heading toward the office. "Those must be the guys. Go. We'll be fine."

Eric turned and saw the men. He stood and started toward them, stopping to look at Ashley and Kylie. "Remember what I said before." He looked at Bobby. "Don't break anything while I'm gone."

Eric grinned and smiled at the girls as he headed toward the office.

Chapter Twenty-Nine

The three men went into the boat store where Rocco sat behind the desk. Eric watched as the boy pointed at him. They turned as he entered.

The older of the men took a step toward him and held out his hand. "Eric?"

"Yes, sir." Eric took the man's hand. He was fiftyish, maybe older but looked in great shape. No middle-aged spread on his six-foot-plus frame. "Mr. Carson?"

"Guilty as charged." The man smiled warmly and nodded.

He turned and gestured to the men with him. They stepped toward Eric. Both looked younger than Carson—ten, maybe fifteen years. And like him they looked as if they'd spent more than a few hours at the gym.

"Dan Richter." The taller one with sandy hair said as he shook Eric's hand.

"Colin O'Brien," the second man volunteered. He was stocky with a neat reddish beard.

"I didn't know you were bringing anyone else." Eric surveyed the three men, hoping they were who they claimed.

A clairvoyant Bobby appeared with the brawniest member of the yard crew. "Everything all right, boss?" He stood in the doorway, stance squared.

Carson looked at Bobby, then at his companions. "Did we happen on something we shouldn't have?" His tone was even, conversational as he watched Eric.

Eric waved Bobby away. "Everything's fine, Bob." He turned toward Carson and his friends. "I'm sorry. We have a…a situation, Mr. Carson. We didn't expect anyone but you."

Carson nodded and showed a casual smile. "Sorry we caused a commotion." He chuckled as he turned toward his companions. "Dan's my wife's younger brother. Spent a few years in the Coast Guard. I thought he could give me some sage advice. I'm a novice when it comes to this boating thing." He nodded at the heavier man. "Colin's a partner in my firm's Edinburgh office. He's here on holiday. You know those folks across the pond. They're always on holiday." He gave the younger man a slap on the back. They all laughed.

"So I've heard." Eric managed a smile, watching them. It was in the high seventies but all wore expensive waist-length cotton jackets—zipped up tightly.

"What does your firm do, Mr. Carson?" Eric asked.

"Import-export," Carson volunteered.

"Sounds interesting." Eric laughed inwardly. Every international hood and intel operative he'd ever known used import-export for a cover. It gave them freedom of movement and didn't require much in the way of specific job expertise.

"Well, how about that sea trial?" Eric gestured toward the door.

"Lead the way, Eric."

Eric picked the keys off the board in the storeroom and headed to the door. "After you, gentlemen."

The four assembled on the Bertram's flying bridge. The sky was a high blue with a few lonely clouds dotting the western horizon. Carson explained again that he wasn't much of a boater but told Eric that he'd always wanted to own a first-class cruiser. A Bertram fit the bill. Carson sat next to Eric while he explained the helm controls.

"What you have to learn first is how to control her. This cruiser has twin engines. That makes it a lot easier. You'll be getting her in and out of tight spots in no time."

Dan stood close by, nodding as Eric gave his customer a brief tutorial.

"She has everything you could imagine in terms of safety and electronics. But for now, let's focus on the throttles and the gear shifts." Eric pointed to the four chrome levers on either side of the wheel. "You want to give it a try?"

"Thanks, son, but I'd feel safer if you got us out of traffic. I'll wait till we're out in the ocean before I give it try."

Dan looked at Eric and winked.

Eric started the powerful diesels and easily maneuvered out of the dock complex. Carson remained next to Eric while his friends stood casually holding onto the stainless steel supports that held the Bimini top in place.

"You know what you're doing," Carson observed with an appreciative nod.

"Thanks. Like I said—it's just like riding a bike. It takes practice and once you master it, you'll never forget. You can turn a boat with twin engines on a dime," Eric repeated as he entered the channel and headed toward Nantucket Sound slowly. "Where do you want to go?"

"Oh, down the river to the sea. Then out a couple of miles. I trust your judgment. I'd like to try the controls when we're safely away from everyone." Carson looked at his companions and chuckled.

"Kinda warm. You want to shed those jackets?"

"Thanks. We're fine," Carson said. The others nodded, wearing easy smiles. The zipped jackets still made Eric uneasy but they'd shown no sign of anything suspicious.

They made the mile to Nantucket Sound at the six-knot speed limit in ten minutes and headed out the channel to the red number two buoy two miles offshore.

"They told me at the coffee shop you're a veteran. Special Forces." Carson said, looking impressed.

"That's right. Five years."

"Thanks for your service. Did a few years myself. They told us you were an officer?"

Eric nodded and punched both throttles simultaneously to bring the Bertram up to twenty knots. He swung the big cruiser to the left and headed east toward Monomoy, a peninsula extending south from Chatham on the Cape's southeast coast.

"Now, this cruiser's equipped with a system to synchronize the throttles."

Carson looked mystified.

"So you use one throttle for both engines. They'll be balanced in terms of RPMs and speed. Makes it much easier to control," Dan explained as he stepped over.

"If you say so." Carson nodded, adding, "You were an officer?" he asked Eric again.

"Yes, sir. An officer and a gentleman," Eric said with a hollow laugh.

"Five years. That's a long time. Guess it was enough?"

"More than enough." Eric found his customer's eyes. They were steel-gray and held no humor. The small hairs on his neck stood up. They'd done nothing to arouse his suspicion, but Eric had a strange feeling about where this conversation was headed.

"You know, I think you were right about these jackets." Carson looked around at his friends. He nodded to them, then stood. They all unzipped their jackets slowly. Each wore a holster in his belt. At a glance, Eric could tell their automatics were 9mm. Glocks like his. The older man maneuvered around Eric and pushed the throttles down quickly while he put the gear shifts in neutral.

"I know what you're capable of, son. Your 201 file and record are here on my iPhone." He held up the device. Eric could see his name and information on the small screen. "But I don't want to pull on you." The man's hand rested easily on the stock of his weapon. "I use hollow points. Kinda messy. And I don't miss." The men with Carson had flipped off the hammer locks on their holsters and had their hands on their weapons. "So if you want to get back to Ashley and Kylie in one piece, I think it's time you let me take over."

Eric studied them. Carson or whoever he was had called it. These men were no amateurs. He could take down the old man, maybe one of the others, but three? No way.

"What do you want with me?" Eric asked searching the bridge and the Sound for an opening or alternative.

"Got a message for you," Carson said evenly, eyes never leaving Eric's.

"Oh yeah?" Eric did his best to sound confident. *Never show weakness to your opponent*…Sun Tsu. "From whom?" he asked quietly.

Carson looked around at his companions. When he turned toward Eric again, he wore a wry smile. "One of our best field operatives."

"Who's that?" Eric asked casually.

Carson watched him, a casual look on his weathered face.

"Okay, enough with the cloak and dagger. Who is it?" Eric demanded.

"Your brother."

Chapter Thirty

Eric stared at the older man in silence. His mouth hung open in amazement. He shook his head. He must have travelled to an alternate universe. That was the only explanation.

"Ralph? My brother?" he blurted. "You've got to be shitting me!"

A look of amusement crossed Carson's tanned face. "I told you this was going to be interesting!" he said turning to his friends. "I know this may ruin a long-standing contempt you had, but yes, I'm talking about your brother."

Eric looked back and forth between the three of them. The others wore the same smug look of satisfaction that Carson did.

"I probably should have shown you this." The older man held his left hand up in a non-threatening manner, reached in his back pocket with two fingers of his right hand and extracted a worn leather case. Carson opened it and threw it on the seat he'd vacated.

Eric studied it. The case held a large gold-plated badge on one side and a plastic covered ID on the other. Carson wasn't his real name. The ID had a photo of the older man taken years ago. Senior Investigator, Special Division, Department of Defense was etched into the badge's surface.

"Stay cool, son," the man said, looking at Eric.

"We're on your side...okay?"

Eric nodded slowly. "Didn't know I had a side."

The man calling himself Carson lowered his left hand, picked up the leather folder with his right, and put it back in his pocket. "I guess you came home thinking you'd left the bad guys behind, Eric." He paused and shot a look at his companions. "There are bad guys everywhere."

Eric's stomach tightened. His mouth had gone dry. But he breathed easier as his adrenaline subsided. They needed him. And assuming they weren't playing trick-or-treat these guys weren't about to shoot him. They had something more useful in mind.

"Okay, I give up." Eric said, giving the men a wry smile. "Thanks for the philosophy. What do you want and why the drama? Couldn't we have met at a coffee shop? Did you have to tease me by letting me think I might earn a $20,000 commission?"

Carson shrugged and returned the smile. "You're my kind of guy." He slapped Eric lightly on the shoulder and looked at his companions. "I told you he was a cool one. You don't get all those medals by shitting yourself when you're in a tight spot."

Eric glanced up. The other men watched him, showing cautious grins. Carson continued. "Well, here's the thing. What I do. What we do"—Carson nodded at the two men with him—"is a little irregular."

"Irregular?"

"Our jobs are special. Low profile." He chuckled to himself. "Actually, damn near invisible. I report directly to the Secretary of Defense."

"That doesn't answer my question," Eric said, feeling more confident. This was a dialogue not an interrogation.

"And why we're here in Nantucket Sound, son. You're being too modest. You're a celebrity. People round here know you. Know what you've done. Scholar-athlete. All-American. Green Beret. Trunk full of medals. Put that together with the rumors that must be flying round about Ashley and Kylie. Who they are? Why they're here? You get my point? So we set up this little meet-and-greet. Sure, we used a bit of theater." Carson gave Eric a broad grin. "To tell you what's goin' on and how you can help us."

"Interesting. You know the cast of characters. But if Ralph's one of yours that makes sense." Eric stared down the older man. "Look, Mr. Carson or whatever your name is—I've done my bit. Five goddamned years' worth. Came home to nightmares and a dead wife."

Carson glanced at his friends. "Okay, Eric." He nodded at his companion. "Every one of us has demons. I've been at this for thirty years. I lost count of the ghosts."

"Nice speech but every war has its silent casualties. What's your point," he demanded of Carson with a touch of the anger that was building.

"Give me fifteen minutes. If I haven't got your attention, I promise we'll leave you in peace and try to find another way to get the people we're after. And believe me…we have to get them." Carson's words were hard, brittle. "No choice about that." Any trace of humor was gone. "I thought knowing your record you might want to help."

As he delivered his patriotic sales pitch, Eric got a hollow feeling in his gut. Was Ashley one of *them*? He hoped to God she wasn't playing games, playing him—that she was what she appeared to be—an innocent victim. Caught in a web of deceit. The thought that she was lying to him, using him was…

"You better throw out the anchor," Carson observed as he studied the water around them. "Our rate of drift and the current are pretty quick. You'll be in the shallows in ten minutes."

Eric found himself smiling. "You've never been around boats?"

"Some time on cruisers and destroyers."

Eric looked at one of the team. The taller man shrugged.

"I have to bend the truth in my position. Part of the job description. Not something I enjoy. But it can't be helped." Carson and the others followed Eric down the ladder and waited in the cockpit until he went forward and released the anchor using the remote foot switch.

Carson gestured toward the door and they went inside the cabin as Eric rejoined them. "Got any beer on board?"

"Don't know. Not my boat." Eric shook his head. He checked the fridge. A dozen bottles of a microbrew cooled inside. "Help yourself. Leave the money on the counter for the owner."

Carson chuckled, took out a twenty, and left it on the refrigerator.

"You were right earlier." The man pulled his shirt away from his ample frame as Eric tossed him and his friends a beer. "It is damn hot today." He looked at Eric, who'd taken a Pepsi. "You're not joining us?"

Eric sat on the counter and stared at the three men. Carson eased onto the couch facing him with the taller man. The second sat on the chair in the corner of the cabin. Eric shook his head. "I want to keep my wits about me to hear this."

"Good idea." Carson nodded.

"All right. You've gone through this charade and got me out here in the middle of the Sound." Eric stared at Carson. "I assume it wasn't so we could exchange war stories?"

"Wish it was." Carson shook his head and glanced at his companions. "This is a hell of a lot more serious."

"Okay." Eric shrugged. "Let's have it."

"First let me really introduce my friends. The tall guy on my right is an expert in terrorism and international crime. Former *company* man. Call him Jack."

The man nodded, gave Eric a smile and a casual wave.

"This burly gent on my left is former CIA, too. Deadly with his fists and about every weapon you could imagine. Like you, Eric. He's a specialist in surveillance techniques and explosives. On lend-lease from MI-6. Call him Ian." The man Carson called Ian reached across and shook Eric's hand. "He can set up an ultra-sensitive parabolic mic that could hear an ant fart on the moon." Carson grinned. Ian sat without moving.

"Great. I'm impressed." Eric tried to hide the sarcasm. "What does any of that have to do with me? Or is it my new roommates you're interested in?"

"Bingo." Carson nodded, pointing a finger at Eric. He looked at his friends again. "I know you're very fond of Ashley and from what we've seen the feeling's mutual, so this may be hard."

"You've been watching us?"

Carson nodded again.

"So that was *you* parked on my street?"

Carson glanced at his companions and chuckled. "No. We're not that obvious. You're gonna laugh but those guys were just coincidence. Guess your neighbor wanted Direct TV. We didn't want to spook Ashley so we…politely asked them to leave. You know, made up a good cover story."

He had to know. "Okay. Is Ashley one of the bad guys?"

Carson found his eyes. "Absolutely not, Eric." Carson looked at his hands then glanced at his friends. "She's just what she appears to be. A sweet, innocent kid who fell into something very bad. Ashley had no idea the hornet's nest she was getting into."

"All right, so how did you guys find us and get into our lives?"

"We're a special ops team. Very special. They call us when something's so dirty, so complicated, and covers so much territory it doesn't fit anywhere else. This is one of those cases."

"How does Ralph figure into this?"

Carson looked around at his companions and sighed. "Everyone figures that field agents are all whiz kids from MIT or Harvard and look like James Bond." He shook his head and made a frown. Pulling out a cigarette, he offered one to Eric. Eric obliged and Carson lit them both using a scarred Zippo. "Some are like that, right out of central casting, but we need tough, street-savvy operatives. Men and woman like Ralph. People no one would suspect or take note of and that fit into situations like a chameleon."

They sat staring each other down, Eric still in disbelief that his brother was an undercover agent for some deep-cover covert agency he'd never heard of.

"Well, your brother was nicely ensconced in the position we'd put him in—maître d' at the base officers club. It's divided into sections and he was assigned to the area where the higher ranking officers ate. You know, the guys with the fruit salad on their cap brims."

Eric was hearing the words but still finding it hard to believe. Ralph, super spy?

"How long had he been doing this?"

Carson grinned. "Well, you know your brother. He didn't come on board easily." Carson opened the cabin door and threw his cigarette into the water. "It's a long story but it must be at least fifteen years. We needed eyes and ears in a sting operation and made him an offer he couldn't refuse."

Eric shook his head in confusion.

Carson held up his hand. "There was a child who'd been crippled by some bad guys. When Ralph heard about that he came aboard right away." Carson wore a distant look. "That was his soft spot. He could be a slippery pain in the ass, but when it came to kids, he took no prisoners."

The other two nodded and wore smiles.

Wow. All those years and his brother had been a good guy. As he contemplated Carson's words, a series of brilliant flashes invaded the cabin through the cabin door. Everyone stood and tensed as they rushed to the cockpit. In a second the peaceful hum of small boats and seabirds was shattered by three thunderous crashes.

Standing on the deck, Eric felt his stomach turn and his throat tighten as the other three pointed toward the river and what lay beyond the small spit of beach that served as a breakwater.

"Jesus," one of the men whispered as he stared at the flames rising into the placid May sky.

Carson took Eric's shoulder. "Get the fucking anchor up and let's get back there."

Eric nodded as if in a nightmare...Ashley, Kylie, Bobby, they were all there. Where the plumes of smoke and fire rose from. He looked at Carson.

"Let's get out asses in gear, son. I don't believe in coincidences and I think the bad guys just sent a message."

Chapter Thirty-One

Instinct must have taken over. Eric only remembered the young harbor patrolman yelling as he sped up to the Bertram. And by then the big cruiser was almost at the entrance to the river.

"Hurry up. You gotta come real quick," the young man yelled. "There's been a bad accident at the marina! Real bad."

Eric steered into the channel behind the Harbor patrol boat. The patrolman violated every rule, driving his Whaler upriver at twenty-five knots. Eric punched the throttles, trying to keep up. His throat tightened as he saw the plume of smoke, dying flames, and ashes rising, funneling skyward from dock three—dead center of his marina. By a whimsical stroke of luck the gods had spared the fuel dock. One spark in a fuel tank and the whole marina would have been blown into dust.

As he pulled abreast of the last dock, Eric threw the Bertram in neutral, letting the tide and current bring the big cruiser against the pilings.

"Take it," he said to his companions as he dashed off the flying bridge and down the ladder, leaving the tie-up to Carson and company.

As he jumped onto the dock and headed to the parking lot he kept asking himself: What about Ashley, Kylie, Bobby—his crew and customers? Were they all right? Had they been hurt? The noise and activity from the emergency vehicles and their personnel turned the scene into organized chaos. Eric ran toward the blackened cinders where dock three had been an hour before. Smoking pilings and the hulks of several badly damaged boats were being sprayed by the Yarmouth Fire Department. Debris stretched halfway across the river.

"Hey, buddy. Get the hell away from here." A police sergeant grabbed Eric's arm. "There's no guarantee something else won't blow. There's a shitload of combustibles over there. Every boat has a fuel tank that could—"

"It's okay. I know. I'm the owner," Eric interrupted, telling the officer through the confusion.

"I don't care who you are. Until they give me the all clear"—he pointed to the firemen aiming high-pressure hoses at the remaining docks and boats—"you stay behind this yellow tape! Got it?"

Eric gave in and nodded as he scanned the parking lot. *What the hell happened here?* Relief washed over him as he glimpsed Bobby and Ashley being attended to by paramedics. But no sign of Kylie. He ran toward them at Olympic speed.

Bobby saw him and waved, managing a weak smile between grimaces. Eric came to the ambulance where his friend was being hovered over by a pretty EMT.

"You all right?" Eric shouted over the din.

"Fine, boss." He nodded toward Ashley. "Go check her."

"Be right back," he nodded to the paramedic and touched his friend's shoulder as he ran toward Ashley.

Arriving next to the stretcher that held Ashley, he

stopped suddenly. She lay motionless. An IV drip was attached to her left arm and the EMT was applying pressure to a wound on her body. Small patches of blood had soaked through her polo shirt. Icy shivers ran down Eric's spine as he thought of the nightmare just a year ago. If there was a God, and Eric wanted desperately to believe, he couldn't be that cruel. Snatching another woman he loved in such a violent fashion.

"What's going on?" Eric demanded. "Is she gonna be okay?"

The young man nodded. "Sure. From what they tell me she was the closest to the blast. Guess she was facing toward the docks that blew when…" He stopped in mid-sentence. The young man looked at Eric's marina shirt. "You work here?"

"Yeah." Eric reached down and took Ashley's cool, damp hand in his, caressing it. "I own the place."

"Sorry. I didn't know." He turned his attention to Ashley who groaned softly and opened her eyes, finding Eric's.

"No sweat," Eric told the EMT and bent over Ashley. Her large eyes looked vacant and unfocused as she stared up him.

"Eric? Is that really you?" She gave his hand a fragile squeeze. Ashley tried to lift her head. "Told you…tried to warn…" Her head fell onto the small pillow as she closed her eyes again.

"We gave her morphine for the pain and Valium to help her relax." He motioned to his assistant. They tightened the restraints and hefted the gurney, placing it in its cradle on the ambulance.

"Relax?" Eric was confused.

The young man nodded on his way to the passenger door. "Yeah. She was really agitated. Kept mumbling something, calling out a name." He shrugged. "You Eric?"

"Yeah."

"She kept calling you. May be the concussion." He shrugged again as he got in. "She'll be at the Cape Cod Hospital. Should be up and around in a couple of days. Just a lot of scrapes from the blast debris. Looks worse than it is." The EMT closed his door and looked at Eric. "Sorry about all this. Good luck," he threw back as they sped away, leaving a trail of gravel.

Eric gave the ambulance an absent wave and got out his cell as he headed back to Bobby. No Kylie, but Louise was going to take her home, wasn't she? If anything had happened to her he'd...

"Lu?" he said quickly when she answered. "Kylie. Is she with you right now? Is she all right?"

"Next to me. We were just heading to the store." Her words sounded hesitant, questioning. "Why?"

Eric gave her a quick description of the chaos he saw in front of him.

Silence, then, "Oh my God, Eric. I'm so sorry." Louise whispered. Kylie asked questions in the background. "Just a minute, honey," Lu said patiently.

"Answer her questions. I gotta talk to Bobby and the police and fire departments to find out what happened here."

"Okay. We'll stay here. I'll try to figure out something to tell you-know-who," she told him. "Ricky, be careful. I got a bad feeling about this."

"Thanks, Lu. I will—be careful, that is." He looked at the chaos, inhaling the pungent fragrance of burned wood coated with creosote. "And Louise. Please. You be careful, too. Go home and lock the doors. I'm calling my friend at the Dennis PD. I'll keep my phone in my pocket. If anything looks out of line, call 9-1-1 right away."

"Should I be frightened?"

"No," he lied. "It'll be fine," Eric promised her. "I'll call if I get anything else."

As Eric closed his cell he saw Carson and his men coming across the parking lot. Carson motioned him over.

"Thanks. For taking care of the Bertram, I mean. You handled the tie-up like a pro." Eric shook his head. "I think your cover's blown."

"Not to these folks. They're too busy trying to keep things under control."

Eric nodded and took the older man's arm. "Look, I got a strange feeling about this. Could have been a spark and a faulty bilge fan but all this damage from one small boat going up?" Eric shook his head. "And Ashley was saying something…"

Carson held up his hand. "Don't bother. I told you. I don't believe in coincidences. This was a message. More dramatic than I would have expected, but I'm on it. I called from the boat. One of our team is already headed to your house and we have someone following Ashley to the hospital."

Eric looked behind him. "I thought this was your team."

Carson looked at the two men behind him. Both wore grins.

"Hell, son, I got more people here and if I need 'em, I'll roust the whole fucking Boston FBI field office. You have no idea what you fell into the middle of." He motioned to his men as he gave Eric a business card. "We're at the Red Jacket. On the beach. My cell is on the back. We'll let you get this mess straightened out. I want you to call me—often. Call your mother-in-law—Louise, right?"

Eric nodded.

"Tell her she's gonna have a visitor." Looking back at the destruction, Carson paused and nodded to Jack. "More likely two."

"Hey," Eric called out. "What about Ralph?"

"He's gone dark." Carson shook his head. "Left a strong trail for these bastards to follow to keep them from the girls."

Ralph was not only a first-class spook, he was a goddamned heroic SOB. This was getting weird.

"Remember, call me." Carson patted Eric lightly on the back and the three men trotted to their Cadillac Escalade. These guys travelled in style.

Chapter Thirty-Two

The two men in gray sweatshirts and camo pants returned to the nondescript Ford sedan hidden near the desolate stretch of beach.

"Everything went off without a hitch, sir," the larger of the two said into his cell.

"Good," the Director whispered.

"The device did exactly as we expected," the man assured his boss as he scanned the deserted section of beach and eel-grass surrounding them.

"Really?" the Director asked evenly. "And how many vessels were destroyed?"

"Two, maybe three. Hard to tell till the smoke clears."

"Two or three." The Director sighed. Was there anyone he worked with who had the vaguest idea of how to carry out an assignment as instructed? "One small explosion would have sent a signal to the girl. We could have used it as leverage. The last thing she wants is to see harm come to her daughter or her new family."

"But, sir, it was hard…"

"I'm sure it was, Captain. Obviously more difficult than you and your partner are capable of!" The Director raised his voice. "Instead of what everyone would interpret as an accident you've created a damn catastrophe. The police, fire marshal, and everyone else who's bored on Cape Cod will be all over this."

"But, sir…"

"Shut up." He did his best to mitigate his anger. These fools may have destroyed any chance of Firestorm bearing fruit. "Their technicians are no fools. If you were as sloppy as I suspect, they may find traces of the sonic detonator and who knows what else."

A long silence ensued.

"By six o'clock this will be everywhere: the national news, the Internet—some bastard probably has video. Your little display will be viral."

There was nothing he could do about it now but regroup, find a way to see their mission was carried out. But not with these fools.

"All right," he spoke quietly into the silent phone. "Get back here ASAP. Independence Day is only five weeks away and we have final preparations to make."

A whispered, "Yes, sir," was followed by a long silence.

The Director hung up in frustration. He needed good people. So far he'd found no one save his inner circle worthy of his trust and except for himself none of the other senior officers were capable of field ops.

****

The two men who'd executed the mission at the marina looked at each other. Both wore doubt on their faces and fear in their eyes. What had begun as a glorious quest to bring the country to its senses had become a one-man crusade, a battle of wits between the Director and a surprisingly bright and resourceful young woman. At first they assumed she may have discovered the Director's plans and identity by accident. Now, this whole adventure was assuming the character of a vendetta.

"Let's get the hell out of here," the larger man said as he backed the car up and turned abruptly. He looked at the other man, his comrade and friend of twenty years. "I don't like this. Not one bit."

"I'm with you. The boss has gone off the deep end." The other nodded. "We've both got some resources stashed in the Cayman Islands. Let's just get the hell out of here and keep on going."

"That's what I'm thinking." He looked at the carnage in the rearview mirror. "I'm up for a crusade, but suicide and murder for no reason is just plain stupid."

His friend nodded.

They headed up the narrow, sandy trail they'd taken in, heading for the pavement. Suddenly, a cell phone rang. They looked at each other. Both had their smart phones in their pockets. The hollow ring tone came from the glove box. A flash lit up the sky for a mile as the Ford exploded into a thousand pieces, taking its passengers and their secrets with it.

Chapter Thirty-Three

"What happened here?" Eric asked as he watched the blond EMT fussing over Bobby. "Tell me about Ashley!" he demanded, his stomach in knots. "How did she get hurt?"

"They said she'll be okay." Bobby placated him as he took Eric's arm and they headed toward the office. His friend had a large wrap around his thigh, and favored the bandaged leg. The young woman tending to Bobby protested as he began to walk away. "I'm fine," he told her, shaking off her attempts at attention. She shook her head as he followed Eric to the picnic bench. "Ashley's a tough lady. She was just in the wrong place at the wrong time."

"I'm not so sure." He watched the emergency personnel cleaning up the mess. "Was anyone hurt badly?"

Bobby's eyes studied the picnic table. "Rocco. The college kid," his friend whispered.

Eric shrugged. "I didn't see him. Is he in the hospital?"

Bobby gripped Eric's forearm tightly. "He's dead."

Eric slumped like he'd taken a shot to the gut. "Dead?" he repeated quietly.

Bobby nodded. "A couple of customers and one of the mechanics were banged around pretty bad, but they're okay." He nodded to the parking lot where another emergency vehicle was serving as s field hospital.

"What the fuck happened, Bob?"

"Damned if I know. Rocco was at the end of dock four, bringing one of the boats over to be hauled out, I heard the engine start, and then all hell broke loose." He shook his head in frustration and anger. "Thought we were back in the Afghani mountains again."

They sat quietly side by side facing the destruction on the docks. No, Carson was right. Whoever had done this was sending a message. *Come to us or all hell's gonna break loose.* But Eric was pretty sure they'd miscalculated. Too much firepower. Way too much. This wasn't a message, it was a damn Federal disaster area.

Bobby sighed and looked away. "Fred Markham asked us to check his prop. The old Larson 26 we had on dock three. Said he hit bottom on Friday and was getting cavitations." He pointed to the smoldering wood and debris.

Eric nodded as he studied the damage. Dock three was history. A few of the ten boats tied up were as well. Too early to tell how many.

"And…" Eric raised his hands.

"It's crazy." Bobby exhaled and looked toward the remains of the dock. "Rocco was always asking to do more than run the fuel pumps so I figured he couldn't do any harm. Hell, it was a hundred yards from the slip to the lift cradle."

"I got it," Eric agreed, patting his friend on the forearm.

Bobby was staring blankly at some invisible image. "I was heading toward the office, about a hundred feet away when he called me. 'Thanks,' he yelled and turned the fucking key." Bobby's head sank. He swallowed. "All the Harbor Patrol guys found was his baseball cap."

Eric studied him. "I don't know what to say. But I know you didn't cause that explosion."

Bobby let out a breath and hung his head. "When I close my eyes all I can see is that kid standing there, waving at me."

"It could have been you, or any of us," Eric whispered.

"I know. Maybe that's what's spooking me. But this isn't Iraq or Afghanistan, Ricky." He shook his head again violently. "He was a kid from town doin' a summer job."

As Eric put his hand on Bobby's shoulder, he looked at the disaster playing out before them. His friend was right. This wasn't a war zone. But what he was witnessing looked familiar. Too damn familiar.

When Bobby turned, his eyes glistened. They wore a vacant look as he studied the horizon. "Just a kid doin' his summer job," he repeated quietly.

Someone approached rapidly on the gravel. "Mr. Montgomery?"

Eric turned at the tap on his shoulder. A tall, middle-aged man with a ruddy complexion and thick torso stood next to an attractive, slender young woman. The man wore dark blue trousers and a white, short-sleeved shirt, the woman the uniform of a State Police officer.

"I'm Eric Montgomery."

"Chief Elliot, from the Yarmouth Fire Department. I've heard your name." The man found Eric's eyes and held out his hand. "Sorry we have to meet like this."

Eric stood. He held out his hand and shook the chief's. "Hello." Eric nodded.

"This is Stacy Birch. A state police inspector. Her team handles investigations in this district when a fire and explosion is involved. They're attached to the state fire marshal's office."

Eric looked closer at the young woman. Her thin face sported a dark tan masking a trace of freckles. Thick auburn hair disappeared under her military-style uniform hat. She studied Eric. Stacy was striking, but Eric's mind was on overload. She pulled a black leather case from her back pocket and let it hang open, showing Eric her badge and ID.

Eric was no sexist but it was hard to reconcile this slim young woman with the tough job and responsibilities he assumed went with it. His mind would have conjured up a grizzled forty-five-year-old. But he'd grown a sixth sense in his previous life. It told him Stacy had her shit wired tight.

"Hi." Eric volunteered his hand. Stacy's shake was firm, her hand rough and calloused. She didn't spend her days baking cookies. He gestured toward the docks. "I hope you can figure out what happened here." He shrugged, words trailing off as he watched the men spraying pungent, burning wood and collecting debris that drifted to shore. The images he stared at brought back bitter memories—eerie similarities to dozens he'd witnessed in Iraq and Afghanistan.

"Chief." Stacy nodded toward the water. He turned. "Tell your men to leave that alone. My team will take care of it."

He nodded, yelling and using hand signals to tell

his men and the marina staff not to touch anything.

Stacy concentrated on the accident site, putting her lips together tightly. "We'll find out what happened." She looked at Eric as she gestured toward the waterfront. "You've got my word on it."

"Stacy's the best. Ex-military." The chief nodded at her. "She'll get to the bottom of what went on here if anyone can."

"The report said there was one casualty and several injuries?" Stacy asked as she watched the smoke plume working skyward from the wreckage. She pulled out a small notepad from her uniform shirt and made an entry.

Eric watched her.

"Every combustible or compound has a signature," she explained.

"What do you see in this one?" asked Eric.

She nodded, putting the notebook away as she watched him. Her face wore a neutral expression. Stacy was the consummate professional. "Not sure. Too early to tell, sir. Can you give us your version of what happened?"

"Well, I was gone. Showing a boat on the Sound. And I just heard about Rocco—the boy who died. I'm sorry." Eric motioned toward Bobby. "Chief Elliot, Inspector, this is Bobby Cochran, chief mechanic and yard foreman. He's an old friend. Been with me for years."

Bobby stood, putting on his game face as he rubbed his eyes quickly, holding out his hand.

"Bobby was here and saw everything," Eric explained. "You should talk to him."

Stacy and the chief shook Bobby's hand.

"May I, Chief?" Stacy asked the older man.

"Sure." He deferred to her. "I'm gonna go see how things are going. I'll leave you in Stacy's hands." He nodded and headed to the dock area.

"Look, Mr. Cochran…"

Bobby sighed. "Please, call me Bobby."

"Okay. If you call me Stacy." She gave Bobby a studied look, then scanned the grounds. "Is there a place we can talk?"

Bobby gestured to the ship store. "Okay, boss?"

"Sure," Eric agreed.

"My K-9 team will be here in a few minutes. We use dogs trained to detect C-4, T-4, nitro—any synthetic explosive residue," she told them.

Stacy looked toward the street and waved. "There they are now."

Eric followed her glance. A spotless black van with a State Police logo and K-9 Unit emblazoned on its side pulled into the parking lot.

"I'll meet you at the office, Bobby. I want to get them started and then change out of these class As." She smiled self-consciously. "I was down the street doing a show-and-tell for the Yarmouth Police and Fire."

Bobby agreed and limped off in the direction of the office.

"When I'm done I'd like to talk with you." She found Eric's eyes again.

"I think I'll be here for a while." Eric shrugged.

Stacy took a few steps toward the van, then stopped, looking over her shoulder. Eric was confused. She kept staring at him and there was something— something very familiar about her he couldn't place.

But a good kid was dead, Ashley was headed to the hospital and Bobby was covered in bandages.

"Sounds good." She broke his concentration and headed to the office. "I'll talk to you later. I expect to be here a while, too."

Chapter Thirty-Four

Dusk. The fires were out. Smoldering wood cooled in the damp air as the marina staff struggled to make order from the crowded tangle of boats. They'd doubled up, rafting some of the orphaned cruisers on the remaining docks while the harbormaster's men helped by dropping half a dozen temporary moorings to handle the overflow. A deputy fire chief and two men stayed to supervise safety as the cleanup continued under the spotlights.

Stacy's team had made a thorough examination of every inch around docks two and three. She'd personally interviewed everyone who'd been close to or witnessed the explosion—except Ashley. Eric's initial impression had been on target. Stacy was no hothouse flower. After changing into a set of faded fatigues, she'd donned hip boots and waded into the water, scraping material and gathering residue from the burned pilings her canines had shown interest in.

"Headin' home, boss." Bobby waved as Eric hit speed dial for the sixth time. The calls were evenly divided between his house and the Cape Cod Hospital to get an update on Ashley.

Bobby stopped at the picnic bench. "But I can stay or do anything you need me to." He gestured toward the remaining staff. "We all can."

"I think everything's under control, but thanks."

Eric nodded. "How'd it go?" Eric hadn't seen his friend since the interview with Stacy.

"Okay. Man, that girl knows her shit." He looked back toward the office with what Eric thought was admiration. Not an emotion Bobby shared lightly.

He approached, still favoring his right leg. "You gonna see Ashley?"

Eric nodded. "Not sure." He shrugged, unwilling to acknowledge the emptiness he felt knowing she lay alone, in pain, and probably terrified. "Gotta talk to Stacy first." Eric made the excuse. "Besides, I just heard from Lu. She took Kylie to the hospital. Ashley's talking ragtime. Probably the concussion. So they sedated her. Lu took Kylie home."

"Level with me, boss. This has something to do with that business you were talking about." It was a statement.

"I'm thinking it did," Eric acknowledged. "We're dealing with some bad guys, here, Bob. Real bad, so stay alert."

"I can go to your house, the hospital, anywhere you need me."

"I think we're okay for now." Eric looked toward the dark sedan and the large Tahoe flanking the entryway. He patted his friend on the shoulder. "Thanks, Bob. I mean it. You're the best."

Bobby nodded slightly with a half-smile, acknowledging his friend's show of gratitude. "Those guys. On the boat. They weren't really buyers, were they?"

Bobby was a quick study.

"Let's say they're here to help us."

Bobby nodded again and grabbed his friend's hand,

giving him a high five. "Hang in there, man. We've been through some bad shit before." His friend headed to his pickup, then turned. "Maybe sometime you'll tell me what the hell's going on!"

Maybe. Eric waved to Bobby. *Not sure you really want to know.*

A pile of plastic bags and Rubbermaid containers rested in the back of Stacy's truck. Her team had labeled them as to location and substance. A team member stood watch over the collection.

Eric closed his eyes for just a moment. His head dipped and his mind shut down for an instant as the sounds and smells brought back a bitter memory.

Two weeks left on his tour in Afghanistan. A pristine village on the banks of the Amu Darya, a river in the north. Intel promised a cakewalk. Eric's team and one other were sent on the Afghan war's version of a meet-and-greet. Twenty-four good men walked into a nest of more than seventy Taliban. The enemy body count was forty-two when they were extracted. The villagers weren't so lucky. Their elders were hung in the village square, women raped then split up the middle like cattle, their men and children cut in half by ritual swords and Kalashnikovs. The two teams held out for fourteen hours until the Blackhawks arrived and swept the insurgents into the river. Ten men came out alive: Eric and five from his team, four from the other.

He jumped as a hand landed lightly on his shoulder. "What is it?"

"Bad memories?" Stacy came around the picnic bench, finding his eyes. "I did two tours as a warrant officer. I get 'em too." She smiled softly. "Especially when you see something like this." She nodded toward the dock area.

Eric came to attention and cleared his throat. "Yeah. You can't relate to someone who's never been there." He sighed. "How's it going?"

"Pretty good, I guess. Depends." She looked toward the men still mooring boats and cleaning up. "I think we've got some good evidence."

"Evidence?" Eric arched his eyebrows. "Sounds like you're leaning toward something intentional. Can you give me a hint?"

"You know better than that." She shook her head as her penetrating eyes focused on his again. She made a poor attempt at hiding a smile. "You don't remember me?" Stacy asked, pushing her lips into a crooked grin.

He shrugged. "There's something there, but it's foggy."

Eric's mind was far from Stacy. It was on the damage in front of him, Rocco's death, Ashley, Kylie, Lu, now Ralph. No matter how good Carson and company were, Eric was frightened. Not for himself. For everyone who'd stumbled into this nightmare. The kind of people who would wreak this kind of havoc to instill fear in an innocent girl were more than dangerous. They were downright crazy.

"Fifteen years ago," Stacy began, her tanned face flushing. "The senior prom. A lovesick sophomore who'd had too much to drink and cornered you to steal a kiss."

Eric concentrated. *Sure.* A cute cheerleader with braces, long red hair, and a healthy figure. It could be. But that girl bore faint resemblance to the lean, tanned woman before him.

A smile crossed his face as he nodded. "It's been a

while."

"Sure has. Never thought I'd see you again. Not like this anyway. I'm so sorry, Eric."

She glanced down at his left hand, staring at the wedding ring he wore. "Looks like you and Elaine made it to the altar."

He still struggled, imagining this lean, tough Stacy as the girl he knew in high school.

"Yeah," he paused, his throat tightening. "We did."

"I had such a crush on you," Stacy admitted, face flushing again. "But I'm glad it turned out all right." Stacy touched his hand lightly and looked away. When she faced him again, her eyes looked moist.

She stood and held out her hand. "Well, gotta cross the river. Meeting a detective over there." She gestured to the Dennis side of the River. "PD got a report of some suspicious activity and there was another explosion right after this." She gestured toward the dock and shook her head. "This is turning into a field day for the fire marshal's office."

Eric thought about Ashley, Lu, and Kylie. Ashley was sedated. Louise and Kylie had two world-class watchdogs with them. He was no good to any of them right now. Too much frustration, anger, and adrenaline. Eric was a warrior. And suddenly he was at war again.

"Can I come?" The words spilled out.

Stacy swallowed and narrowed her eyes. "Don't you want to get home to Elaine?"

Eric hesitated, not sure how to answer.

"She's… not with me anymore," he managed in a whisper.

Stacy let her hand fall. "Sorry. I didn't know. You…you want to talk about it?" She stumbled over the words.

He sighed. "If you take me along."

"Shit, Eric, this is an open investigation. I can't. I don't know what the hell's going on here, but we both know this was no accident." She tilted her head. "And if this wasn't an accident, everyone's under suspicion..." She hesitated and frowned. "Including you."

He shook his head slowly. "Please."

"I told you. I can't," Stacy repeated, throwing her hands in the air.

"For old time's sake?" he asked in a soft voice as he found her eyes.

"I can't do that. It violates every rule in the book." She turned and headed toward her pickup.

"Stacy," he called after her.

She stopped and turned, her face hard. "All right, damn you! Get in the fucking truck."

Chapter Thirty-Five

They sat in Stacy's truck next to a looming trophy house that faced the marina. Her eyes glistened in the fading sun as she took Eric's hand gently and squeezed it. He let her.

"I'm so sorry. I..." She rubbed her eyes. "I had no idea. I went to NYU and then enlisted. Mom kept me up on everyone's life. She was better than the *Cape Cod Times*, but she moved to Maine a while back. So I've been out of touch."

"Don't apologize. There's no way you could have known." He turned to watch her. The glow of the setting sun glistened on her tanned cheeks.

"NYU, then the Army?" he asked. "Interesting."

"After 9/11 we were all patriots." She shrugged with a wry expression. "My younger brother Gary joined up on the twelfth. I come from a long line of soldiers. What could I do?" She sighed. "Besides, look at you. Williams, then the Special Forces. Anyway, I got my degree in psychology. They wanted to train me as a shrink. But I didn't want a commission. I wanted to be where the action was not listening to some poor kid with PTSD."

"Looks like you made warrant officer," he said seeing the bars on her worn fatigue collars.

"Yep. My dad was the fire chief. I was a sparky. You know, followed fires like a Dalmatian." She laughed softly. "Combustion was in my blood." Stacy tilted her head and drew a deep breath. "I led a BDU—a bomb disposal unit. Learned my craft well enough to qualify for this job when I was discharged."

Eric looked down and realized they were holding hands. He slowly took his away.

"Sorry," she whispered. "Guess I'm still the silly sophomore."

"No." He paused. "You're a friend. I needed one tonight. But since we're doing true confessions, where did the name Birch come from? You used to be Stacy Resnik."

"That's a story for another time." Stacy looked in the mirror, brushed aside the trace of a tear and fiddled with her hair. "Right now, our detective's here."

"What do you want me to do?" Eric asked.

"You wanted to come along. *Come along*," she ordered. "But keep quiet and let me do the talking."

They dismounted the pickup.

"Detective Hallgren?"

He nodded, watching Eric with narrowed eyes. "Inspector Birch? You fit the description. Who's your friend?"

"It's Stacy." She offered her hand. "And this is Eric Montgomery. His marina had that serious explosion this afternoon."

Hallgren studied Eric, then offered Eric his hand. "Sorry about that." He turned toward Stacy. "But what's he doing *here?*"

"He's former Special Forces," Stacy began. "And we go back a long way." Her eyes pleaded. "Asked to come along. Can you cut him some slack?"

The detective drew his lips into a crooked line. "I

don't think my chief or yours would like citizens hanging around, but...I heard about you," he said to Eric. "Did some heroic shit over there. Saved a buddy of mine—Joe Kelleher."

Eric nodded slowly. "I remember. Joe's a good man. And Buzz Russo's a good friend, too."

Stacy tilted her head coyly and parted her lips, showing the detective a smile that could start its own fire.

The double-teaming worked. Eric couldn't be sure if it was him or Stacy's charm but Hallgren shrugged and gave in. "Okay." His lips twisted upward. "Just remember. Eric stays in the background. And if it comes up, he's attached to the fire marshal's office."

They headed to the house, knocked on the massive wood door and met the homeowner. He described the scene just before the explosion. A dark sedan—he thought it was a late model Ford—had parked on a small side path directly across from the marina. Two men got out and stood watching the marina. Both wore khaki shorts and navy polo shirts. Nothing unusual.

"Did you get a look at their faces?" Stacy asked.

"No." The man shook his head as he stared across the river. "Nothing I could swear to. They were a long way off and their faces were hidden by baseball caps and sunglasses. I couldn't figure why anyone would be there. Odd place for tourists or fishermen."

"But they did nothing suspicious?" It was Hallgren's turn.

"They talked to each other, pointing across the river. Nothing weird that I saw. But just before the explosion, they stared toward the marina."

Hallgren glanced at Stacy.

"Like they were looking for something?" Stacy shot a look at Eric.

The homeowner nodded. "Maybe. I looked, too and a couple of seconds later—boom. Never heard anything like it."

"Then what happened? Can you be more specific?" Stacy pressed, eyes narrowed.

The man shrugged. "More specific? Well, they turned and headed back to their car, spent a few seconds doing something. Could have been talking on a cell. I was about to call the police 'cause after the explosion I figured something suspicious was going on. But while I was dialing, they got in their car and in a few seconds they blew sky high."

"Did you notice anything about the color of the flash or how loud the blast was?" Stacy asked.

The man shook his head. "So bright I had to squint. Almost white I'd say and loud. I served in the artillery in 'Nam and this was as loud as a 155mm howitzer."

Stacy paid strict attention and took copious notes. She looked at the detective. He took the lead.

"Thanks for calling us and telling us what happened. You were a big help. We may have to talk again," Hallgren told the homeowner.

They all nodded and shook hands.

Stacy, Hallgren, and Eric returned to their vehicles.

"Simple trigger device set off by something electronic. Explosive was most likely something simple and volatile like nitro." She looked in the direction of where the vehicle had blown up. "Part of my team is coming over to comb the site but judging from the debris field I doubt they find anything significant."

Hallgren nodded. "Makes sense. These guys had

something to do with the marina explosion and were expendable."

"I agree," Stacy confirmed. "But we found something interesting at the marina I want to check out. Something I've never seen before."

They shook hands all around as Stacy and the detective exchanged cards.

"I have some work to do at the lab. But let's keep in close touch." She looked at Eric. "This was no accident. Somebody was sending you or someone you're close to a message."

Eric looked across at the thin column of smoke and debris still floating on the river. "I figured that out." He paused. "But when I'm through with them they'll be damn sorry they did."

Chapter Thirty-Six

"Long day, Officer Birch. Now where to?" Eric whispered above the engine after Stacy started the truck.

"Back to your Jeep so you can get home and get some rest. One hell of a day," she said quietly. "I have something I want to check out."

Eric's life had been torn apart and Stacy thought of this as a jigsaw puzzle. He wanted to see Ashley desperately, but these people had violated his world and put lives at risk. Eric wanted to tag along and watch Stacy put the pieces together as he had faith she could. Her expression told him not to push it. Her patience was wearing thin.

Stacy put the truck in gear and they headed back toward Route 28, the main road that hugged the Cape's South Shore. The trip took ten minutes more than it should have. The bridge that crossed the river going west was a bottleneck.

"You know we have company?" she asked, looking at Eric. "They've been following us since we left the marina."

"They're the good guys," he said, hoping he was right.

She nodded, looked in the mirror and raised her eyebrows. "What's going on here, Eric?"

"I need to talk to someone before I tell you.

Knowing this guy he's already talked to your boss, the fire chief, and the governor by now."

"Sounds like a good man to know." She nodded in approval. "I'd like to meet him."

"Oh, I'm sure you will." Eric agreed as he thought of Carson sitting in his room, fuming and barking orders, wheels spinning, surrounded by his men and equipment. "You'll like him. He's probably listening to us right now on some $100,000 parabolic mic."

After three changes they made it through the lights at Route 28 and Old Main Street. Two minutes later they pulled into the marina's parking lot.

Stacy fidgeted with her lip again and tapped the steering wheel. "Where are you going? You seem wired," she asked.

"I got a couple of calls to make, but I'm gonna head over to the hospital and see how Ashley is doing."

"She's the girl who ran your office?"

He nodded.

"Bobby told me about her. Sounds like she's pretty special." She sighed. "They took her to the hospital."

"She's…" He paused, searching for the right words. "Real special. Like no one else I've ever met."

"Wow, that's quite an endorsement," she whispered, staring straight ahead. "Well then. You better go see that she's all right."

He took her hand and gave her a warm smile. Her eyes had a moist look again but she returned the smile. "See you first thing in the morning. By then I hope I'll have some answers I can share."

****

Eric closed his cell. Kylie and Lu were watching TV, surrounded by a security detail that would have made the President blush. But he was glad. They were both so special. Eric squeezed the steering wheel so tightly it hurt.

He started the Jeep and pulled out of the parking lot with the expected shadow doing its best to look inconspicuous. As he got to Route 28 he fumbled in his shirt pocket and found Carson's card. As he waited at the light, Eric used his thumb to dial the number.

"Eric," Carson greeted him evenly. "Did you have fun playing detective with the fire marshal?"

"It was informative, but I'll bet you're two steps ahead of me."

"If you mean do I know a couple of guys were eyeballing the marina just before the explosion—yeah." He paused and put his hand over the phone, calling to someone nearby. "Sorry. If we can get enough of them to find some dental work or prints we may figure out who they are. If not, Ashley's still our only lead."

"Shit," Eric whispered into the phone. "So she wasn't just imagining things."

"Well, you got that call this morning. Did that sound like they were playing games?"

Eric was about to ask how Carson knew about the call to his bedroom when he realized their lives had probably been public for weeks.

"Don't worry, son," Carson said, as if reading Eric's mind. "We aren't voyeurs. What happened or didn't happen between you two is none of my business unless it involves national security."

"Good to know." Eric smiled self-consciously. "Look, I'm going over to the hospital to see Ashley, but I want to meet...afterwards. I want to know what the hell's going on here."

"You want to help, be a soldier again, protect your pretty little lady and her daughter?" Carson asked. "You suddenly want to make the world safe for democracy?"

It required no thought. From the moment he saw the smoke rising from the marina and thought about what might have happened to Ashley, Kylie and Bobby, he knew the answer. "You're fucking right I do. I'll call you when I leave the hospital."

Chapter Thirty-Seven

Eric pulled into the hospital parking lot at 8:10. He'd just spoken to Louise again. Poor Kylie had cried herself to sleep. He hated leaving them alone but they were safe with a complement of Carson's watchdogs. Those guys were no rent-a-cops.

A Barnstable police cruiser hid behind a small grove of trees as he parked his Jeep and got down. Eric sneaked a glance toward the vehicle. Two men in plain clothes sat inside as he entered the main building. A uniformed officer stood concealed in an alcove near the door as he entered. *Damn!* Was this all for Ashley or was Whitey Bulger in the building? The big question he kept asking himself was why? Were they here to protect Ashley or keep her prisoner?

Stopping at the information desk, Eric grew concerned when the volunteer on duty told him she was in intensive care on the third floor. The woman shot a glance at the policeman near the entrance. Eric nodded casually to the man who immediately put his 230 pounds between Eric and the hallway.

"Can I help you?" the officer asked.

"Sure." Eric was frustrated and angry, itching for a confrontation but held himself in check. "Here to see Ashley Fitzhugh. In intensive care. She's family," he lied.

"May I see an ID, sir?" the officer asked in nonconfrontational tones.

When Eric reached for his wallet the man's hand slid to his holster. The hammer lock had been removed.

"Here." Eric pulled out his wallet with two fingers. The officer held it up, eyes never leaving Eric while his hand wrapped around the grip of his SIG-Sauer. This guy was no amateur. Experienced and sharp. Ex-military. Hand-picked for the job. Carson knew his talent and chose the best.

The officer smiled and handed Eric back the license.

"Thank you, sir." He nodded.

Eric looked around.

"Take the first elevator on your right," the man volunteered.

"Thanks again." Eric returned the nod and headed down the long hall.

When he reached the third floor he was amazed to see Jack, Carson's right-hand man and former CIA operative, talking to another uniformed officer. Jack nodded and approached, holding out his hand.

"Mr. Montgomery," he said with a look of quiet assurance. Despite confidence in his own martial-arts skills, if this man's handshake was an indicator of strength, Eric was glad they were on the same side. "She's in here. The Admiral said to expect you." His smile stretched thin across his lips. Jack looked alert but tired. Eric was sure his boss was a taskmaster.

"The Admiral?" Eric must have looked curious.

"Yes, sir. That's his rank and title." For a brief moment Jack's thin smile grew. It disappeared quickly.

"Is Ashley all right?" Eric asked with concern as he studied the rooms. The others were surrounded by clear glass enclosures with a dizzying collection of technology arrayed inside. Patients lay immobile, some with concerned looking visitors. Ashley's room was more conventional, hidden anonymously behind a massive wooden door.

"She's fine. Just sedated. It's a contained environment." Jack gestured as he looked around. "Easier to control."

"She must be valuable to justify this much security. What the hell did she stumble onto?" Eric inquired as they stepped into her room.

Jack waited till they were inside the door. "The Admiral will have to explain that. He put this whole operation together."

"Okay," Eric agreed. He still wondered what Ashley knew or had seen to create this much commotion. His team had been assigned to guard some visiting political heavyweights, but he could never remember this size detail. "Are you expecting trouble?" he asked.

"Can never tell." The man shrugged casually. "Comes when you least expect it." He pulled the massive door shut, adding, "But you know that."

Eric shot him a look. He felt a mixture of pride and irritation at being grouped with these men whose lives were characterized by death and secrecy.

"Can I sit with her?" he asked.

"Be my guest." Jack turned and let himself out. "She's not a prisoner."

Eric surveyed the room. It was like so many others he'd witnessed. Soft, electronic pulses droned in the background while a sterile, antiseptic odor permeated the room. Eric approached the bed on tiptoes. His face flushed as he saw her, eyes lingering on each feature. He relaxed as her regular breathing kept pace with the monitor that stood next to the bed. As he reached her bedside, Eric touched her hand. It was warm, sending shivers up his arm. She responded immediately, smiling as if she knew he was there.

"Ashley," he whispered as he bent down to examine her injuries. The paramedic had been on target. Everything looked superficial. One of the wounds on her forehead might be deep enough to leave a small scar. It didn't matter to Eric. He just needed to know she was all right. He breathed deeply and gripped her hand more tightly.

Her eyes opened slowly—the same velvet-brown he saw in his dreams. Her face took on a contented look as she recognized him.

"Hi." She squinted, her lips forming a weak smile as her eyes washed over his face.

"Hi," he whispered back.

"I'm so sorry," she managed, the hint of a tear forming as she studied him. "About everything."

"Not your fault."

Ashley licked her lips. Eric quickly searched the nightstand and found the water pitcher. He poured half a cup. He let go of her hand and directed the cup carefully to her mouth after placing a straw in it.

He stroked her tousled dark hair. It could be unruly. Tonight it looked in a state of chaos. But to Eric she looked wonderful. A smile crossed his lips as she reached out for his hand again.

"You're all right." His throat tightened. "That's all I care about."

"Kylie?" she asked hoarsely, eyebrows arched.

"She's fine. Lu brought her here earlier, but you were sleeping." He smiled. "I'll bring her by tomorrow if you're all right."

He put her hand on the cover sheet and turned to get a chair.

"No! Don't leave," she pleaded in a scratchy voice as she found the tray with her cup. *"Please."*

"I won't," he promised and pulled his chair close enough so he could hold her hand. He took a deep breath inhaling a trace of the intoxicating fragrance that surrounded her.

She sighed gently and closed her eyes again.

All the security? What didn't he know? If Ashley was in this much danger, he wasn't going to leave her. She'd become more than an important part of his life. She was his life. Eric would never let anything happen to her. But something wasn't right. Eric couldn't put his finger on it. The guards, the agents, his brother? What was he missing?

Ashley dropped into a light sleep, snoring softly. He let his eyes close for just a minute. Eric needed sleep. Needed it badly. In the field fatigue was expected—SOP. It went with the job. Back in the world it was different. He tried, fought against it but his eyelids refused to stay open. Eric couldn't…give…in…

He had no idea how long he slept, but it was filled with strange, frightening images. Ashley cried out. Eric sat bolt upright.

"No," she mumbled, fighting with her sheets as she threw the top one off. "Too dangerous…" She continued her rant, eyes staring at some invisible specter. She collapsed on her pillow again, closing her eyes for a minute.

Suddenly she rose again. He'd seen it before in men with severe concussions or PTSD. Eric pressed the call button. "Eric...danger." She fought, yanking at the IVs just as the first nurse appeared. "Can't stay…have to get away…*to leave!*" she yelled.

Get away? Leave? Eric's mouth went dry as he watched the nurse inject something into her IV drip. He stared, terrified at the thought she might run away—stop being part of his life.

Suddenly he understood the intense security surrounding Ashley. She was the lynch-pin, the vital cog or...what? He didn't want to think about the suspicion that lurked in the back of his mind. Jack had assured Eric she was no prisoner. Had he lied? And if so, why? What were these people really after? What was so important, so damning she had to be protected like the crown jewels?

The sedative had taken effect. Ashley rested quietly again.

Eric pulled out his cell and found the number he wanted. He hit dial.

"Hi," Carson said quietly.

"We need to talk." Eric stood and headed for the door.

"Okay," the man they called the Admiral agreed. "There's a place just off…"

He gave Eric directions to a small, out-of-the-way coffee shop.

"Got it. See you in twenty minutes." Eric took two steps toward the bed and kissed Ashley on the lips gently. He backed away and watched her for a long moment. "God as my witness, I will never let anything happen to you," he said as his throat grew tight. He squeezed her hand.

"Love you..." She moaned softly and grew an innocent smile in her sleep.

I love you too, Eric mouthed the words as he threw open the door, pushed past Jack and the guard, and headed toward the elevator without another word.

Chapter Thirty-Eight

Eric sat in his Jeep in the hospital parking lot. The car with the plainclothes officers huddled inconspicuously behind the large maple tree.

Eric couldn't spot the tail behind him as he sped down Route 28 toward the rendezvous. He knew the place. Traffic had evaporated. But that was Cape Cod. Despite being one of the prime vacation getaways in the East, Eric always marveled at the fact that they rolled the sidewalks up at nine p.m. The meeting spot was a mile down the street from Lu's house. Good place for quiet conversation. Also a good place for an ambush but that made no sense. If they'd wanted to waste him they had ample opportunity. No, he'd calculated that he must have some integral role in this complex scenario.

On the way he gave Louise another quick call.

"Hi. Everything okay with you and Kylie?" he asked.

"Yep. We're all snuggled in with our own private police force." Eric wasn't sure. Was she annoyed or pleased?

"Good. Stay that way," Eric ordered. "Do what they say and try to stay cool!"

Right, he thought.

Eric arrived at the coffee shop and parked next to a utilitarian Dodge pickup. He got out and scanned the parking lot and the dimly lit interior. He walked toward the door and through it. Four customers sat in booths or at the counter. Since the placard said that closing time was ten p.m. and it was five past Eric assumed they were Carson's people.

Carson nodded casually and showed what passed for a smile as he motioned for Eric to join him. The fact that he sat in the center of the small shop reinforced Eric's belief that the "customers" belonged to the Admiral.

Eric studied the small interior. It had the feel of one of those film noir scenes—poorly lit, ceiling fan thumping overhead, and everyone apparently minding their own business. Despite the noisy rattle of the overhead AC unit and the few inhabitants, it held a damp, musty feel. He quickly scanned the others and slid in across from the older man.

"Admiral," he said with an even tone.

A faint smile crossed Carson's thin lips. "Who gave you that title? Jack?"

Eric nodded. "Yep," he managed before a rotund young waitress approached them. She was working at chewing her gum and had a cherubic face. Eric wondered if she was part of the cast or had been recruited to give the place a semblance of normality.

"Anything else?" she asked in a soft Midwestern drawl that confirmed she was more than part of scenery.

"Another black coffee for me and...you?" he looked at Eric.

"A Pepsi if you have it?"

The girl nodded and gave him a flirtatious smile as she turned and headed toward the counter adding a special sway to her generous hips as she left. Eric knew it was window dressing though why Carson and company were role playing he had no idea.

"How's Ashley?" Carson asked with a look of concern.

"Okay," Eric said quietly as he studied the older man. "Let's skip the pleasantries and get to the point? Someone is stalking her. Trying to scare the hell out of her and me, too, I guess. They've killed at least two people, probably more if you include the guys across the river. What does she know that would put her at the center of this whirlpool?"

"Nothing," the older man said casually.

Eric pushed back in the booth and stared. "What the hell do you mean, nothing?"

"Just what I said. Nothing," Carson repeated. A half-smile teased his thin lips again.

Eric watched him as a cold fear swept over him. So that was it. What had his father always told him? Everything is perception, appearance. Like the pretty waitress, Ashley was window dressing. Only the waitress wasn't lying in the Cape Cod hospital scared out of her wits.

"So all the smoke and mirrors are just that—smoke and mirrors?"

Carson nodded.

"Does she know that?"

The older man shook his head. "Nope. Wouldn't work if she did." Carson looked around casually. "Ashley thinks she's discovered a clue to the next 9/11."

So that was it. Ashley and by extension Kylie were decoys. Pawns in a game of cat and mouse. And Carson, the Admiral, or whatever the hell he was called was standing by with dozens of agents just waiting for the bad guys to pounce—make a move. Then they'd go into action. If Ashley was caught in the crossfire, tough luck.

"You son of a bitch," Eric whispered through tight lips. He started to reach across the table. The "customers" who remained stood. They were next to him in a split second.

"Hold on, son. I know what you're thinking, but I'm not the cold-hearted bastard you think I am."

Eric sighed deeply and sat back in his seat as he raised his arms in a gesture of surrender. He was outmatched.

Carson motioned the men away and leaned toward Eric. "You don't know what we're dealing with here. You think I wanted to put that innocent young woman and her daughter in harm's way?" He grabbed Eric by the forearm. "You know what real loss is. Combat deaths, your wife. I know it too, Eric." He looked around and lowered his voice. "I can't even count the good men and women I've lost." His gray eyes found Eric's. "But I can remember every face. And I had a daughter at Cantor-Fitzgerald on 9/11. Ring any bells?" Carson released Eric's arm. He slumped in his seat.

A large lump formed in his throat. "Sorry, Admiral."

"I want to put an end to terrorism. Once and for all. Be done with it. But what's happening now...the situation we're dealing is worse by a factor of ten."

"Worse?" Eric was confused. "How so?"

"After 9/11 everyone went scalp hunting. Wanted somebody to blame. In the end we discovered that like most everything in life, it was a series of mistakes, oversights, and coincidences. A lot of fingers got pointed. Some higher-ups got whitewashed, others got fired."

Eric nodded. "Okay, so…?"

"Have you ever heard of Firestorm?"

"Yeah," Eric answered. "Ashley mentioned it. It's the reason everyone's chasing her."

"Yep." Carson nodded. "The other thing that happens when there's a terrible tragedy like 9/11 is you'll usually find some folks who think they know what's best for the rest of us. They're smarter and better than the system."

Eric nodded back. "Some geniuses who've figured out how to protect the world and prevent the next crisis?"

"You got it." Carson sighed and closed the space between them again. "But the guys we're after have taken that to a whole new level. They have a new technology and intend to use it to show us how vulnerable we are."

"Shit." Eric felt cold fear creep into his body as he looked into Carson's face. "How?" he asked.

"They're going to scare us straight—show us how badly we need their leadership and guidance by blowing up thirteen small towns during their Fourth of July celebrations."

Eric was hearing but not believing this. It was straight out of Ludlum or Lee Child. "What?" he whispered incredulously.

"We're still not sure what their real goal is. Ralph infiltrated the mid-level operation. Anarchy, martial law, a military coup? They're all possibilities. We only know they're a powerful cabal of highly placed officers from all the service branches. They think we need their leadership because we're all such stupid shits. But then every egomaniac and fanatic I ever met thinks that way."

"What does this have to do with Ashley?"

Carson sat back and wore a reflective look. When he spoke he wore a soft smile. "Ashley is a genius of sorts. You could call her a savant. You know, like the five-year-old who can play Rachmaninoff's piano concertos or beat the world chess champion. But her talent is much more practical. She's a genius with technology—computers and the Internet to be specific."

"I knew she was good, but I didn't know she was that good."

"Good?" The older man chuckled. "She's beyond good, Eric. If there was a competition for hacking she could be the world champion."

"Then why was she still living with Ralph? Why isn't she working for you or the CIA or Microsoft making six figures a year and driving a Lexus?" Eric asked.

Carson sighed deeply. "She attended Norfolk State University. Full scholarship to the College of Science, Engineering, and Technology. In her junior year she was working the graveyard shift in the data center. Stupid, boring shit she could have done in her sleep. There was a problem. They said she was changing student grades for money."

Eric shrugged as he watched Carson. Had his angel lost her halo? He swallowed. "Did she?" he asked.

"If she had they'd never have caught her. Ashley's too good." He shook his head disdainfully. "But she lost her scholarship and it went on her record. Not many places want to hire someone who's been thrown out of college for cheating at that level. Poor kid couldn't even get a job as a bank teller after that."

"All right, so what does all this have to do with what's happening now?" Eric asked.

"Here's the bottom line. The lunatics behind Firestorm know she hacked into their secure data base. She did it in a misguided attempt to help Ralph. They have no idea what she saw or downloaded. We know most of the supporting cast of Firestorm but there are three men at the top who run the operation. Ralph was able to worm in far enough to get that. Those men are terrified she might have information or pictures that could identify them."

So that was it. It was what Eric had been afraid of, but it made perfect sense…if you didn't care what happened to the girls. He found Carson's eyes and fixed on them. They had that cold, impassive look. The ceiling fan rattled, breaking the tense silence as the two watched each other.

"So, you're using her as bait. Hoping that the big fish come after Ashley." He shook his head. "And you've set up this whole charade, even sending them to me hoping to draw them into the open?"

"We've got four weeks till they execute their plan." Carson stared back. "If you think I like doing this, you're as crazy as the guys we're trying to find. But we're out of options, so yes, I don't like it but we're going fishing. And we're using Ashley as bait."

Chapter Thirty-Nine

The Director sat in his office, staring absently out at the landscape of his nation's capitol. The cradle of liberty, hallowed ground for which so many of his brothers in arms had sacrificed their lives. What would they think of our nation today? Embassy bombings, the Cole, 9/11, two more endless wars they could never win? Was that what their lives had bought?

No! He'd dedicated his life to service. Enlisting as a youth, working his way up the chain of command from private to the rarified status he now occupied. For what? So the bureaucrats and bean-counters could hamstring the country once more? His family had served America since the days of Lexington and Concord. His grandfather many times removed had stood on that green, outnumbered and outgunned, facing down British regulars. Over the intervening centuries he and his family had lost countless friends, family members, and fellow patriots too numerous to count.

Now, on the eve of his greatest triumph...his graphic, frightening demonstration that would awaken his countrymen to the ever-present threat that confronted them had been placed in jeopardy. And by whom? A world-class intelligence operation? A crack team of capitol insiders? No! An upstart girl. An arrogant and irreverent young woman whose frightening skills had all but destroyed his years of planning and work.

No matter.

The Director had no intention of abandoning his grand scheme. Postpone it until a more fortuitous time? Maybe. And if his plans were laid bare he would not go down without a fight. He knew the price. It was a devastating one—sacrifice his fellow leaders, take their vast war chest, and live to fight another day.

He pulled himself to his feet and turned toward his long window one last time, studying the magnificent obelisk of the Washington Monument. The Director picked up his briefcase and the tools he would require from behind his desk and headed to the door. Firestorm would have to wait for a better time, but his identity could never be revealed. He must survive. And for her whimsical treachery, the Fitzhugh bitch would pay the price for her interloping. As a bonus he would take down her new guardian angel and her spawn.

When he got to the limousine that would take him to the airport and Boston, he took out a disposable cell, dialed the number he knew well.

"Hello. I'm calling to make you aware of a deadly threat to national security. I have only a few minutes, but this is a matter of life and death and I must speak with your supervisor…"

When he had finished betraying his most trusted companions, he opened the window. The phone fell casually from his hand at Dupont Circle, where the steady stream of traffic guaranteed its life would be measured in seconds.

He smiled.

One more task to complete and like all the others it

had fallen to him to bring it to fruition.

Tomorrow at this time he'd be on a jet to safety and Ashley Fitzhugh and company would be close to death.

Chapter Forty

Eric headed toward his house on a deserted Route 28. An occasional vehicle passed, but he took only casual notice. His mind was fixed on the task at hand. He knew what he had to do—first go home and make sure that Lu and Kylie were safely tucked in for the night. Pick up a selection of weapons and then head back to the hospital ASAP. No matter what the "Admiral" said, Eric would be the primary protection for Ashley.

When Eric had asked about Ralph, the older man shrugged noncommittally. There was an ambivalence when he thought about his brother, the ne'er-do-well, the bad seed who'd turned out to be living a double life, had uncovered a sinister plot and more importantly, had probably saved Ashley and Kylie from torture and death. The sudden transition in his brother's status was complicated to say the least. Ralph a hero and one of the good guys. Maybe he'd gone dark but perhaps these people were keeping him under wraps, which brought Eric to the question of Lip. Was he all right? Had he given up thinking this was a wild goose chase, a misadventure? When he talked to Carson next, he'd try and find out what had happened to his friend. Lip would never abandon a friend and teammate in trouble. Worry gnawed at Eric.

The warm, damp breeze blew in through the open

window as he sped along at fifteen miles per hour over the speed limit. The trail car was a hundred yards behind, populated by two of Carson's team.

He reached the back road that led into his street and took the turn onto the dirt road. The house was lit up like it was Christmas. Every window and all the outdoor spots were blazing brightly.

He parked, descended, and made his way quickly to the porch and the back door. Save the light show, the house was a picture of normalcy. No extra vehicles, no agents with MAC 10s or shotguns burst out at him as he trotted up the stairs and knocked lightly on the door.

Louise appeared in the casual outfit she wore to bed—loose gym shorts and a faded T-shirt extolling the Red Sox 2004 World Series Championship. Her pleasant face grew a wary smile when she saw him. Lu opened the door and ushered Eric inside.

As soon as he was safely into the kitchen and the door was double locked, she threw her arms around Eric and gave him a hug that took his breath away. The faint aroma of something Italian and spicy hung in the air. When he pulled free, he saw a trail of tears from her large, pale-blue eyes.

"Thank God you're all right," she whispered emphatically and hugged him a second time, resting her head on his chest.

"I'm fine, Lu, and so is Ashley," he assured her, searching the downstairs for signs of the protection he expected. "We just have to stay calm. I know it's asking a lot but I need you to…"

She pressed her fingers to his lips. "Don't you dare apologize. I think of the girls as family. So whatever you need, I'm with you. Already called the hospital and told them I needed time off."

Louise, he thought. How would he have ever travelled the long, bitter months since Elaine's death and the weeks since the girl's arrival without her? Eric had no idea.

She searched his eyes. "The people here couldn't or wouldn't tell me anything. What's happening—with Ashley, with you?"

He directed her to one of the kitchen chairs and took her hands. "We both figured that Ashley had a…a history. You spoke about it the other day."

Louise sat and nodded, eyes wide and fixed on him.

"Well," he continued. "We were right. But we couldn't have imagined how much trouble she was in."

Lu squeezed his hands as her face took on a wary expression. Eric caught sight of a shadowy figure in the hallway. Ian. He nodded. Eric returned the gesture.

"Ashley is very smart. She's a whiz at computers. Some time ago, by accident she found some information about a project that was secret and threatened our safety."

"You mean like…like 9/11?"

Eric nodded. "The men who planned the operation found out about it and are trying to frighten her into revealing what she discovered. And you were right. Someone was here last night." He nodded toward the hallway. "There are some high-level government security people who want to find and arrest them." He sighed deeply. "In the meantime, while they're looking for these men, there will be plenty of people to protect all of us."

He took her hands and rose. "I'd like to see Kylie."

Lu wiped her cheeks and nodded.

He headed upstairs and tiptoed into Kylie's room. She slept restlessly, pulling at her covers and holding her giant pink teddy bear as if her life depended on it. Eric sat on her bed and studied her angelic face, brushing stray strands of her unruly hair reminiscent of her mother's. He bent and kissed her cheek tenderly, then squeezed her tiny hand, and picked it up, laying it on the sheet.

Eric rose with a purpose and headed to the basement and his workout room where his weapons were kept. He unlocked the door and studied the array before him. The Glock and two boxes of hollow points, the eight-inch commando knife with the serrated blade, the twelve-gauge and shells he'd keep in the back of his Jeep.

He locked up and took his arsenal to his Jeep before Lu could see him, then ran back inside.

"Planning on starting World War III, mate?" asked Ian, in his thick Scottish accent.

"Something like that," Eric offered defiantly.

Ian put his hands up. "No argument from me, laddie. We're dealing with some real bad people," he said.

Lu appeared and Eric gave Ian a cool look. No need getting his mother-in-law in any more of a frenzy than she already was. Ian nodded and backed away.

"Lu, I'm going to sit with Ashley. They should have some preliminaries on the explosives soon, too, so I may be gone for a while." He took her by the shoulders firmly. "But if you need anything, anything at all or if Ian needs help. Call me. Right away!"

She pulled him close and held him tightly for a

split second. "Promise me this will all be over soon. Real soon." Her words had the ring of a plea.

He gave her a squeeze then backed away, finding her eyes, the ones that recalled Elaine's. "Promise," he whispered, crossed his heart, took Ian's hand and shook it firmly, then ran out to his Jeep, wondering how he would keep that promise.

Chapter Forty-One

Eric sat, eyes closed in the reclining chair next to Ashley's bed. The slow rhythmic hum of the air conditioning sounded pleasant, restful. He'd been here for—Eric opened his eyes and studied his watch—two and a half hours. One forty-five p.m. The duty nurse had brought him a blanket since the rooms in ICU were kept cooler than most—the result of the additional technology needed for the patients.

He leaned back and studied Ashley. After her earlier outburst the nurse assured him she'd slept deeply. Now, as he stared at her face, half covered by the mop of unruly dark hair, he smiled. Despite all the threats, the endless sinister possibilities, Eric was at peace as he heard her softly purring, keeping time with the electronics that monitored her vitals.

Eric had spent the last hour working out why he loved Ashley so deeply and so unconditionally. He needed her, of course. Needed her desperately, like a cool spring to a man dying of thirst. And finally, he'd understood why. Elaine was the embodiment of perfection itself. Beautiful, brilliant, beloved. Ashley was flawed. As a result she needed him. It was that simple. She was pretty, full of life, and held an appreciation for everything around her that Eric had never seen in anyone. But it was her vulnerability and her need for him that made him want her so much.

Eric took one more look, letting his gaze wash over her face as his lids grew heavy. The slow regular beeping of the monitors, Ashley's deep breathing, the peaceful murmuring of the air conditioning, then a small noise behind his chair, a sudden prick in the neck and…

Ashley stood next to him, walking on the beach, her hand warm in his. Turning toward him she found his eyes. It began slowly, starting as the corners of her mouth turned up, growing into a smile, then a grin.

She laughed, letting her slender arms surround his waist, pulling him close as their shoulders bumped.

"Eric, we're free. No one will ever bother us again."

"Free?" Could they be.

"Of course." Ashley nodded and tightened her grip on his hand. He prayed she was right.

"Uncle Eric." He turned toward the voice calling from the shoreline.

"Kylie," he called to the child in the flowing white dress as she ran through the surf.

Ashley pulled him to a stop and waved at the little girl. "Come up here, you, before you ruin that new dress."

The child's face mirrored her mother's: pale, flawless skin, enormous eyes, picture-book smile surrounded by deeply carved dimples.

Kylie ran, shoes in hand, heading toward them, squeezing into the small space between them as she giggled. Her laugh was lyrical—intoxicating.

She snuggled tightly between them. The three joined as if they were one.

Eric laughed.

Ashley released her hold on Eric and ran a hand through the child's flowing hair.

"Eric." Suddenly, another voice called from the bluff above. He shaded his eyes, looking into the sun.

"Eric." The voice called again. He felt more than heard it.

When he squinted he could just make out her face. She stood on the shallow rise. He scrambled up the dunes. From this distance he could see her. He moved toward her, taking hesitant steps while looking back at Ashley and Kylie.

Waves of emotion engulfed him as she drew close. Her hand reached toward him but suddenly drew away. A delicate smile came to her lips—the special one he loved so much. Eric closed his eyes. He could almost feel her embrace.

She whispered in his ear. "I always loved you. I always will. The first time I saw you something took hold of me. It never let go." She sighed deeply. "But please, I'm begging you. Move on. Don't spend your life worshipping someone who only exists in memories."

The wind blew her sweet fragrance around him. He inhaled deeply, wanting to hold it and her inside him forever.

Eric opened his eyes. She backed away slowly. "I know how much you loved me. It's all right, Eric." Her eyes looked past him to where Ashley and Kylie laughed, chasing each other, unaware of the reunion a few yards above them. She smiled softly. "It wasn't your fault. It was simply my time to leave."

She turned.

Tears filled his eyes and burned.

She stopped, facing him for the last time. "The most difficult person to forgive is yourself," she said as she blew him a kiss and waved, looking toward the beach. Eric knew he'd heard that somewhere before. Her lips parted. "Time for both of us to move on. Good-bye, Eric."

He brushed the tears aside and watched her image fade and disappear. "Good-bye, Elaine."

"Hey, where'd you go?" Ashley called to him. She and Kylie lay in a heap, still giggling on the soft sand. "I thought you'd left us."

He swallowed, looking back for the last time to where her spirit had been.

"Never. You two are stuck with me. Forever."

It was dark. Eric needed to open his eyes. They refused. He pushed himself forward in the recliner. He tried a second time. They cooperated reluctantly.

The room was as quiet as...death. A frightening analogy. It was dark. Very dark. Eric grabbed the arms of the large chair and stared. He checked his watch: 3:10 a.m. It came back to him—slowly. He'd been thinking about Ashley...then a pinprick in his neck. Barely noticeable. Where was Ashley? Her bed was empty. The electronics had gone dark. The covers looked neat, well-ordered—as if she'd slid out of them to use the lavatory.

Eric stood. He swayed but kept his feet. He scanned his surroundings once more. Cold terror engulfed him as he staggered to the door. He pulled it open quietly. The policeman on watch sat in his chair, facing away from Eric.

"Officer," he whispered, not wanting to disturb the other patients or alert the bad guys if something sinister was going on. No response.

Closing the small distance between them, he touched the man's shoulder lightly. Still nothing. *Asleep*, Eric thought as he moved close, facing the man. The cop sat, eyes wide open, staring straight ahead, a blank look on his round face. His forehead was pierced neatly by a large, single bullet hole. As Eric watched the young officer fall forward, a large exit wound appeared in the back of his skull. The wall behind him had been split by the large caliber bullet.

He pulled out his cell as he spotted a second victim slumped at the nurse's station. The young woman who'd been so concerned, so helpful. The one who reminded him of Elaine. Was it true? Only the good died young? He found Carson's number on his cell. Eric was about to hit dial when the phone jumped to life.

"Eric?" Carson asked, his voice sounding subdued, heavy with stress.

"Yeah," Eric answered. "I'm at the hospital. We've got serious trouble."

The older man exhaled deeply. "You don't know the half of it."

Chapter Forty-Two

"I need you to meet me at your place—*ASAP!*" It was an order. "No time for debate. Just get there!"

"All right," Eric answered, desperate to know what was going on.

Eric hurriedly shared his part of the story. Ashley's disappearance, the dead cop, and night nurse he'd found. *Enough talk*, Eric thought. He needed to find the girl he loved.

"Eric," Carson whispered. "Stay in control. Don't do anything crazy."

"You gonna tell me what the hell is going on?" Eric demanded.

"I'd love to, but I'm still assessing the situation."

"The situation," Eric said, voice raised in anger. "You're *assessing the fucking situation!* I lost one woman I loved. I don't intend to lose another! How did this get so far out of control?"

"I don't have the answer. It shouldn't have. Look, you're a pro. I need you to stay in control," Carson repeated. "Get to your house. Now." He added a quiet, "Please."

Eric closed his cell. After his frustrating, abbreviated conversation with Carson he was boiling. But the old man was right. Stay in control. That was the mantra. He ran down the stairs to ground level two at a time, stopping to throw open the second floor door.

Nothing. A few nurses and a cleaning man. Eric needed to find Ashley, Jack, or some sign of where they'd gone.

Eric held out hope. Jack was the consummate pro. Maybe he'd surprised the intruder and taken him out, or frightened him off, since there was no evidence of a struggle or blood. He could have taken Ashley downstairs in hopes of protecting her and finding backup. But Jack had his phone and a walkie-talkie. And if they'd left ICU, would they leave him unconscious in Ashley's room? Not likely. But, Eric rationalized, even experienced pros do strange things under stress. Eric prayed he'd find them on the first floor.

When he arrived in the lobby it was deserted save another big cop on watch. This one looked as imposing, fit, and professional as his predecessor. But his stare blanched, and he sat open mouthed when Eric described the grisly scene in ICU.

Eric rushed outside, quickly interrogating the other police and agents on site despite Carson's instruction to the contrary. Thanks to Carson's team, all had been notified by the time Eric saw them. They were as confused as he was, swearing they'd seen nothing suspicious.

Double-timing it to his Jeep, Eric speed-dialed Carson again, probing, hoping for more information.

"Are you gonna tell me what the hell's going on?" Eric demanded again as he continued scanning the parking lot.

"Look, son. Just get your ass over here." Carson stone-walled him again. "And stop playing detective at the hospital. We have agents who can handle that. I need you *now!*"

His phone went dead as he hopped into the Jeep. He reached into the back, unlocking the special cabinet under the rear seat that housed his weaponry. Eric took the Glock, chambered a round, and shoved it into his waistband. He added the commando knife.

As he sped the eight miles that separated him from Lu and Kylie, the icy fear that had begun in the hospital continued to spread. Eric knew it all too well. He practiced a technique that he'd learned and had served him well in the Middle East, a TM thing, refusing to allow any negative images into his consciousness.

So many questions and loose ends: Ashley, Ralph, Carson, and the one that continued to nag at him despite his attempts to avoid it. His friend Ron Lipton. Where was he?

The questions grew and festered. Answers did not.

As he pulled into the small gravel side road that his house fronted on, a local policeman held up his hand. Eric brought the Jeep to a halt. He was growing impatient, very impatient.

"Mr. Montgomery?" the officer asked, shining a powerful flashlight in Eric's eyes and raising his voice to be heard over the engine.

"Yep." Eric nodded.

"They're expecting you." The man stepped aside and waved him on with military precision. *Former MP*, Eric thought as he passed. Eric spotted a cruiser hidden in the small grove bordering his house. He could just make out another officer with a heavy weapon—an M-16 or shotgun.

Carson's massive SUV was parked next to two others. All were flanked by two Dennis Police cruisers and...an ambulance.

Eric turned off the engine and dismounted the Jeep at warp speed. The outside lights blazed and several people moved in the bright white halogen glare. Eric knew none of them.

Ian approached and put his hand on Eric's chest. "Can you wait here a minute, laddie? I think *he* wants to speak to you."

Eric strained to catch sight of Lu, Kylie, or Ashley. No luck.

Carson approached rapidly. For someone into his fifties, the large man moved with a fluid grace despite a slight limp. Carson hadn't spent his years of service riding a desk. Eric felt a grudging admiration.

He moved across the wide front lawn toward Carson. The older man held up his hand. "Stay put, son. No one hurt that you know." He looked back, then found Eric's eyes again. When he did Eric saw a mix of anger and regret in Carson's face.

"Wish I could say the same," he said as he swallowed hard and exhaled.

"Where are they?" Eric demanded. Any remnants of patience draining as he scanned the scene.

Carson gave him a stare that hovered between anger and concern. Deep concern. "I honestly don't know. That's why you're here."

"What do you mean. How would I...?" Eric stopped as he followed Carson's eyes. A gurney appeared on his back porch. His throat grew tight at the sight of a body covered by a sheet. Eric thought he'd left this behind, half a world away. Yet it kept coming back to haunt him.

Carson took his arm as they met the stretcher. The

old man pulled back the sheet. A stranger. Dead. A pretty woman Eric had never seen. Carson's breathing took on a labored, shallow sound as he studied the young, dark face staring up at them.

"Phoebe. Phoebe Wells," Carson whispered. His eyes clouded over as he touched her limp hand. She'd been shot three times, twice at close range in the chest. Her head rested on dark residue. Another blood stain.

"Execution style," Carson observed coolly with a light cough. He swallowed hard again. "She was the best," he said. "That's why she was here."

The older man shook his head. "It never gets any easier." Uncharacteristically, he rested a hand on Eric shoulder. "But you lost your share, didn't you, son?"

"Yes, sir. I did and no, it never gets any easier," Eric agreed as the gurney rumbled down the three steps to the brightly lit lawn and worked noisily across the uneven ground to the ambulance.

The sound of another stretcher's wheels caused both men to turn toward the back porch and the kitchen door again. As Eric caught sight of Carson, he could see the older man's eyes glistening. They held a sadness he hadn't seen in Carson before.

Carson mounted the steps and stopped the gurney as he lifted the sheet and looked down for a long moment. He sighed and descended while the EMTs moved their sad payload toward the waiting ambulance. Its bright rotating lights competed with the illumination from the stark halogen bulbs in Eric's spots.

As he stood watching this strange, poignant scene, someone tapped on Eric's shoulder. Ian stood behind, staring at Carson, then followed the second gurney. He shook his head as it passed. "Jake Connelly." He whispered. "A fine lad. One of the best field agents I've ever seen."

All Carson's agents were apparently the best.

"But then the Admiral doesn't suffer fools. All our people are top notch," Ian observed in answer to Eric's thoughts. "The old man was very close to him. Trained him personally. Took the kid under his wing and…"

Ian's explanation stopped abruptly as Carson approached. "Great kid," the older man offered softly, shaking his head slowly.

"Sorry, Admiral. Real sorry," Eric sympathized. "But where are Louise and Kylie?" Eric asked. He knew Carson had lost agents. Good people he was close to. But he needed to know what was going on and where the people that he cared about had gone.

"We got a call about an hour ago," he nodded toward his second in command. "From Ian. When the team didn't call in on the half-hour, he came to check. He discovered this." Carson's thick arm made a sweeping gesture.

"But where are Lu and Kylie?" Eric repeated with growing anger and frustration.

Carson looked at Ian then back at Eric. "That's the problem, Eric." For the first time Carson's face showed his age. "I have no damn idea!"

Chapter Forty-Three

Eric checked his watch: 4:40 in the morning. The ambulance had departed on its solemn mission a few minutes earlier. Carson had just hung up after having an abbreviated talk with Stacy. She was on her way to Eric's house. Carson did his best to explain what she'd discovered after a night's work on the debris from the explosion.

Carson paced back and forth, raising his eyes toward the entry road every time a car went by.

As Eric watched, Ian came up behind him. "Never seen the old man like this," he whispered as his eyes studied Carson. They showed a mixture of admiration and sympathy. "Blames himself for the way this got bollixed up." Ian sighed and shook his head.

Eric wasn't feeling the love. After discovering that Carson's massive team had no idea what had happened he'd lost all sympathy. "If the shoe fits," he offered with no attempt to hide the sarcasm. "Why are we just sitting here doing nothing, for God sakes?"

"I don't think you understand the import of this mission. These blighters were determined to blow up thousands of people across the country. Men, women, children…all innocents just watching the Fourth of July fireworks."

Eric must have looked quizzical.

"They have a device—a detonator that's incredibly

sensitive. It uses sound waves to set off an explosion. We've been working on that technology for years. Like the glass-break detector in your home alarm, only a hundred times more sensitive and with the ability to discriminate. It can actually be set to detonate based on the frequency and sound quality of a noise." Carson had said that this was one of Ian's special skills. He sounded like a high school quarterback watching Tom Brady. "Amazing technology."

"Very exciting," Eric said with a definite edge to his voice. He heard Ian's grudging admiration. All he cared about right now was doing something, anything to find Ashley, Kylie, and Louise.

Carson had been talking to one of the agents in the back of a Tahoe. For the first time in this endless night, the older man's face showed a glimmer of what might be hope. He showed Ian thumbs-up as he closed the thirty feet between them.

"We picked up her signal!" he told Ian like a happy child on Christmas Eve. A smile spread across Carson's creased, broad face.

Could it be? Was there something they'd kept from him? Something that held out hope? "What are you talking about?" Eric demanded. He wanted action.

Carson reached them. Ian's face wore a smile, too. "That's great, Admiral." He paused and looked at Eric. "Knowing that something like this could happen we had an implant placed in Ashley's arm. Did it when she was in the hospital a few weeks ago. She doesn't even know about it."

Eric was hearing but not believing. "So you can track her. Like a GPS in a cell phone?" he whispered, shifting his gaze between Ian and the Admiral.

Carson nodded, looking tired but pleased. "Within fifty feet they tell us."

"So, when do we get going?" Eric asked anxiously.

"Not so fast, son." Carson chided.

"What's the holdup now? I'm assuming that when we find Ashley we'll find Lu and Kylie. With any luck, Jack, too."

Carson and Ian exchanged an anxious glance.

"I think it's a good bet that Jack is either dead or gone to the dark side," Carson pronounced evenly, without emotion.

Ian nodded in agreement.

"Okay. I still don't get it. What's the holdup?" Eric asked.

"We can't go in there like cowboys. We have to scout the location, find out the opposition's strength and come up with a game plan. Plus, if Jack is on their side, it gets complicated." Carson shrugged. "Very complicated."

"Why?" Eric asked.

"Because he knows about the chip we implanted. They'll certainly try to remove it and…" Carson looked at Ian and stopped in mid-sentence.

Eric looked back and forth between them. The enthusiasm of a minute before burst like a party balloon. He understood. They'd be in a hurry and not worry about their captive.

"Then it sounds like there's no time to waste," Eric said, watching the two men.

Carson nodded and looked at Ian. "Go get everything we need. There's a team on the way there now to scout the area."

Just as Eric headed for his truck Stacy pulled up.

She nodded to Eric as she ran over to Carson. "Going hunting, Admiral?" Her thin face looked fatigued.

Carson nodded. "We think we've found out where Ashley is. Hopefully her daughter and Eric's mother-in-law, too."

Stacy sighed deeply and bit her lip. "All right. But we have to be careful. Very careful. If this detonator is as sophisticated as I suspect, they can set it to blow at any range."

"So what?" Eric shrugged. "Why would they do that?"

"Their leader turned in his team. Gave them up. They think he's gone over the edge…like certifiable." Stacy shook her head.

"But if we've got them, we know who he is," Eric asked, confused. "Right?"

"No, I just got the same intel." Carson had been at the Tahoe command vehicle again. He approached and broke in. "They have no idea who the mastermind is. They never met with him. No one has. All their communication was done by phone. But they all agree on one thing. He has definitely gone over the edge." He repeated Stacy's warning. "He has only one goal in mind."

Eric felt the cold fear grip him again and tighten in knots as he looked at Carson's cool gray eyes. He knew what the older man was going to tell them.

Carson looked at Stacy, then back at him. "Making Ashley pay for destroying his plans."

Chapter Forty-Four

The Director sat on the small stool watching Ashley Fitzhugh across from him. She was gagged and handcuffed to a two-by-four. She looked terrified. But not for herself, he thought. No, she was frightened for her daughter and the older woman, Montgomery's mother-in-law.

Ashley had surprised him...again. She was more than he'd expected. Far more. He liked that. It was a perverse turn-on. He enjoyed a worthy adversary but had never considered her that. Until now. She deserved his enmity but she also deserved a measure of respect.

He walked over to her. She fixed his eyes with hers. She had beautiful eyes...just like his daughter. He put that thought out of his mind. Ashley might have his daughter's eyes, but she'd stolen any chance to exact his revenge. At least for now. He pulled the duct tape from her mouth.

She made no sound but continued fixing him with a stare. "You're never gonna let me go," she whispered as she watched him. "I've seen your face. I can identify you!"

"Don't be so sure. You interfered with my plans. Created a setback but..." Why not tell her. She was right. Ashley and the others would never leave this place alive, but he'd tease her into thinking otherwise. "I have a fortune, a private jet picking me up at the

Hyannis Airport, then a trawler to someplace safe." He gave her his best smile. "I'll be back to finish the job I started."

"Then why do you care about me, about us? We can't do any harm to you now."

"You're right." He placated her momentarily. It was the path of least resistance. "I just need one more thing from you.

"Here." He thrust a cell phone at her. "Make the call to your boyfriend. Tell him to come alone. He can pick you, your daughter, and his mother-in-law up."

"Eric's not stupid. He won't come here for us. He knows…"

The Director gave her a violent backhand to the cheek that sent her reeling. She bumped into the wall of the filthy little shack and slumped, hanging by her handcuffed arm.

"Do it!" he commanded. "Or your daughter and Louise will stay in that hole and suffocate slowly. Very slowly…and you'll hear every agonizing gasp." He held up the small walkie-talkie he'd programmed. She could hear her little girl whimpering in fear as the older woman attempted to soothe her.

He pulled Ashley roughly to her feet. The Director unlocked the handcuffs he'd placed on her and gave her the phone. He held an index card in front of Ashley. "Read this exactly the way I told you."

Chapter Forty-Five

The group in front of Eric's house was about to load into three Tahoe SUVs when his cell phone rang. Eric pulled it out. *Caller unknown* flashed across the screen. He had a bad feeling. His stomach churned as he pushed send to answer.

"Eric." His throat tightened when he heard Ashley's voice. He scanned the group and moved a few feet away.

"Ashley. Where are you? Are you all right?" he whispered as he watched Carson.

"I'm…okay," she managed, sounding anything but. "I'm gonna text you some directions. You have to come alone." Eric was sure she was terrified but doing her best to hold it together. "And do exactly what the text says…*please.*"

He heard her grunt as someone else took the phone. "You heard her, Mr. Montgomery. Do exactly what the text says. I have the little girl and your mother-in-law. And I have hidden cameras on your property. I want to see you get into your Jeep and leave, alone. The Admiral and his team must stand down."

"Even if I agreed to that they never would," Eric protested, trying to buy time. He wanted to alert the others, but if this man was telling the truth about the surveillance, it could mean death for his three captives. He looked at Stacy.

"I just saw you look toward the fire marshal," the man said evenly.

Eric took a deep breath. He had cameras watching or he was taking a gamble. Either way, he'd won. "What do you want?"

"You. I want to have a talk," the man whispered into the phone. Eric had no idea what the man's real motive was.

"All right." He headed for his Jeep. "What am I supposed to tell these people?"

"Tell them the truth. You come where I direct you or Ashley and the others die a very slow death. Add this as an incentive. I have several of the Firestorm sites already programmed to detonate. If my orders aren't followed to perfection, I'll kill the women and walk away. You can wait till Independence Day to see if I'm telling the truth."

Eric tried to think of an argument, some protest to even the odds. He was exhausted, mad as hell, and terrified for Ashley, Kylie, and Lu. Nothing came to mind.

"Oh. I forgot to tell you." The man paused. "The older woman and the child are buried alive. They have about two hours of air left so I suggest you get moving."

The phone went dead.

"What the hell am I supposed to do?" Eric asked Carson as he rushed for his Jeep.

"Slow down. We have our people surrounding the signal from Ashley's GPS chip."

"I can't slow down. He said Kylie and Lu are buried alive. I have to assume they are. There's no time to waste."

Carson took his arm. "Okay. I understand. Follow his directions. We'll be in place when you meet this guy." He smiled broadly and slapped Eric on the back. "Piece of cake. This is what we get paid the big bucks for!"

Carson's false bravado did nothing to assuage Eric's fear for Ashley, Kylie, and Lu. As soon as he turned onto Route 28, he heard his phone beep. The text instructed him to head west for four point three miles, then north on Route 134 to Route 6A. His heart raced as he calculated the time it would take. He looked at his watch. Thanks to the time of day there was no traffic. But the trip would still take him at least twenty minutes. If Lu and Kylie really were buried alive that left little time for error. The last line warned: commit to memory. Erase immediately. Eric had no idea what technology this maniac had at his disposal. He did as instructed.

The mastermind holding Ashley seemed clairvoyant. As soon as he hit Route 6A his phone beeped again. It was 5:15 a.m. Thank God, the roads were still empty. The text told him to follow the main road for three and a half miles then turn into the entrance to Fallon State Park.

He followed the orders. It was what he would have expected. Almost too obvious. If you were going to kidnap and hide three people in an out of the way secluded spot, the park was the place he would have chosen.

Suddenly his phone rang. It was Carson. Eric shifted uncomfortably not knowing whether or not the bad guys could hear or see him. He shook his head. This guy had to be smart...no, brilliant. But there was no way he could have locked into his cell or have a listening device in the Jeep. He risked it and pressed send.

"Hi," Carson's voice sounded calm, almost confident. "We've found an old shed. No sign of activity outside but there's a light on inside and we can hear voices coming from the building."

"Where are your people?" Eric asked tentatively, hoping for the answer he wanted.

"Someplace called Fallon State Park. Up on the north side."

"Good. I'm almost..."

His phone beeped.

"Gotta go," he whispered.

The next text told him to follow the asphalt road for two point three miles then turn off onto a side trail—for one mile, then...

He focused on the directions, committing them to memory. From what Carson had told him, his agents should be in place by now.

In ten minutes he was where the directions told him to dismount and walk east toward the sunrise, over a long low hill. From there he should be able to spot the shed where the man was holding Ashley.

He kept his weapons, the Glock and the knife, despite knowing that the man would likely search and disarm him.

Five minutes of brisk walking and he was on the rise, perspiring, more from tension and fear than the light exertion. Eric looked down on the small cabin. He'd expected to spot some of Carson's troops but had seen no one. Probably just as well. He took a deep breath and focused, hoping desperately that in ten minutes, Ashley would be in his arms and the others would be safe.

As he double-timed it down the low rise to the shed, a man stepped out of the door. Ashley was with him, hands cuffed behind her and duct tape over her mouth. She still wore the hospital gown, now torn and dirty, that she'd been wearing when he fell asleep. He clenched his fists when he saw that her face was bruised and swollen.

"Good job, Eric. May I call you Eric?" the man offered politely as if they'd met at a social gathering.

Eric nodded, trying to placate this guy till Carson's men showed themselves.

The man pushed Ashley roughly in front of him. She stumbled and groaned through the gag but kept her feet. In his right hand, her captor held a large caliber automatic. In the other, a thin, cylindrical device that had a small button on top and tiny red light that glowed on the side.

"Of course you're armed, Eric. You'd be a fool not to be." The man paused and gave him a placid smile. "Please remove any weapons you're carrying, take off your jacket and pull out your shirt so I can see you're being honest with me."

Eric threw the Glock and the commando knife on the ground five feet in front of him. He threw his jacket aside, pulled out his shirt and spun around to satisfy the man.

"Good... now your pant legs so I can see you have no ankle holsters or weapons there either. Do it very slowly with two fingers."

Eric complied.

"Good. Now we can finish our business here, and I'll be on my way."

"What do you want? I'm here now. Our deal was that they can go." Eric nodded toward Ashley.

The man shook his head slowly. Eric kept glancing around, expecting momentarily to hear a bull-horn telling this maniac to put down his weapon and move away from Ashley. What the hell were they waiting for?

"You seem nervous. Expecting someone perhaps. Help? The cavalry to charge in and save you and your lovely lady friend here?"

Eric shook his head. "I don't know what you talking about. I..."

"Well, that's good to hear." The man interrupted. "Because I'm afraid you'll be disappointed. And I know how much we all hate disappointment."

He showed a sickening, self-indulgent smile.

"You see, I suspected that your friends might have done something to keep track of your little friend here. Jack wouldn't tell but..."

"Where is Jack?" Eric broke in, partly to keep the man talking and partly in hopes that he might be alive.

"I'm afraid he met with an accident. He wasn't very cooperative so I had to do away with him."

Eric saw the fear in Ashley's eyes. She must have witnessed it. *You bastard*, Eric thought. *Torture, murder, beatings, burying a child alive...* Eric wanted five minutes alone with this piece of shit before...

"Anyway," the man continued. "I discovered that my friends put a tracking device in Ashley and I had to...extract it.

Ashley closed her eyes. Tears streamed down her cheeks. This son of a bitch must have cut it out while she was awake. Eric clenched his fists and took a tentative step toward her captor.

"Careful," the man warned sternly. "I not only have a powerful weapon here but I have a detonator in my other hand. But of course you knew that. One movement of my index finger and we'll all be blown into the stratosphere. At this point I have little to lose, but you, Eric…" He nodded toward Ashley.

Eric held his place as Ashley opened her eyes. He thought she was trying to smile.

"Oh and that small tracking device…" He looked at his watch.

Suddenly an explosion cracked through the damp morning air as it lit up the sky. "I think Mr. Carson's men just found it."

Chapter Forty-Six

Eric looked down at the weapons lying on the ground five feet in front of him.

The man holding the gun shook his head slowly. "Don't even think about it. One twitch and I press this button."

"I don't think so." Eric called his bluff. "You're after something. Revenge, justice, glory? I haven't figured it out yet but if you just wanted Ashley dead, why all the theatrics?"

"You really haven't figured it out?" The man looked amused. "I'm surprised. You may run a marina now, but you're a warrior, Eric. Always have been. I've done my homework."

"I suppose that's your idea of a compliment." Eric was trying to think of some alternative, a way to gain leverage. He saw none. He could charge the man having no idea of his self-defense skills or his agility. He could try surprise: dive for the Glock, hope to catch the man off-guard enough to give himself some chance...even a slim one.

"Yes, it is." The man answered. "You see, I needed to get Ashley and gain the advantage to get the evidence she had."

"You mean the flash drive?"

"Yes. It's the only thing that can tie me to Firestorm. Her daughter and your mother-in-law provided me with the leverage I needed to get that."

"So you took it when you were at my house?" Eric asked. The longer he kept the man talking the more relaxed he'd become. It also meant that maybe, just maybe Carson would find them.

The man nodded. "But don't you see? If I simply kidnapped and killed your lady friend here—" He thrust the large handgun into Ashley's side. "I'd never be rid of you. And you, Eric, you're a man to be reckoned with. Between you and that old bastard Carson I could never draw an easy breath, so I lured you here and now, as part of her punishment before I take Ashley back to die with the other two..." He raised the weapon and pointed at Eric's chest. Ashley squealed from under her gag and closed her eyes.

"You've got ten seconds to put that weapon down and back away from the girl," a voice called from a small grove of trees twenty yards away. It was a voice Eric knew well. A mixture of relief and amazement swept over him as he found Ashley's eyes. His friend Ron Lipton hadn't deserted him.

"You heard him," said another voice that had a familiar ring. Ralph? It came from behind the wall of the shed nearest to the kidnapper.

The man was caught completely off-guard. He'd never expected this. As he turned in surprise toward the voices, Eric saw his chance. He lunged for the Glock. As the man spun, facing him again, finger poised on the detonator, Eric took quick aim and shot him in the chest three times. Two more rounds caught the hand with the detonator. High caliber hollow points, Eric thought since they blew his hand and device into splinters. Eric braced himself for the explosion, pushing Ashley to the ground and shielding her. It never came.

He stood and pulled Ashley up, gently pulling the tape from her mouth. "Oh, Eric," was all she could say as she fell into him. Lip ran up to them and fished through the man's pockets, producing the keys for the handcuffs.

Suddenly, Eric heard a groan. A loud noise was followed by a warm feeling in his back. Ashley cried out as she pulled her hands away. They were bloody.

"Bastard," Eric heard his brother say as his weapon fired three times into the bad guy.

Eric felt no pain but was light-headed as he found Ashley's enormous eyes. They were soft and filled with tears. "*Eric...*" she whispered, reaching for him in slow motion as he lost consciousness.

Chapter Forty-Seven

Eric had vague memories of voices...Lu's and Bobby's, Carson's he thought, but Ashley's was the voice that filled his thoughts as he drifted in and out of consciousness. Its gentle drawl kept him grounded, her hand would find his, connecting Eric with the outside world. Her musky fragrance tempted him, leading him toward dreams of pleasant things that lay ahead.

Daylight would come and go in fits and starts, accompanied by the constant, ever vigilant beeping of electronic monitors. He recalled being moved and jostled, the confinement of some device or another, an MRI or CT scan, perhaps. Once in a while he would open his eyes to find her asleep in a chair touching his hand. He would dream of her eyes, her smile, the feel of her lips on his. The thought occurred more than once that if death was going to come he would welcome it if she was with him and her hand was in his...

****

"Well, Mr. Montgomery. Welcome back." The man smiled down at him. His nametag read *Head of Internal Medicine*. He was surprisingly young, had a shock of red hair, and a sparkling smile. "For a while we thought you might be leaving us."

Eric licked his lips.

One of the younger doctors standing nearby smiled at him and offered him a spoonful of ice chips.

"Thanks," Eric acknowledged and tried to move. Pain shot through his right side while the array of tubes and sensors attached to his chest and arms held him prisoner.

"Please, just lie still," the doctor in charge said kindly and touched his arm. "We want you to get better as quickly as possible. But you've given us quite a time, and it's going to take a while."

The man whose nametag described him as Chief of Internal Medicine explained Eric's condition to those surrounding him. Eric assumed he was a case on rounds for the medical students and interns, all of whom looked like high school students.

"Mr. Montgomery sustained a serious gunshot wound. He was very fortunate. The high caliber bullet found its way around his vital organs." The man squeezed Eric's shoulder as he continued with more doctor-speak. Some simple tests of his reflexes and cognitive skills brought the session to an end.

The doctor nodded toward the door. "I think"—a broad smile showed on his freckled face—"there's a young lady who's going to be very glad to see you awake and alert." The smile grew into a grin. "I'll be back later with a team from physical therapy so we can begin the discussion of your recovery. There's a very influential gentleman who seems intent on seeing to it that you get absolutely top-notch care. But I explained to him that's the way we treat all our patients."

The doctor chuckled and gave Eric a tap on the leg. Turning, he and his entourage headed to the door. Some engaged in casual conversation while other typed notes into their tablets and smart phones. As soon as they opened the door, Ashley pushed past them. She stood staring at him.

"Please, Ms. Fitzhugh. Now just a few minutes. He still needs plenty of rest," the doctor cautioned.

Ashley stopped, apparently glued to the floor. Eric wanted so much to touch her, hold her close, inhale her scent but she stared, unable to move.

He did his best to hold out his arms. "Please, come here," he whispered.

Suddenly, like a projectile shot from an artillery piece, she exploded across the final five feet bending as she got to the bed so she could embrace him gently.

"Oh…Eric." She broke into sobs. Mammoth tears washed over and flooded her cheeks. "I was afraid—so afraid you'd never wake up." Ashley swallowed loudly and backed away. "Don't you ever do this to me again!" she scolded in a hoarse whisper.

Suddenly she was next to him again. Her full, soft lips found his forehead, his eyes, his mouth. He groaned as he did his best, lifting himself to meet her.

Ashley backed away wearing a frustrated look. "Are you okay?"

He nodded.

"I'm sorry. But I can't help it! I just can't bear being away from you."

He took her hand. "I'm fine—now," he said, reaching for her hand. "And I don't want you to stay away from me. Not now, not ever."

****

Eric waited impatiently for Ashley's daily visits. She'd come after lunch and stay late into the evening. It was like a shot of adrenaline laced with morphine when he saw her come through the door—excitement laced with intense pleasure.

But the most emotional moment of his hospital stay came when Ralph appeared at noon two days after Eric had awakened.

"Hey, bro. How you doing?" Ralph asked quietly. He stood in the doorway studying Eric. He looked scruffy, unshaven, uncomfortable, and older than Eric remembered. Much older.

Eric stared back unsure what to say. His entire adult life had been spent vilifying the man who leaned casually in his doorway. Suddenly his world had been turned upside down. Ralph had been thrust into the unlikely role of hero. Eric had spent long hours thinking about what to say when they met. How should he handle this predictably awkward moment—grab Ralph, hug him, and offer profuse apologies for degrading him?

No, that made no sense. Eric knew next to nothing about Ralph or his life. He had no way of knowing his real story and that, apparently, fit Ralph's cover to perfection. Whatever transpired in the future, Eric gave himself a pass. There was no conceivable way he could have called this one.

"I…I don't know…" Eric offered softly in answer to his brother's inquiry.

Ralph held up his hand. Eric could see it in his eyes. His brother was experiencing the same uncomfortable loss of words after spending a lifetime built on fabrication.

"Don't worry. You don't owe me anything, kid," Ralph assured him.

Eric thought his brother's eyes were filling up. The emotion passed quickly.

"But so much has happened. Ashley, Kylie,

Carson…and you." Eric picked at the bedclothes then found his brother's hard blue eyes again. "If I'd known. If you'd have given me the slightest tipoff, a hint…"

"Look, Eric. I knew what I was getting into when I signed on for this." Ralph shook his head. "Funny. I was always trying to hustle someone. It was Melissa. When I met her, the hustle lost its magic. It made no sense any more. I decided to try the good guys for a while. Sounds like a cliché but it's true."

"Did Melissa know? I mean about the deep cover…what you were doing?"

Ralph sat down next to the bed. He looked out the window to the leaves, now fully green and open. Then he cleared his throat. "Yeah. There's a little kid in all of us, Eric. You know, the need for recognition—to have someone you really care about know you're doing the right thing." Ralph's face grew dark; his eyes wore a distant look. "Someone like her…so special, so kind, and so sweet. I told her. Guess I had to." He sighed deeply. "It was worth seeing the glow in her eyes, the look of pride on her face until she..." His words trailed into silence.

Eric stretched out his hand. Ralph took it and squeezed it tightly. "Gotta go, kid."

"You just got here," Eric protested. "You've been MIA for years. And now…there's so much more I want to…"

"Don't worry, kid. I promise. I won't be a stranger."

Ralph stood, let Eric's hand go, and gave him a confident nod. Then he was gone. Eric wondered if Ralph would keep his word. Suddenly he wanted to have his older brother in his life. Wanted it badly.

****

It was Lip's turn the next afternoon.

"How are you doing, buddy?" he asked.

He had to ask, to hear the answer to the question that had haunted Eric since he'd returned to the world. "How did you and Ralph end up at the park the night Ashley and I were there?"

"Simple," his friend said as he sat down. "We both work for the same man. Your ole buddy, Mr. Carson." Ron Lipton allowed himself a smile.

"What?" Eric couldn't believe what he was hearing. "Is there anyone who doesn't work for him?" he asked with a mixture of amusement and cynicism.

Ron Lipton looked toward the window, then back at Eric. "I know this must be hard for you to take. It didn't go exactly the way we expected."

Eric swallowed. Carson had given him an answer but he no longer knew what was true and what wasn't. So much of this adventure had been theater or it seemed that way. "Did Ashley know anything about this?"

"No. Sometimes you just get lucky."

"Lucky?" he said with incredulity. Ashley, Kylie, and Lu had been kidnapped, *he'd* almost been killed. Others had. His mind pictured Rocco, that poor college kid just doing a summer job. Eric had no idea how many others. Were there other innocent bystanders, what the spook world euphemistically referred to as collateral damage? He wondered what Carson and company defined as *lucky*.

"Yeah." Lip gave him a wry smile. "I mean the whole thing with Ashley. Ralph said she'd had a schoolgirl crush on you for years. Sending her up here. How perfect was that?"

"Sending her up here? As a decoy?"

"C'mon, buddy. You must have seen that one coming." Lip watched him. His smile faded. "Ricky. We live in a complex world. None of us like the things we're forced to do. We all make tough choices. Sometimes downright ugly ones. After what we've been through. Don't go high-handed on me. You spent five years in the Middle East. Can you sit here, putting on this smug, self-righteous act and tell me you never had to make a no-win choice, a choice you knew could lead to some people dying so you could save others?"

Eric sighed and stared at the freshly painted ceiling, listening to the low drone of the AC as it pushed cool air through the ductwork. "No," he admitted in a reluctant whisper.

"The difference is that you didn't love your team in the all-consuming way you love Ashley and her daughter. I know. You thought you could find a pure, pristine place where you and Elaine could build Utopia."

"Yep. Least I hoped I could."

"Well, this is the real world. This time it was a powerful man gone over the edge. A paranoid who'd suffered a mind-numbing tragedy. He'd lost his whole family—wife, two sons, and two daughters on 9/11. They were at Windows on the World waiting for him when the first plane struck. He was a top-level guy, a genius who worked for NSA. He snapped. He wanted to terrorize us into submission. To offer some sort of fear-based anarchy as an alternative." Lip shook his head violently. "Sometimes I wake up in a cold sweat, knowing that for every Osama Bin Laden or Saddam Hussein there may be a hundred of these self-righteous maniacs. They frighten me a lot more. And they usually have powerful friends, alliances, and the kind of resources most of these third-world overseas types can only dream of."

Lipton stood. "Sorry for the lecture. Go back. Run your marina with your adopted family."

Eric reached for his friend's hand. Lip turned and grasped Eric's in a firm handshake. "It's okay, Rick. Trust me. If I need you, I know where to find you."

Like Ralph the night before, Lip showed a coy smile and let go of his friend's hand.

When the door opened Ashley stood there, waiting. Eric wondered how much she'd heard. Nothing, he hoped. It was terrifying stuff, and she'd already had far more than her share of reality for a lifetime.

"Oh, sorry," she offered. "I didn't know you were in here, Commander. I can come back later."

Lip stood for a moment and shook her hand. He gave his old friend one final nod and salute. "I think we're done here. Take good care of this guy. I'm leaving you in good hands," he said looking back, giving Eric a wink. "He deserves it."

"I agree," Ashley said in a whisper as she smiled pleasantly, releasing Lip's hand.

"Take good care of him, Ms. Fitzhugh," Lip repeated and bent to give her a peck on the cheek. And as quickly as Ralph the day before, his old comrade was gone.

Carson had appeared at Eric's bedside for a couple of days, but once the crisis passed they never saw him again. *Spooks*. That was what deep-cover operatives were called. For good reason.

Other than the vague references from Lip, no one

ever explained the down and dirty details of Firestorm. But then, this wasn't Agatha Christie, there was no Hercule Poirot who lined the suspects up and revealed the fiendish plot and villain to the audience. This was reality. It was dark, it was dirty, and often left more than a few question marks.

****

Eric was close to discharge. He'd been through rehab and could do everything he had before the gunshot. Not as fast or as well, but that would come in time. At least he hoped it would. He refused to talk to newspaper reporters though they continued to hound him for weeks. Carson and company had orchestrated a plausible cover story about sadistic kidnappers, once again positioning Eric as a hero—the small-town savior and rescuer of three women. The explosions had been described as accidents. The public seemed satisfied. Local police and other savvy observers knew better but kept their mouths shut. That was the way of it.

On a day trip before his discharge, Ashley had driven Eric to the marina where a group representing his customers had appeared to congratulate him on his latest heroic adventure and assure him that they were with him to stay, no matter what the inconvenience.

Ashley grinned when Bobby came over to show the boss the new docks. After spending time showing Eric the improvements the havoc had wrought, he left. When Eric asked Ashley why she was beaming from ear to ear she pointed to Bobby's small cruiser. Stacy lay sunning herself on the foredeck.

"No more Gwen," she explained. "Those two have become quite an item."

"Like you and me?" he asked as he found Ashley's

hand.

She turned and put her arms around him tightly.

"Oh," he groaned, teasing her.

"No, nothing like you and me," Ashley whispered. She backed away so she could find his eyes. "There never will be anyone like you and me, darlin'."

"My goodness. *Darling.* We are getting intimate aren't we?"

"Damn right!" She squeezed him. "Your buddy Carson called and offered me a job with DOD by the way. Said you recommended it."

Eric watched her. "And?" he asked, hoping she was teasing.

"Lots of money, nice condo in Georgetown. Private school for Kylie." She sounded smug. "This whole thing may have a silver lining."

"So..." The words stuck in Eric's throat. "Does that mean..."

She put her fingers to his lips. "Shhh. Have no fear." She beamed, pleased with herself for having caught him. "How could I ever leave this place? Great scenery, best seafood in the world, even good company—sometimes."

It was his turn. "I think I can do something about that." He winked at her.

She turned and backed away. "Are you saying that...?"

Eric stepped toward her and kneeled clumsily. "Ashley Fitzhugh. Will you do the honor of marrying me?"

Ashley stood, hand clasped tightly over her mouth as tears of joy rolled down her cheeks.

Eric had alerted the marina staff. Bobby raised a

cheer as Kylie and Lu appeared from the office door, smiling broadly.

"Well," Eric held out his hands. "I'm waiting."

Ashley composed herself and put her lips together. "I just may do that, but I'll have to think about this for a while." She giggled, brushed her tears away as she opened her arms, and ran into Eric's.

A word about the author...

Successful author, college faculty member, president of one of the Northeast's most respected writing organizations, and sought-after public speaker, Kevin Symmons has a new romantic thriller set near his Cape Cod home. *Out of the Storm* is a page-turner snatched from today's headlines.

Rite of Passage, his paranormal romance, was a resounding success when released by the award-winning Wild Rose Press in 2012. His other efforts include *Voices*, a sweeping women's fiction work that brings to light the tragic problem of domestic violence in contemporary America, and collaboration with award-winning screenwriter, playwright, and Professor Barry Brodsky, who has adapted one of Kevin's story ideas to the screen.

He is an active member of the National Writers Union, Mystery Writers of America, and both the New England Chapter and National RWA. Kevin is currently at work on his next novel, *Chrysalis*, a new adult thriller also set near his Cape Cod home.